More praise for

Cockroach

"The book is misanthropic and highly allusive—with the addled but endearing tone of *Notes from Underground* and a clear nod to Kafka. . . . Hage's language can queasily bring the inanimate to life."
—*The New Yorker*

"Most fiction writers are primarily either stylists or plotters, but Hage is clearly both. There's a slight jolting sensation as the narrative shifts gear from poetic to cinematic, with guns and knives and elaborately contrived set-ups replacing the earlier evocations of drains and flesh and wintry streets, but it's all managed with great brio and expertise."
—James Lasdun, *The Guardian*

"[A] strange, powerful story. . . . Hage writes brilliantly of the hidden lives teeming in a modern city."
—Kate Saunders, *The Times*

"The novel's gritty back-alley world gives rise to a host of glorious rogues, each swindling the others at every opportunity, and yet each is capable of great empathy under just the right circumstances."
—*Publishers Weekly*, starred review

"Hage sounds a new note in immigrant fiction . . . [he] is a devastatingly precise writer."
—Boris Fishman, *London Review of Books*

"Hage stalks his readers with a shrewd understanding of their conflicted moral sensibilities. As the narrator moves toward a final act to vindicate himself, the reader (now a queasy accomplice) has no time to equivocate or judge, only to watch."
—Ron Slate, On the Seawall

"Hage owes something to Camus and more to Kafka but what he makes of them belongs distinctly to himself."
—*Globe and Mail*

"[A] dark and uncompromising vision. [*Cockroach*] offers a version of an émigré underground which is original, raw and brave."
—Colm Tóibín

"A dark Dostoevskian fable, which lowers the reader into the sewers of immigrant Montreal to confront an underground world teeming with sex, crime and greedy insectoid life."
—Hari Kunzru

"Searing, affecting, misanthropic."
—Mohsin Hamid

Cockroach

RAWI HAGE

W. W. Norton & Company
New York   London

For information about permission to reproduce selections from this book,
write to Permissions, W. W. Norton & Company, Inc., 500 Fifth Avenue,
New York, NY 10110

For information about special discounts for bulk purchases, please
contact W. W. Norton Special Sales at specialsales@wwnorton.com
or 800-233-4830

Manufacturing by Courier Westford
Book design by Laura Brady
Production manager: Louise Mattarelliano

Library of Congress Cataloging-in-Publication Data

Hage, Rawi.
Cockroach / Rawi Hage. — 1st American ed.
p. cm.
ISBN 978-0-393-07537-3
1. Thieves—Fiction. 2. Immigrants—Fiction. 3. Montréal
(Québec)—Fiction. 4. Psychological fiction. I. Title.
PR9199.4.H33C63 2009
813'.6—DC22
2009019612

ISBN 978-0-393-33787-7 pbk.

W. W. Norton & Company, Inc.
500 Fifth Avenue, New York, N.Y. 10110
www.wwnorton.com

W. W. Norton & Company Ltd.
15 Carlisle Street, London W1D 3BS

For Ramzy, Jenny, and Nada, who bring me smiles; for my brothers; for Lisa, as once promised; for Madeleine, who loves the East; and for my exiled friends: may they go back.

What we call species are various degenerations of the same type.

— Isidore Saint-Hilaire,
Vie d'Étienne Geoffroy Saint-Hilaire (1847)

Then Satavaesa makes those waters flow down to the seven Karshvares of the earth, and when he has arrived down there, he stands, beautiful, spreading ease and joy on the fertile countries.

— *Avesta*, the ancient scriptures
of Zoroastrianism

I

I AM IN LOVE with Shohreh. But I don't trust my emotions anymore. I've neither lived with a woman nor properly courted one. And I've often wondered about my need to seduce and possess every female of the species that comes my way.

When I see a woman, I feel my teeth getting thinner, longer, pointed. My back hunches and my forehead sprouts two antennae that sway in the air, flagging a need for attention. I want to crawl under the feet of the women I meet and admire from below their upright posture, their delicate ankles. I also feel repulsed — not embarrassed, but repulsed — by slimy feelings of cunning and need. It is a bizarre mix of emotions and instinct that comes over me, compelling me to approach these women like a hunchback in the presence of schoolgirls.

Perhaps it's time to see my therapist again, because lately this feeling has been weighing on me. Although that same urge has started to act upon me in the shrink's presence. Recently, when I saw her laughing with one of her co-workers, I realized that she is also a woman, and when she asked me to re-enact my urges, I put my hand on her knee while she was sitting across from me. She changed the subject and, calmly, with a compassionate face, brushed my hand away, pushed her seat back, and said: Okay, let's talk about your suicide.

Last week I confessed to her that I used to be more coura-geous, more carefree, and even, one might add, more violent. But here in this northern land no one gives you an excuse to hit, rob, or shoot, or even to shout from across the balcony, to curse your neighbours' mothers and threaten their kids.

When I said that to the therapist, she told me that I have a lot of hidden anger. So when she left the room for a moment, I opened her purse and stole her lipstick, and when she returned I continued my tale of growing up somewhere else. She would interrupt me with questions such as: And how do you feel about that? Tell me more. She mostly listened and took notes, and it wasn't in a fancy room with a massive cherrywood and leather couch either (or with a globe of an ancient admiral's map, for that matter). No, we sat across from each other in a small office, in a public health clinic, only a tiny round table between us.

I am not sure why I told her all about my relations with women. I had tried many times to tell her that my suicide attempt was only my way of trying to escape the permanence of the sun. With frankness, and using my limited psychologi-cal knowledge and powers of articulation, I tried to explain to her that I had attempted suicide out of a kind of curiosity, or maybe as a challenge to nature, to the cosmos itself, to the recurring light. I felt oppressed by it all. The question of exis-tence consumed me.

The therapist annoyed me with her laconic behaviour. She brought on a feeling of violence within me that I hadn't experienced since I left my homeland. She did not understand. For her, everything was about my relations with women, but for me, everything was about defying the oppressive power in the world that I can neither participate in nor control. And the question that I hated most — and it came up when she was frustrated with me for not talking enough — was when she leaned over the table and said, without expression: What do you expect from our meeting?

I burst out: I am forced to be here by the court! I prefer not to be here, but when I was spotted hanging from a rope around a tree branch, some jogger in spandex ran over and called the park police. Two of those mounted police came galloping to the rescue on the backs of their magnificent horses. All I noticed at the time was the horses. I thought the horses could be the answer to my technical problem. I mean, if I rode on the back of one of those beasts, I could reach a higher, sturdier branch, secure the rope to it, and let the horse run free from underneath me. Instead I was handcuffed and taken for, as they put it, assessment.

Tell me about your childhood, the shrink asked me.

In my youth I was an insect.

What kind of insect? she asked.

A cockroach, I said.

Why?

Because my sister made me one.

What did your sister do?

Come, my sister said to me. Let's play. And she lifted her skirt, laid the back of my head between her legs, raised her heels in the air, and swayed her legs over me slowly. Look, open your eyes, she said, and she touched me. This is your face, those are your teeth, and my legs are your long, long whiskers. We laughed, and crawled below the sheets, and nibbled on each other's faces. Let's block the light, she said. Let's seal that quilt to the bed, tight, so there won't be any light. Let's play underground.

Interesting, the therapist said. I think we could explore more of these stories. Next week?

Next week, I said, and rose up on my heels and walked past the clinic's walls and down the stairs and out into the cold, bright city.

WHEN I GOT HOME, I saw that my sink was filled with dishes, a hybrid collection of neon-coloured dollar-store cups mixed with flower-patterned plates, stacked beneath a large spaghetti pot, all unwashed. Before I could reach for my deadly slipper, the cockroaches that lived with me squeezed themselves down the drain and ran for their lives.

I was hungry. And I had little money left. So it was time to find the Iranian musician by the name of Reza who owed me forty dollars. I was determined to collect and I was losing my patience with that bastard. I was even contemplating breaking his santour if he did not pay me back soon. He hung out in the Artista Café, the one at the corner. It is open twenty-four hours a day, and for twenty-four hours it collects smoke pumped out by the lungs of fresh immigrants lingering on plastic chairs, elbows drilling the round tables, hands flagging their complaints, tobacco-stained fingers summoning the waiters, their matches, like Indian signals, ablaze under hairy noses, and their stupefied faces exhaling cigarette fumes with the intensity of Spanish bulls on a last charge towards a dancing red cloth.

I ran downstairs to look for the bastard at the café, and god behold! Two Jehovah's Witness ladies flashed their Caribbean smiles and obstructed my flight with towering feathery straw hats that pasted a coconut shade onto the gritty steps of the crumbling building where I live. Are you interested in the world? they asked me. And before I had a chance to reply, one of the ladies, the one in the long quilted coat, slapped me with an apocalyptic prophecy: Are you aware of the hole in the ozone above us?

Ozone? I asked.

Yes, ozone. It is the atmospheric layer that protects us from the burning rays of the sun. There is a hole in it as we speak, and it is expanding, and soon we shall all fry. Only the cockroaches shall survive to rule the earth. But do not despair, young man, because you will redeem yourself today if you buy this magazine — I happen to have a few copies in my hand here — and attend Bible gatherings at our Kingdom Hall. And afterwards, my handsome fellow, you can go down to the basement and listen to the leader (with a cookie and a Styrofoam cup in hand) and he will tell you that transfusions (be they administered through a syringe, a medical doctor, or perverted sex) are a mortal sin. Then and only then will you have a chance. Repent! the woman shouted as she opened the Bible to a marked page. She read, The words of the Lord my son: *Therefore will I also deal in fury: mine eye shall not spare, neither will I pity: and though they cry in mine ears with loud voice, yet will I not hear them.* Buy this magazine (the word of the Lord included), my son. Read it and repent!

How much? I asked, as I liberated my pocket from the sinful weight of a few round coins sealed with idolatrous images of ducks, geese, bears, and magisterial heads. They were all I had.

Give me those coins and pray, because then, and only then, you will have the chance to be beamed up by Jesus our saviour, and while you are ascending towards the heavens, you can take a peek down at those neighbours of yours who just slammed their door in our faces. You can watch them fry like dumplings in a wok, and I assure you that our Lord will be indifferent to their plight, their sufferings, their loud cries of agony and regret and pain — yes, pain! And may God save us from such harrowing pain.

I kissed the Jehovah's Witness ladies' hands. I asked them to have mercy on me in that sizzling day to come. Dying from fire is a terrible thing. If I had to choose, I would certainly want something less painful, quicker, maybe even more poetic — like hanging from a willow tree or taking a bullet in the head or falling into a senseless eternal slumber accompanied by the aroma of a leaky gas stove.

I left the ladies and ran down to the Artista Café on St-Laurent, still hoping to find Reza in a circle of smoke and welfare recipients and coffee breath. As my feet trudged the wet ground and I felt the shivery cold, I cursed my luck. I cursed the plane that had brought me to this harsh terrain. I peered down the street and hesitantly walked east, avoiding every patch of slush and trying to ignore the sounds of friction as car wheels split the snow, sounds that bounced into my ears, constant reminders of the falling flakes that gather and accumulate quietly, diligently, claiming every car windshield, every hat, every garbage can, every eyelid, every roof and mountain. And how about those menacing armies of heavy boots, my friend, encasing people's feet, and the silenced ears, plugged with wool and headbands, and the floating coats passing by in ghostly shapes, hiding faces, pursed lips, austere hands? Goddamn it! Not even a nod in this cold place, not even a timid wave, not a smile from below red, sniffing, blowing noses. All these buried heads above necks strangled in synthetic scarves. It made me nervous, and I asked myself, Where am I? And what am I doing here? How did I end up trapped in a constantly shivering carcass, walking in a frozen city with wet cotton falling on me all the time? And on top of it all, I am hungry, impoverished, and have no one, no one . . . Fucking ice, one slip of the mind and you might end up immersing your foot in one of those treacherous cold pools that wait for your steps with the patience of sailors' wives, with the mockery of swamp monsters. You can curse all you wish, but still you have to endure freezing toes, and the squelch of wet socks, and the slime of midwives' hands, and fathoms of coats that pass you on the streets and open and close, fluttering and bloated like sails blown towards a promised land.

I am doomed!

When I entered the café, I peeled myself out from under layers of hats, gloves, and scarves, liberated myself from zippers and buttons, and endured the painful tearing Velcro that hissed like a prehistoric reptile, that split and separated like people's lives, like exiles falling into cracks that give birth and lead to death under digging shovels that sound just like the friction of car wheels wedging snow around my mortal parts.

I spotted Professor Youssef sitting alone at his usual table. That lazy, pretentious, Algerian pseudo-French intellectual always dresses up in gabardine suits with the same thin tie that had its glory in the seventies. He hides behind his sixties-era eyeglasses and emulates French thinkers by smoking his pipe in dimly lit spots. He sits all day in that café and talks about *révolution et littérature*.

I asked the professor if he had seen Reza, the Iranian musician, but he did not respond. He just gave me his arrogant smile.

I knew it, I knew it! The professor wants to shower me with his existentialist questions. The bastard plays Socrates every chance he gets. He has always treated the rest of us like Athenian pupils lounging on the steps of the agora, and he never answers a question. He imagines he is a pseudo-socialist Berber journalist, but he is nothing but a latent clergyman, always answering a question with another question.

Is it a yes or a no? *C'est urgent*, I shrilled at him, intending to interrupt his epistemological plot.

Non! J'ai pas vu ton ami. The professor pasted on his sardonic smile again, puffed his pipe, and changed the position of his legs. He leaned his body into the back of the chair and looked at me with an intellectual's air of dismissal, as if I were a peasant, unworthy of the myopic thickness of his glasses. He does not trust me. He smells me through his pipe's brume. I know he suspects me of stealing his last tobacco bag, which I did. But he cannot prove it. Now whenever I approach him, he acts as if he is repositioning himself in his chair in order to say something valuable and profound, but I can see him through his pipe's smog, gathering his belongings closer to his body, hugging his bag like a refugee on a crowded boat.

I turned away from the professor, thinking that I would like to choke Reza, the Middle Eastern hunchback, with the strings of his own musical instrument. He owed me, and I was in need. He always managed to extract money from me, one way or another. He either gave me long monologues about Persia and the greatness of its history, or he re-enacted the tears of his mother, whom he will never see again before she dies because, as he claims, he is an unfortunate exile. But I know that all Reza cares about is numbing his lips and face. He is always sniffing, and if it's not because of a cold, it is because of an allergy, and if it is not because of allergy, it is because of a natural impulse to powder his nose with "the white Colombian," as he puts it. But there was nothing I could do now except dress again in my armour against the cold and go back to my room and wait for Reza to call.

At home I lay in bed, reached for my smokes, and then for no reason became alarmed, or maybe melancholic. This feeling was not paranoia, as the therapist wrote in her stupid notes (notes that I had managed to steal); it was just my need again to hide from the sun and not see anyone. It was the necessity I felt to strip the world from everything around me and exist underneath it all, without objects, people, light, or sound. It was my need to unfold an eternal blanket that would cover everything, seal the sky and my window, and turn the world into an insect's play.

A FEW HOURS LATER, in the early evening, I decided to pay Reza a visit at his home. I walked through the cold to his house, rang the bell, and waited. Matild, a French beauty of a waitress and Reza's roommate, opened the door. As soon as she saw me, she tried to slam the door in my face.

I put my foot in the corner of the door frame and whispered tenderly: I am worried about Reza.

Alors, appelle la police, quoi, bof. Ah moi, alors, je ne veux pas me mêler de cette affaire. He did not pay his share of the rent last mooonth. *J'en ai marre là de vous deux.*

Can I come in? I said.

I told you, he eeezzz not herrrreh.

I just want to take a look at his room, I said.

Mais non là, tu exagères.

Please, I begged. And I showed Matild what my droopy, bashful eyes were capable of.

You can only go in hiz rrrroom, she said. No kitchen, and no toilet-paper stealing, *d'accord?* When you worked with me at the restaurant zerre, everyone was saying that it was you who was stealing the toilet paperzzzz, and they all look at me bad because I was the one who recommended you forrr zee job.

I watched Matild's firm ass bounce towards the kitchen. I shrunk into myself and hunched my neck into my shoulders, and my teeth felt as if they were growing points as I stared at her magnificent, majestic, royal French derrière — studied it, surveyed it, assessed it, and savoured it to the last swing. She was still in her nightgown, which ended right above her thighs. And she was barefoot!

I sighed. Still hunched, I scratched my legs against each other. Then, with the desperation of the displaced, the stateless, the miserable and stranded in corridors of bureaucracy and immigration, I turned and fled to Reza's room.

His room smelled of old socks and a troupe of enslaved chain-smokers. It had barely any light, but still I recognized the old black and white TV that he had inherited from his friend Hisham, a Persian computer programmer who had moved to the United States because, as he said, there is more money there and no future in Canada — too many taxes. At least, that is how the empty-headed technocrat of an *arriviste* put it to me the night I was introduced to him at an Iranian party. The party was full of Iranian exiles — runaway artists, displaced poets, leftist hash-rollers, and ex-revolutionaries turned taxi drivers. That was also the night I met Shohreh. Oh, beautiful Shohreh! She drove me crazy, gave me an instant hit of metamorphosis that made me start gnawing on paper dishes, licking plastic utensils, getting lost inside potato-chip bags (bags that crunched with the sound of breaking ice and snapping branches). She was dancing with a skinny, black-clad Iranian gay man named Farhoud. He danced and rubbed himself against her firm body. Like him, Shohreh was dressed in a tight black outfit, and her chest was bouncing in time to the peculiar, menacing cries of a cheap immigrant's stereo. When the music stopped for a moment, I trailed behind her in the crowded hallway and followed her to the kitchen. I made my way through plates, forks, and finger food until finally, as she dipped a slice of cucumber in white sauce thick as a quagmire, I made my move. I want to steal you from your boyfriend the dancer, I said.

Shohreh laughed and exclaimed, Boyfriend? Boyfriend! And she laughed even louder. Farhoud! she called to the man in black. This guy thinks you are my boyfriend.

Farhoud smirked and walked towards us. He put his arm around my shoulder. Actually, I am looking for a boyfriend myself, he gently whispered, and swung his hips. The drink in his hand took on the shape and the glow of a lollipop. Shohreh laughed and tossed her hair and walked away.

All night I followed Shohreh; I stalked her like a wolf. When she entered the bathroom, I glued my ear to its door, hoping to hear her eleven-percent-alcohol urine plunging free-fall from between her secretive, tender thighs. Oh, how I sighed at the cascading sound of liquid against the porcelain-clear pool of the city waters. Oh, how I marvelled, and imagined all the precious flows that would swirl through warm and vaporous tunnels under this glaciered city. It is the fluid generosity of creatures like Shohreh that keep the ground beneath us warm. I imagined the beauty of the line making its way through the shades of the underground, golden and distinct, straight and flexible, discharged and embraced, revealing all that a body had once invited, kept, transformed, and released, like a child's kite with a string, like a baby's umbilical cord. Ah! That day I saw salvation, rebirth, and golden threads of celebration everywhere.

I asked Shohreh for her number. I won't give it to you, she said, but I don't mind if you put in an effort and get it on your own. It is more romantic that way, don't you think? As she danced she looked at me, and sometimes she smiled at me and other times she ignored me. I could tell how flattered she was by my look of despair. She knew perfectly well that I was willing to crawl under her feet like an insect, dance like a chained bear in a street market, applaud like a seal on a stool, nod like a miniature plastic dog on the dashboard of an immigrant cab driver. I wanted so much to be the one to swing her around the dance floor. I wanted to be the one who dipped her and took in the scent of her breasts flooding over her black lace bra.

For days after the party, I begged that asshole Reza to give me Shohreh's number. He refused. That selfish, shady exile would only say, in his drooling accent, You are not serious about her. You only want to sleep with her. She is not that kind of girl, she is Iranian. She is like a sister, and I have to protect her from dirty Arabs like you.

But, Reza, maestro, I said, sisters also fuck, sisters have needs, too.

This upset him and he cursed, Wa Allah alaazim. I will prevent you from meeting her again!

But I did meet Shohreh again. I got her number from Farhoud, the dancer. One day I saw him walking down the street, bouncing happily, trotting like Bambi. I had a large scarf around my face that day, and I flew across the street and stood in front of him, my hands on my hips like Batman. Farhoud recognized me right away, through my mask and all. He pulled down my scarf and kissed me on the cheeks and laughed like little Robin. Right away I told him that I was in love with Shohreh and needed her number.

I will have to ask her first, he said, and his hands gestured in sync with his fluttering eyelashes. But she is not the in-love type, my love, he added.

Give me her number and I will love you forever, I promised him. I put my arm around his shoulder and gave him a kiss on the forehead.

He laughed. You are so bad! he exclaimed, and pulled a pen with a teddy bear's head from his purse and wrote out both his and her numbers.

NOW I SEARCHED Reza's room for money, food, hash, coke — anything I could get from the bastard. I opened his drawers, sniffed under his bed, reached under the dresser and scanned with my finger for the small plastic bags he usually tapes there, upside down. I would have settled for a bus ticket — anything to get back what he owed me. But there was nothing. That impoverished restaurant musician blows everything up his nose.

I shouted to Matild, but she did not answer me. I went to her room. She was lying in bed, half-naked, reading *un livre de poche*, smoke rising from behind its pages. She felt my heavy breathing and my eyes sliding over her smooth shaved thighs. From behind a scene in the book, she whispered, I thought we agrrrreed that you would not enterrrr herrrre.

Will you call me if you hear from Reza?

Matild puffed and did not answer.

It is important.

D'accord. I will call you. Leave now. Pleeeezzzz.

I walked to the apartment door, opened it and closed it loudly, then snuck back inside to the kitchen and opened the fridge slowly. I grabbed whatever I could — food and sweets — and then I left for good, shuffling home through the high snow. At home in my kitchen, the cockroaches smelled the loot in my hand and began to salivate like little dogs. I moved to the bedroom, away from their envious eyes, and sat on my bed and made myself a sandwich. Now, I thought, I have to get some money before the end of the month, before I starve to death in this shithole of an apartment, in this cold world, in this city with its case of chronic snow. The windows whistled and freezing air drifted through cracks; it was a shithole of a rundown place I lived in, if you ask me. But what was the difference? Nothing much had changed in my life since the time I was born. At least now I lived alone, not crowded in one small bedroom with a sister, a snoring father, and a neurotic mother who jumped up in the night to ask if you were hungry, thirsty, needed to go to the bathroom (or if you were asleep, for that matter). I was no longer in the same room as a teenage sister coming of age, dreaming of Arabs with guns, ducking her left hand under the quilt, spookily eyeing the void, biting her lip, and rotating her index finger as if it were the spinning reel of a movie projector beaming sexual fantasies on the bedroom wall. And here comes the cheering, like that of the men in the old Cinema Lucy, where clandestine dirty movies quickly appeared and disappeared between clips of the Second World War, Italian soap operas, cowboys and Indians bouncing on wild horses. Cinema Lucy, with its stained chairs glowing and fading with semen, and its agitated men dispersed across the floor in the company of their handkerchiefs, which they held in their arms like Friday-night dates. Like guerrillas at night, these men waited impatiently for the porn clips to appear between the irrelevant worlds of the main features, circuses of jumping mammals and falling buffoons, fantasies of high seas and sunsets that faded and darkened into invading European armies stomping high boots over burned hills and cobbled squares, frozen at the sight of a few saluting generals and their fat-ankled women.

Inside Lucy we sat and waited for flesh to appear on the screen. We were like angels. And then, when the older men became afraid that too much time had passed or was being wasted on the projection of old memories, wars, and aging stars, they shouted and banged on the bottoms of the old chairs: *Attcheh* (a porn cut) *Abou-Khallil! Attcheh, Abou-Khallil!* And succumbing to the pressure of the drumming palms, a bosom would swell on the screen, the back of a head would veil a voluptuous thigh, and some of the men would stand up, cheer, and whistle until the swelling in their pants burst their zippers open, and their shoulders tilted forward like the silhouettes of fishermen against crooked horizons scooping fish by the light of a sinking sun, and they blasted their handkerchiefs with the bangs of expelled bullets, wounding their pride, and finally folding up images of past lovers and their own unsatisfied wives.

A joint will warm my bones, I thought, or at least numb my brain just enough so that I won't feel my misery and the cold. I slipped inside my closet and reached for the secret hole beside the top shelf. I arrange my cupboards precisely: the towels and sheets on the bottom shelf, the untouchables like opium and dreams on the top. I pulled out a plastic film canister and the thin white papers that went with it. Only a small amount of hash was left — a small ball, enough for one thin roll to lift me up like a rope and swing me down into a calm descent. I cut it and tried to roll it, but my fingers were cold and, as usual, shaky. Besides, I had no tobacco to mix with the stuff. Cigarettes are bad for one's health, I consoled myself.

I lay in bed and let the smoke enter me undiluted. I let it grow me wings and many legs. Soon I stood barefoot, looking for my six pairs of slippers. I looked in the mirror, and I searched again for my slippers. In the mirror I saw my face, my long jaw, my whiskers slicing through the smoke around me. I saw many naked feet moving. I rushed to close the window and draw the curtains. Then I went back to bed, buried my face in the sheets, and pulled the pillow and covers over my head. I closed my eyes and thought about my dilemma.

My welfare cheque was ten days away. I was out of dope. My kitchen had only rice and leftovers and crawling insects that would outlive me on Doomsday. I was lucky to have that bag of basmati rice and those few vegetarian leftovers from Mary the Buddhist's party.

Where there is music there is food, I say! A few nights ago around seven, after the sun had left to play, I heard shoeless feet pressing against my ceiling from the floor above me, little toes crawling under the brouhaha of guests and the faint start of a jam session that sounded both menacing and promising. The drums were calling me.

I cracked my door open and I saw feet ascending to my neighbour's place. Mary? I thought. Yes, that was her name. I remembered once meeting her down in the basement. She complained about the absence of recycling bins. Or was it compost? In any case, she wanted to fill the earth with dust from the refuse of vegetables, and she had a strange kind of theory about reincarnation. One look at her guests and I knew what kind of party it would be — one look at the braids, the drums, the agonized Rasta lumps of hair on bleached heads, the pierced ears and noses that would make any bull owner very proud, and I knew. What to wear, was the question. A bedsheet wrapped around my waist and nothing else? Or my pyjamas? Yes, yes! Everyone in the southern hemisphere fetches the newspaper at daybreak in pyjamas fluttering above flat slippers and vaporous feet, everyone drinks coffee on dusty sidewalks, their wrinkled morning faces staring out from between the fenders of bedridden cars. But I decided not to overdo it. The exotic has to be modified here — not too authentic, not too spicy or too smelly, just enough of it to remind others of a fantasy elsewhere. In the end, I kept my jeans on and took off my shoes and left my socks in my room to air a bit more, and I climbed barefoot through the walls.

Mary was welcoming. A peaceful smile wafted my way. I wasn't sure if it was the effect of the ever-burning incense in the room or maybe the effect of the hallucinatory fumes that I myself had been pumping through the years, into her walls.

I had helped myself to food at her party while everyone else sat on the floor with folded legs, eating. I could hear their chewing, like an incantation, as they floated on Indian pillows, the humming inside their throats synced to the sound of Mary's old fridge and the cycles of the world.

I despised how those pale-faced vegans held their little spoons, humbling themselves. Who do they think they are fooling, those bleached Brahmins? We all know that their low-sitting is just another passage in their short lives. In the end, they will get bigger spoons and dig up the earth for their fathers' and mothers' inheritances. But it is I! I, and the likes of me, who will be eating nature's refuse under dying trees. I! I, and the likes of me, who will wait for the wind to shake the branches and drop us fruit. Filth, make-believers, comedians on a Greek stage! Those Buddhists will eventually float down, take off their colourful, exotic costumes, and wear their fathers' three-piece suits. But I will still recognize them through their strands of greying hair. I will envy them when they are perched like monarchs on chairs, shamelessly having their black shoes shined, high above crouched men with black nails feathering and swinging horsehair brushes across their corporate ankles. At the tap of the shoeshiners, the Brahmins will fold their newspapers, stand up and fix their ties, scoop out their pockets for change, and toss a few coins in the air to the workingmen below. And they will step onto ascending elevators, give firm handshakes, receive pats on their backs, smooth their hair in the tinted glass of high-rises. Their radiant shoes will shine like mirrors and their light steps will echo in company corridors to murmurs of, "See you at the barbecue, and give my regards to your lovely spouse." No, none of these imposters was chanting to escape incarnation; they all wanted to come back to the same packed kitchens, to the same large houses, the same high beds, the same covers to hide under again and again.

I was out of toilet paper, but who cared? I always washed after defecating. Though I must admit, during the water shortages in wartime in that place where I come from, there were periods when I did not wash for a long time. You could hardly brush your teeth. Oh, how I once gave priority to that which was most visible — I would wash my face, and deprive everything else, with the little water I had. Every drop of water that ran through the drain inspired me to follow it, gather it, and use it again. As a kid, I was fascinated by drains. I'm not sure if it was the smell, or the noises and echoes that were unexpectedly released after the water was gobbled, or if it was simply the possibility of escape to a place where the refuse of stained faces, infamous hands, dirty feet, and deep purple gums gathered in a large pool for slum kids to swim, splash, and play in.

I got up and went to the window and opened the curtains. The burning coal on top of my joint shone, lustrous and silvery, against the backdrop of Mount Royal. There was a large metal cross right on the top of the mountain. I held out the joint vertically, stretched my hand against the window, and aligned the burning fire on the tip of it to the middle of the cross. I watched its plume ascend like burning hair. The smoke reminded me that it was time to escape this permanent whiteness, the eternal humming of the fluorescent light in the hallway, the ticking of the kitchen clock, and my constant breath — yes, my own breath that fogged the glass and blurred the outside world with a coat of sighs and sadness as the vapour from my tears moistened the window. My own breath was obstructing my view of the world!

I reminded myself that I can escape anything. I am a master of escape (unlike those trapped and recurring pink Buddhists). As a kid, I escaped when my mother cried, when my father unbuckled his belt, when my teacher lifted the ruler high above my little palm. I disappeared as the falling blows glowed across my hands like thunder across land-scapes of lifelines — long journeys, and travellers' palms. I watched the teacher's ruler as if it wasn't me who was receiv-ing those lashes across fingers extended like noontide red above beaches lit by many suns. I alternated my six cock-roach hands and distributed the pain of those blows. And when my palms burned and ached, I fanned my cockroach wings. I let the air cool off my swollen hands as I stood in the corner, my face and a tender belly to the wall.

But I escaped most when I stole sweets, pens, chewing gum, and, later on, cameras and cars. Primitive and uneducated as I was, I instinctively felt trapped in the cruel and insane world saturated with humans. I loathed the grown-ups who were always hovering above me and looking down on me. They, of course, ruled the heights: they could reach the chandelier, the top of the fridge; they could rumple my hair anytime they pleased. But I was the master of the underground. I crawled under beds, camped under tables; I was even the kind of kid who would crawl under the car to retrieve the ball, rescue the stranded cat, find the coins under the fridge.

When I was a teenager I met my mentor Abou-Roro, the

neighbourhood thief. He realized I had the capacity to slip through anything. To help me reach the heights, he would fuse together his fingers and I would step on his locked and open palms, and he would lift me up to small windows that only vermin can go through. Once I was inside a house, a church, or a school, I would go straight for the valuables. I stole them all. You name it and I stole it. I crawled through windows and holes and gathered silver sets, crosses, change, watches. I even took my time to nibble leftovers and kitchen-counter crumbs.

The underground, my friend, is a world of its own. Other humans gaze at the sky, but I say unto you, the only way through the world is to pass through the underground.

OVER THE NEXT FEW days I called Reza's place in vain. I banged on every door at every place I thought he might be, with rhythms that he himself could never replicate — a few *tat-a-tats* here and there. Once I even experimented with a *bouwang!* and a *bou-doum!* But I could not find him. Forty dollars he owed me. Just imagine the soap I could buy, the rice, the yards of toilet paper I could line up, use to sweep the counter, mark territory and divide nations, fly like kites, dry tears, jam in the underground pipes and let everything subterranean rise to the surface. I would share it and cut it and divide it among the nation's poor, fair and square. You name it, I would do it!

Reza, that charming compulsive liar, was a master charlatan who for years had managed to couch-surf in women's houses, bewitching his hosts with his exotic tunes and stories of suffering and exile. His best and favourite story was how he almost lost all his fingers performing for the Ayatollah Khomeini. He usually told this story in bars after some fusion gig with an Anglo with an electric guitar or a Caucasian Rasta with a drum. He would tell the women gathered around him at the table how he was afraid and nervous when he was asked by the Iranian Hezbollah, the Guards of God, not to play anything subversive for the holy man, meaning no fast or nonreligious tunes. Then, when he was finally pushed behind the door where the great leader of the Iranian revolution was sitting, he was so nervous that he forgot to kiss the great mullah's hand, and even forgot to bow and murmur *Al-salaam alaikum*, which made the guards angry. He would relate how he'd sat on the floor tuning his instrument while sweat dripped down his spine, but once he started playing, he was transported (true to his art, to the artist that he was!). He forgot himself and played faster and faster. And here Reza would usually pause to gauge the women's reactions and keep them in suspense, until one of them would ask: And then what happened? (And the woman who asked this was usually the one who would invite Reza to sleep over that night.)

Reza would continue his story, telling the women that he started to play fast and non-religiously and shook his head left and right, because when he plays he can't help it, until one of the guards ran over to him and broke his instrument with one stomp of the foot and held Reza's index finger in the air, bending it backwards, trying to break it, promising that this was the first of many broken bones to come. And if it hadn't been for the Ayatollah Khomeini himself, who gave a slight wave of his hand and liberated Reza from the brute's clutches, all the musician's fingers would have been broken by now. And then the Musician of Love would end his story with a question: And you know what the consequences are for a musician like myself to have broken fingers, right? Gullible heads would nod, compassionate eyes would open, blankets would be extended on sofas and beds, fridges would burp leftovers, and if the rooster was lucky, it would all lead to chicken thighs and wings moistened by a touch of beer or wine, and hot showers seasoned by pizza pies delivered to the bedroom and gobbled in front of trashy movies on TV.

Once, when Reza and I were having an argument, and the topic shifted to each other's lives and each other's decadent methods of survival, I confronted him about his schemes and lies. He leaned his long face towards me and said: Brother, think of me as a wandering Sufi. I spread love and music, and in return I accept hospitality, peace, and love. Love, my friend — it is always about love. As he said this, his eyebrows danced and he swayed his musical head, dimmed his eyes, and smiled. I give something in return, he continued, while you are nothing but a petty thief with no talent. All you can do is make the fridge light go on and off, and once the door is closed you're never sure if the light inside has turned to darkness like your own dim soul.

I cursed him to his face and told him that the day would come when all my power would surface from below. I shall bring up from the abyss the echoes of rodent and insect screams to shatter the drums of your ears! I told him. And then you won't need to cut trees to carve music boxes, and no wire will be stretched, tuned, or picked, and all melody will come from the core of the beings whose instruments are innate inside them — insect legs making tunes as fine as violins, rodent teeth more potent than all your percussion, millions of creatures in sync, orchestrated, marching to claim what is rightly theirs . . .

Reza laughed at me and walked away, humming. I knew it, he said. You are a lunatic. I always knew it — a loonnneyyyy.

FINALLY, I REACHED Matild again, Reza's housemate, the beauty who still works at the French restaurant where I used to work. Lately I find the city is being invaded by whining Parisians like Matild, who chant the "Marseillaise" every chance they get. They come to this Québécois American North and occupy every *boulangerie*, conquer every French restaurant and *croissanterie* with their air of indifference and their scent of fermented cheese — although, truly, one must admire their inherited knowledge of wine and culture. These are skills to be secretly admired. Indeed, the Parisians are highly sought after and desired by the Quebec government. Photos of *la campagne rustique, le Québec du nord des Amériques*, depicting cozy snowy winters and smoking chimneys, are pasted on every travel agent's door; big baby-seal eyes blink from the walls of immigration offices, waiting to be saved, nursed, and petted; the multicolours of Indian summers are plastered across every travel magazine; and *le nouveau monde français* is discovered on every travel show. The Québécois, with their extremely low birth rate, think they can increase their own breed by attracting the Parisians, or at least for a while balance the number of their own kind against the herd of brownies and darkies coming from every old French colony, on the run from dictators and crumbling cities. But what is the use, really? Those Frenchies come here, and like the Québécois they do not give birth. They abstain, or they block every Fallopian tube and catch every sperm before the egg sizzles into *canard à l'orange*. They are too busy baking, tasting wine, and cutting ham and cheese, too occupied intimidating American visitors who play the sophisticates by tasting and nodding at every bottle of French wine wrapped in a white cloth.

When I worked as a dishwasher in the French restaurant, I heard the Frenchies laughing behind swinging kitchen doors, making fun of the cowboys who gave a compliment to the chef with every bite and hummed approvingly at antibiotic-laced hormone-injected cows ruminating ground chicken bones, all the while quietly starving from the small portions and becoming disoriented by the potions of those French Druids. It was Matild who got me the job. And so, for a whole year I splashed water on dishes and silverware. Sometimes when I picked up a spoon or a fork, I swear I could still feel the warmth of a customer's lips. By the shape of the food residue, I could tell if the customer had tightened her lips on the last piece of cake. I would take off my gloves and pass my thumb across the exit lines of a woman's lips. When she is happy, delighted with the food, a woman will slowly pull the spoon from her tightened mouth and let it hang a while in front of her lips, breathe over it, and shift it slightly to catch the candlelight's reflection. It saddened me to erase happiness with water. It saddened me to drown sighs and sparkles with hoses. And then it saddened me to bring back the shine and the glitter.

One day, I was promoted to busboy. I picked up dishes from under the clients' noses and poured water in their glasses while always, always keeping an eye on Maître Pierre, who stood in the corner, hands clasped in front of his crotch like a fig leaf in a fresco. He hardly ever talked. His job was to monitor employees, to answer clients' questions, and with the gold braid on his sleeves to give an air of luxury and aristocracy to the place. When he approached the clients, he would never kneel an inch. His back and shoulders were always erect and proud, and he was always calm and composed. He spoke little. And when he spoke in English, the bastard accentuated and exaggerated his French accent. He sang his words, and when he snapped his fingers you could detect a small vibration in his neck. The employees nearest to him would instantly sweep, fill, offer, pick up, fetch, change, bend, call a taxi, open a door, pass a torch over a cake, and make their way past the fancy tables singing "Happy Birthday" in many languages.

Once I approached Maître Pierre and told him that I would like to be a waiter. He looked at me with fixed, glittering eyes, and said: *Tu es un peu trop cuit pour ça* (you are a little too well done for that)! *Le soleil t'a brûlé ta face un peu trop* (the sun has burned your face a bit too much). I knew what he meant, the filthy human with gold braid on his sleeves and pompous posture! I threw my apron in his face and stormed out the door. On the way out I almost tripped over the stroller of a dark-complexioned woman with five kids trailing behind her like ducks escaping a French cook. Impotent, infertile filth! I shouted at Pierre. Your days are over and your kind is numbered. No one can escape the sun on their faces and no one can barricade against the powerful, fleeting semen of the hungry and the oppressed. I promised him that one day he would be serving only giant cockroaches on his velvet chairs. He had better remove the large crystal chandelier from the middle of the ceiling, I said, so the customers' long whiskers wouldn't touch it and accidentally swing it above his snotty head. And you had better serve crumbs and slimy dew on your chewable menu, Monsieur Pierre, or your business will be doomed to closure and destruction. And, and . . . ! I shouted, and I stuttered, and I repeated, and I added, as my index fingers fluttered like a pair of gigantic antennae. And, I said . . . And you'd better get used to the noise of scrabbling and the hum of fast-flapping wings fanning the hot food, my friend, and you had certainly better put up a sign: No laying eggs and multiplying is allowed in the kitchen or inside cupboards or walls. And, and, I added . . . And you will no longer be able to check your teeth in the reflection of the knives and silverware; there will be no need for utensils in your place anymore. Doomed you will be, doomed as you are infested with newcomers! And your crystal chandeliers, your crystal glasses, your crystalline eyes that watch us like beams against a jail's walls, all shall become futile and obsolete, all shall be changed to accommodate soft, crawling bellies rolling on flat plates. Bring it on! Bring back the flatness of the earth and round surfaces! I shouted. Change is coming. Repent, you pompous erectile creatures! And, and, I continued, my voice shaking as I stood on the sidewalk, I can see the sign coming, my friend, and it shall say: Under new management! Special underground menu served by an undertaker with shovels and fangs! Ha! Ha! Ha!

And I laughed and walked away, to no end.

WHEN I CALLED and asked Matild about Reza, she said again that she had not seen him around the house for several days.

I need to come and look in his room one more time, I told her. Maybe he has fallen under the bed and decided to crawl on his belly and hide. You know that he owes me money, and those who owe, they usually hide.

You just want to come here so you can make your usual sexual advances. *Il n'est pas sous le lit.* Matild hung up the phone on me.

I felt my teeth grinding. That mysterious, mutant urge was coming over me again. So I called her back immediately and confessed. Matild, I said, I dream of you every day. Do you know that soon the ozone will burst open and we will all fry, and only a few chosen people will be saved by the Lord? We shall all fry and only the cockroaches and their earthly kingdom shall survive that last deluge of fire. We will all melt like fondue, and all I want on that day is to melt next to you.

You are not seeeerious, she said.

Believe me, I said, I am seeeerious. I have a magazine to prove it.

Quel magazine? C'est un article, ça?

Well, yes indeed! The article is approved by the Grand Minister of the Ascending Temple himself. He has even pasted his photo onto the first page. Let me come over and show you his meticulously combed hair, his thick glasses that are a testament to his diligent reading of the scriptures, his sincere smile that is proof of his inner happiness, his guaranteed salvation, his family devotion, his anticipation of the long celestial journey on the back of Jesus the saviour.

N'importe quoi, bof, en tout cas les religions me font chier, moi.

I do not care about religion either, I wanted to say to her, but she had hung up the phone in my ear.

The last time I thought about religion was when I chose the tree to hang myself on. I was pissed with the gods, or whoever is responsible for sprouting the trees around here and making them either thin and short or massive and high. I didn't think about religion too hard, but I did not take my decision lightly either. It was not deceit, depression, or a large tragedy that pushed me to go shopping for a rope that suited my neck. And it wasn't voices. I've never heard any voices in my head — unless you consider the occasional jam sessions of Mary, the neighbour above me. No, the thing that pushed me over the edge was the bright light that came in my window and landed on my bed and my face. Nothing made any sense to me anymore. It was not that I was looking for a purpose and had been deceived, it was more that I had never *started* looking for one. I saw the ray of light entering my window and realized how insignificant I was in its presence, how oblivious it was to my existence. My problem was not that I was negligent towards life, but that somehow I always felt neglected by it. Even when

I rushed over to the window and drew the curtains, I could feel the ray of light there waiting for me. Waiting to play tag and touch me again. Flashing and exposing all there was, shedding itself and bouncing images in my eyes, a reminder that this whole comedy of my life was still at play.

I opened and closed the curtains compulsively, many times, that day. Just like death, I thought to myself, just like death it is always there, and it will eventually reach me. I became obsessed with escaping the sun. I thought: What if I live only at night? I can sleep all morning and have a nocturnal existence. But even the next morning, in bed, even when I was asleep with the curtains drawn, I knew that the sun was still there. Then a brilliant, luminous idea came to me. I thought: It is precisely because I exist that the light is still there. What if I cease to exist?

I pulled open the curtains and ran downstairs. I found a store and looked for a rope thick enough to hold my weight and fit around my neck. I consulted with the store employee about matters of weight and height. I convinced him that I was moving and the rope was for dangling a fridge through a window that would be held by a pulley, and to make the story more real I went to the pulley section and chose a suitable one. Then I put the pulley back when the employee turned his back and I bought only the rope.

AFTER MY CONVERSATION with Matild I went back to bed and woke up around noon, in a daze, not sure what day of the week it was. These days, the sun wasn't bothering me anymore. Those questions that had consumed me so much before my suicide attempt somehow seemed irrelevant. Well, to tell the truth, they come and go from my mind. But today the most stressful question in my head was wondering what day of the week it was. From the low volume of traffic down the street and the absence of delivery trucks outside the stores below me, I suspected it was a Sunday, full of empty churches and double beds with couples waking up slowly after a long night of drinking and open booze flooding St-Laurent Street and golden beer gushing from fire hydrants and bar tabs.

It was all coming back to me — but yes, of course! I remember now! Last night I had strolled down St-Laurent, hopping from one bar to another, hoping to meet someone drunk and generous enough to offer me a beer, but all I encountered were schools of garishly painted students hurrying to underground rave parties animated by spotlights and ecstasy pills. Girls walked through the cold in their diminutive skirts and light jackets, shivering and hiding their hands like turtles' necks inside shells or sleeves. I encountered solitary middle-aged hockey fans exhaling smoke through their noses, hypnotized by screens and sticks, filling bar stools that had for many years hosted the regulars' exposed arses and baseball hats. Towards midnight I entered Le Fly Bar on St-Laurent. Like an insect I was drawn to the bar's lantern shapes and the dim light through the window. I like faintly luminous places with invisible tables that just sit there and listen to the defeated moans of conquered chairs. I like dark passages that lead you to where everything comes from (the cases of beer, the milk for the coffee, the crates of bread). I like dirty places and sombre corners. Bright places are for vampires.

A live bluegrass band with a banjo, a guitar, and a harmonica wailed about lost lovers in tunes that sounded like those of wandering gypsies from conquered Spain. I balanced my feet on the edge of the rail below the bar, hoping that the bartender, busy swiping the inside of a glass, would not come my way and snap, What will it be, pal? And just as my feet were tapping the wooden floor, whether from thirst, hunger, or the fast plucking of the banjo, and just before my urge for dancing got strong enough to make me go down to that empty space between the stage and the drinking crowd, I said to myself: You'd better leave, my friend, before you turn yourself into a dancing horse galloping off the walls or a slaughtered chicken with a banjo around its neck. You'd better leave and not be dragged into a solo performance. Haven't you learned your lesson from those Sunday weddings when your aunts pushed you into the village circle to perform the horse dance, and where you, with the promise of a few coins from your uncle the hairdresser, willingly pounded your child's feet on the dust to the tunes of the Bedouin drums made of camel's skin and bended oak?

Shaking my head to dispel the memories of the night before, I lifted the phone to call Shohreh. There was no dial tone. I hadn't paid the bills in a few months and finally the phone company must have kept its promise and cut me off. When they cut the line, I wondered, do they send big guys in overalls down underground to locate it and slash it like an open wrist? Does it wiggle for a while like a lizard's tail? Does the last word of a conversation escape and bounce along those long tunnels and transform into the echo of a curse, or just fall into silence? But really, it doesn't matter. Except for Shohreh and a few newcomers to this land, I don't care to talk to many people. Besides, in this city there is a public phone on every corner. In the cold they stand like vertical, transparent coffins for people to recite their lives in.

Hungry, I walked to the kitchen and opened the cupboards. A miracle indeed! A forgotten can of tuna was floating at the back of the shelves. I captured it, opened it, watched it quiver against the stillness of the oil, waited for the rice to boil, and ate sitting at the window, looking down at the white seagulls gliding above the blue French snow.

After my meal I wanted to do the dishes, but then I thought that maybe I should take a shower first. I feared that the hot water might run out if I wasted it on the dishes. I would have to go down and visit the janitor, like I had many times before, and knock at his door with only a towel around my waist, and complain to his Russian wife about the pipes that gurgle with thirst and hollowness. I would give her my lecture about her absent-minded husband who is always hiding in basements, always entangled in extension cords and mumbling to the sound of menacing drills. When he sees me, that brooder, that chain-smoker, he always manages to erect a ladder and, before saying a word to me, climb the metal steps and talk to me from above, through a dead light bulb or an endless line of fluorescent tubes that will eventually, if you look at it long enough, lead you to your dead forefathers, who as soon as the doctor declares you dead and the line on the monitor goes flat with that long green beep, will show up to greet you in long robes, and just before you ask them for the meaning of life, just before you are introduced to the illuminated gods and an orgy of spirits, just before you dip your toes in a peaceful pool, you will get sucked in reverse through the long tunnel and land on the hospital bed and hear the nurses above you, welcoming you back. So now, every time I see that janitor with his head just below the ceiling, I talk to his shoes, addressing the pair by his family name. Mr. Markakis, I say. Your highnesses, I say.

Talking about shoes, I once saw the janitor on the sidewalk walking the dog of a neighbour, an old lady in our building. The janitor's wife would bring the old lady food, and on summer days, when the branches of the neighbourhood trees were full of maple leaves, she would drag the old lady out to the sidewalk to bathe in the sun. She took care of the old lady, and also stole her china and the clothes from her youth. When I saw the janitor that morning, he was scraping the ground with one of his feet, rubbing his shoe along the edge of the sidewalk. He had stepped in another dog's shit. He was cursing people who do not pick up after their dogs. And the old lady's dog was barking, bewildered, its feelings hurt. It would bark and jump at the janitor's feet, and sniff, growl, and pull on its leash in protest.

I laughed at them. And the janitor saw me laughing. He looked me in the eye and cursed me in Macedonian, calling me a filthy Turk, or maybe a dog, or perhaps a filthy Turkish dog. And ever since, when he sees me in a hallway or in the basement, he climbs the high steps on his ladder and dangles a wire towards my neck like an executioner. I always remind him of his faux pas, and once I even told him to watch his step because the world is filled with . . . but I paused and added . . . Well, because you know how dangerous heights can be. And I laughed under the bright new light of a fresh bulb.

I like the janitor's wife. I like how she is always hiding in her basement apartment and trying on the old lady's clothing. Once when I knocked on her door, she opened it wearing one of those large straw colonial hats.

Ready for afternoon tea? I asked her.

What do you want? she said in her thick Russian accent. My husband is not here. You can leave him a message in the box outside if you need to fix something.

I heard classical music coming from behind the dark walls of her apartment.

Stravinsky, *The Rite of Spring*, I said.

You know your music, she said.

And you know your hats.

What do you want? She started to swing the door closed, but before she could widen her arm and expose her smooth, sweaty armpit and fling the door in my face, I bluffed and said that I knew the hat belonged to the old lady.

Yes, she said. The old lady gave it to me. What do you want?

And what else did she give you? I winked at her.

She almost smiled. You're very observant, she said. The lady is very old and she does not have anybody, and she does not need anything. Her husband died a long time ago, in China during the war, so . . .

Oh, yes, yes, I interrupted. He must have died from the plague or the typhoon, or maybe from carrying too much tea and antiques.

She barely smiled and said, I don't know. I do not care. Maybe he was killed in the war. I read his letters to her. Very romantic. He was an officer in the British government. A respected man. Handsome, too. I ask the old lady, but she does not remember anything.

Talking about respected men, did your husband step outside to walk the dog? I asked. And I giggled because I had given the word "step" a high, flat note.

No, he went to buy paint. He will be back in an hour.

Ah, then maybe I can come in for music and tea, I said.

The janitor's wife did not answer me. Instead, she turned and went inside and left the door open.

I stepped into the apartment. The janitor's wife was in the kitchen, filling the kettle with water and smoking. As she moved, her large hat bumped against the cabinets on both sides of the kitchen. The straw of her hat rustled, the water in the kettle bubbled and boiled, the jars, the cups, the sugar came down, little spoons made small triangle sounds, and then the pouring and stirring inside china cups lifted my sprits. I was going to sit on the dog-walker's chair, converse with his wife, and have a warm drink inside his house. What a triumph!

Do you want a drink, or just tea? the janitor's wife asked me.

Tea, please.

Tea, she repeated with irony and disappointment, and I could hear the rustling straw of her hat again as she advanced with the tray and laid it in front of me on a low coffee table that I immediately recognized. I had seen that table once before, on the sidewalk outside our building. In the moving season, people throw out what they do not need. I was hesitant to pick up the table at the time. Low and round, chipped on one side to show its layers underneath, layers more orderly and refined than all the rocks and stones below gardens and fields. Each metal leg branched out into a triangle that fastened with screws to the bottom of the table's surface. I had hovered around it for a while, had done a little dance, looked around for tenants or trotting dogs, but then I changed my mind. The white surface was too shiny, I decided, and if I let it sit in the middle of my room, light from the sun might strike it, bounce off, and paste a luminous square on my wall. And I, like a moth, would be drawn to it.

The janitor's wife took off her hat and leaned over the table. Her eyes looked bigger now, lit by the table's reflection, shining like a lake (I had been right not to take that piece of furniture). She turned, poured, and waved her spoon at me like a conductor. And then the little china cup came shimmering above my lap, and gold traces on the inner rim of the porcelain were lapped by golden tea, subtle, austere, and expensive tea, now surrounded by a delicate saucer and the elaborate high handle of a white cup that made my pinky tingle and stand erect, a nation's pride.

Nice china, I said.

Okay! the janitor's wife exclaimed. The lady is old and dying, okay? Just drink your tea. She poured the tea brusquely as if it were hard liquor that would land in your stomach and make you happy to stand up, dance, chant, and drink from a lady's shoes.

Those shoes look a bit small on your feet, I whispered with my mouth inside the china cup.

These are mine, not hers, my companion answered, raising her voice. If you want to speak like that, you can go outside now. Anyhow, the old lady's husband stole everything from the Indians, or the Chinese. Maybe he paid nothing, or very little.

Oh yes, I agree, I said. And what high culture did not steal, borrow, claim, or pay very little?

Yes, she said. I have a master's degree in anthropology from the best university in Russia, so I know. Do not talk about that. I know more than you.

Well, yes, I said. I am glad you are taking all these things and giving them a new life.

A new life here in the basement, the janitor's wife added, and surprised me with a loud laugh that made her sound like a pirate. She continued: The old lady has a beautiful big trunk, maybe from China or Japan, but my husband is . . . he is afraid. No, not afraid. He believes in the gods. He is Greek!

Oh, is he? I smiled. But he seems so fearless, always walking with his eyes on the horizon, not looking at where his feet land.

Well . . . he is half Spartan and very proud. Anyway, it is none of your business, but the trunk is heavy.

Well, I could help you transport it, I said. And you don't think anyone would notice?

The old lady has a niece, but she never comes to visit.

But when the old lady dies, perhaps the niece will want to claim back the family belongings?

No, she does not know anything about the house or the furniture, not to worry. I will call you when my husband is away, and you can help me carry the trunk. I told him that I wanted to bring the trunk here and we had a big fight. He wanted to break all the china . . . Still, I told him I would bring the trunk here. He does not believe me.

Well, yes, just knock at my door anytime you are ready, I said.

What do you want in payment?

Oh nothing, I said. I am just doing it for history's sake.

You mean to see things go from one culture to another?

No, to watch the loot of war buried, the stolen treasure put back where it belongs, in the underground. I laughed loudly. The underground!

The basement! The janitor's wife laughed with me. History is coming to the basement, she laughed. Okay, now you can go, she said, and chuckled, and then she remembered my historical words again, and hysterically she laughed.

As I walked out of her apartment and past the sombre cement walls of the basement, I heard the janitor's wife's locks and bolts closing the door on the last movement of *The Rite of Spring*, and I hummed the symphony's tune, graceful as Snow White.

DURING MY SHOWER, I collected the small pieces of soap that were stranded on my tub's edges and lathered myself. I am fascinated by the flow of water. It never ceases to amaze me, how all is swept away, how everything converges in the same stream, along the same trajectory. And what really fascinates me is the bits of soap foam floating down the drain, swirling and disappearing. Little things like this make me think. I start to assess my existence based on these observations.

Soon I was clean and dressed. I even did the dishes — against the roaches' will, depriving them of a wealth of crumbs. A rare feeling of accomplishment, of self-esteem descended upon me. I assured myself that a good, clean, hard-working man such as me could not possibly be left out to burn on that last day or be subjected to the rule of cockroaches in the world to come.

A good day indeed! I proclaimed to the seagulls gliding like falling maple leaves outside my window. Now all I need is to get myself a package of cigarettes and a good cup of morning coffee. I remembered how on that day not so long ago, just before I walked to the park and looked for the tree with a rope in my hand, I had a good cup of coffee. I enjoyed that cup the most. Of course, you might think I enjoyed it because it was my last and I made the effort to enjoy it, savour it slowly, wrap my palms around it, brood over it a little, and pay more attention to it. But no, you are wrong; it really was a good cup of coffee. When I had finished my coffee and decided on a tree, I tried to throw my rope over the branch. But I found the task impossible and I realized I lacked some basic cowboy skills. Then I tried to climb the tree, but it was a cold day and my exposed fingers became so frozen that I could not keep from slipping. I changed trees, found a lower branch. I mean, everything was pathetic.

The plan did not work — the branch broke. I tried. I failed.

II

A FEW DAYS PASSED, and then it was time again to climb the stairs of the public health clinic and sit in my interrogation chair.

This time, the therapist was interested in my mother.

My mother, I said, has kinky hair.

What else? she asked.

A long face and pointy teeth.

What does she do?

Well, I said, when she was not dangling clothing by the arms or the ankles off the balcony she would stir her wooden spoon around a tin pot, in a counter-clockwise motion, and if she was not busy doing that, she was chasing after us with curses and promises that she would dig our graves.

Can you elaborate? the therapist asked.

Can you be more specific? I asked in return.

Yes. Did you like her? Was she nice to you?

Yes, I said, she was wonderful, even when I was hanging on to her apron begging her not to leave us, even when I was hiding behind the dresser, watching her jeer in my father's face, betting with my sister which of her eyes would get the first punch (I always bet on the left side), even when I was chasing a few flying dollar bills as she screamed, What am I supposed to buy with this? I am leaving you, Joseph. You feed the kids. Let your mother come and cook for them if you do not like my food, let her cook for you and your dumb, square-headed, filthy, retard kids. Or better yet, let the midget jockey of your losing horse come and feed them.

I told you not to mention the horses in front of the kids, Manduza, I continued, mimicking my father this time. I told you, my father huffed as I was losing my bet, watching my mother's kinky hair flying like the hair of a pony on the run.

So, do you love your mother? the therapist asked, pasting on her usual compassionate face.

Yes, I do, I said, thinking that if I told her anything more, I wouldn't leave this place for two hours. The shrinks are all big on mothers in this land.

The therapist nodded, leaned her chin on her fingers, cracked a spooky smile, and asked, Can you tell me about a happy incident with your mother?

Well, I cannot think of any now, professor. Excuse me. Maybe I should call you doctor?

Genevieve. Genevieve is fine.

Genevieve, I said. Well, if you give me some time for a long walk, maybe in the park across the street, among the trees, I will light a cigarillo somewhere around the war-hero statue, and consult with the pigeons and the begging squirrels. I might be inspired and be able to get back to you next time with wonderful stories.

Was your mother nourishing? Genevieve asked.

With food, you mean?

Well, okay, food. Let's talk about food.

I like food, I said. Though I worry about food shortages lately.

Did you have enough food in your youth? For now I am interested in your past.

Yes.

A lot of food? she asked.

Yes.

Hmmm. No shortage of food?

No.

You were always skinny like that?

Yes, yes, always.

Listen, she said and leaned my way, I am here to help you. You have to trust me. I am here because you need help. You have to tell me more about your childhood. Who did you play with? Did you have a dog? Did you climb trees?

Yes, I said. I climbed everything, trees, stairs, into windows and cars, whatever it took to . . .

To what?

To get things.

Like what things?

Like silverware, wallets, lipstick, whatever would sell, you know. I winked at Genevieve, but I must have aimed a little to the left because my wink bounced off a cheap reproduction of a Matisse painting of a vase and flowers.

You stole things.

Well yes, I did, I guess. But what kid does not steal?

Do you steal now?

I looked around, left my chair, opened the door, peered outside the room, waited for an African family with a feverish crying baby to pass down the corridor and shake hands with a pediatrician, and then I returned to my seat and said: Yes, sometimes. I said this in a low voice.

That's okay, Genevieve said. She cracked yet another big smile. That's okay. This is all confidential.

Confidential, I repeated.

She nodded, and reached out to take my hand, and squeezed. You can, and should, tell me anything and everything. I am here to help.

I held on to her fingers, and as our hands began to get warm, she pulled hers away slowly, fixed her glasses, straightened her skirt, shifted her legs, and sighed with what I hoped was triumph and relief. For no apparent reason, this made me curious about her past, her childhood of snow and yellow schoolbuses, quiet green grass and Christmas lights, her Catholic school that forbade flames, cigarettes, and orgasms. Had she waited for the bus like those girls I saw walking in short plaid skirts in forty-degree-below temperatures? Had she giggled when she saw cute boys? Had she, like my sister, played with herself under her bedclothes, had she bitten her lower lip as she ejaculated rivers of sweaty men?

But really, how naive and innocent this woman is, I thought. If she only knew what I am capable of.

AFTER MY THERAPY SESSION, I passed by the Artista Café and looked for the professor. He was just getting out of the bathroom, shaking his wet hands. I pulled a few napkins from a container on the counter and went over to him. There is never any paper to dry the hands, I said, and that blower is worse than a dying desert wind. I smiled in his face. He took the paper and dried his hands, not grateful but proud. *Vingt-cinq sous, mon professeur,* I said, and laughed and extended my hand towards him.

The professor paused and looked at me, not sure whether I was the joker, the beggar, or the bogeyman. Then I laid my hand on his pile of wet napkins and pulled one of them slowly, taking it back, gently but intensely, and I laid my other hand below his moist knuckles and put my mouth against his ear and whispered, Twenty-five cents or I shall make these napkins sweep up blood and tears from under our feet, professor.

The professor slowly reached inside his pocket and looked around and pretended to laugh, as if he had just heard a joke made while standing on luxurious carpet between opera acts, below large chandeliers, between the whites of two tuxedos. When he handed me what I had asked for, I became giddy and full of love, and I ran out into the cold looking for a city phone that was not too far away and not too noisy from which to call my beloved.

Shohreh answered the phone and agreed to meet me in a café for a coffee that afternoon.

In the café I made Shohreh laugh by imitating Reza's nasal voice and wobbly walk. I told her that the conservative coke-head had refused to give me her phone number because, as he put it: She is not that kind of girl. She is Iranian, she is like a sister to me.

Sister! Sister! That hypocrite! Shohreh exclaimed. He was

so desperate to sleep with me he even offered to marry me. I refused his offer, of course. No, no Iranian men for me anymore. I am sick of them, they are all mama's boys; they want their houses to be cleaned and their meals on the table. She lit a cigarette and slammed the package onto the table next to her coffee cup.

I can live in filth and hunger, I assured her. My mother lives far away, and if we ever get married, no one has to clean because I can tolerate filth, cockroaches, and mountains of dishes that would tower above our heads like monumental statues, like trophies, testifying that we value lovemaking and a hedonistic existence, and that all else can wait! And even if you were my sister, I wouldn't mind hearing your most intimate fantasies.

Shohreh laughed and called me crazy. You are so dirty, she said softly, and suddenly her long, black hair fell away from her face, her thick, arched eyebrows smiled at me and pierced my chest, her laugh escaped her and slapped me in the face, kicked me in the gut, mopped the floor with my hairy chest, dipped me in sweat and squeezed my heart with unbearable happiness. I will sleep with you, said Shohreh, but you have to tell Reza all about it. Reza and his like need to understand, once and for all, that I am not their virgin on hold, not their smothering mother, not their obedient sister. I am not a testament to their male, nationalistic honour.

I will! I will! I shouted, and I mimed Reza's reaction upon hearing all about it. I stood up and did his baffled eyebrows, his itching armpits, and his squeaky voice like a mouse in a trap. Shohreh laughed again.

I took her home, showed her my tiny place, and we both removed our shoes and hunted cockroaches down the sink, swimming and sliding in mildew, and slapping them with the heels of our shoes, and I told her how, when Jesus comes and kills all us sinners and beams up the faithful towards his immaculate kingdom, only those insects will survive. They shall inherit the earth, I said. The two ladies with the hats assured me of it. This made Shohreh enraged by the unfairness of it all. It reminded her of how her country had also been left to the cockroaches, and this inspired her to pound and kill more of those eternal minuscule beasts as if they were the cause of her lost life, her imprisonment, her executed uncle, her tortured friends, her own exile. These are the filth of the land, she shouted as she pounded away. They should be eradicated!

Then we rolled in dirt and made love in dirt until dirt became our emblem, our flag to pledge allegiance to, and we got drunk and composed new anthems with groans and the heavy exhaling and inhaling of breath. Yes, baby, yes, slap away! escaped our throats, and between every scream Shohreh reminded me to take notes and tell Reza how she welcomed me in her mouth, how she closed her eyes and glutted herself on me with the appetite of a clergyman, how naked we were as we danced. My underwear! I almost forgot! she shouted. Make sure you describe it to that musician: its colours, the sturdy thong that stretches like one of his strings and vibrates with sublime acoustics that resonate inside my chamber. Tell him how I undressed you, and how I sucked on your nipples like grapes, and how warm, gummy drips crept down my thighs like lava. Here, lie down so I can take hold of you and print it all in your psyche so you will remember it for the rest of your life. Let's rush and do it before those crawling creatures surface again and forbid me from showing my hair, from holding my lover's arm in public, from singing on the roof a lullaby to my sleeping nephew, from dipping my naked youth in clear rivers, from savouring with my lips my grandmother's Shiraz. Do not forget anything, tell him all about it. Maybe I should leave you with a scar. Hand me that knife so I can cut your arm, so I can suck some of your burgundy blood and mix it with wine, so I can stomp on the heart of that melody to the rhythm of villagers stomping in forgotten pools of grapes and tears.

A WEEK LATER, I found Reza at last. He was walking down the street, sniffing left and right for a filling tune or an inspiring meal. I ran towards him and grabbed his hand and pulled on one of his fingers, and before he had a chance to pull it away I said, I am hungry as well, you drooling beast. And one day I will snap your finger and let you pluck those strings with your yellow teeth.

Reza shouted at this, warning me never to touch his fingers again. He lifted them up against the cold and stuck his thumb towards the sky and pointed and shouted at me, If you touch them again, I will take you back to your goat dunes!

Then we walked along the street together and ended up at my place. I made some tea and asked him for my money. He promised and whined and puffed cigarettes and had the gall to ask me for food. And so, filled with revenge and spite, I told him about my tryst with Shohreh.

That made him furious. He accused me of going behind his back. He said that I was not his friend. Then he smiled and charged me with fabricating lies. If you talk like that, he said, you will ruin the girl's reputation. A good Iranian woman like Shohreh would never do that kind of thing.

I ran to my closet and pulled out her underwear. Smell it, I said. Smell! It is still warm, sizzling. Hot! I added. It smells like her. Here, bring your fat nose closer.

Disgusting liar, Reza shouted, and tossed the underwear out of my hand.

I threw myself onto my bed and flipped the pillow over. Here, I shouted back. That long, black, straight hair could only have come from a Persian princess. Reza turned red with rage and stood up and left, calling me a liar and a looooney.

I STILL HAD NO MONEY, and therefore I had no food. When one is hungry, one should steal. That's what Abou-Roro the thief, our neighbour back home, used to tell me. He taught me the trade. I am not sure how he became so good at it. He was the son of a shoemaker and his father had a tiny place between two old buildings, just big enough for the metal last, a hammer, a few leather pieces, glue, and the tiny nails he stored in his mouth. As a kid, I looked up to Abou-Roro. I watched him filling his fists with pistachios when the grocer was grinding the coffee. I watched him slip lettuce inside his jacket and cheat little kids on the street out of their marble balls and allowances. I admired him even though I knew he was a coward. He always avoided direct confrontation. During the war, he befriended a few militiamen for protection. He did them favours, washed their cars, cleaned their rifles, fetched them food. The bastard had a square head, flat feet, and googly eyes. He looked like a mini-Frankenstein, but he could detect power and kneel to the powerful. When the port went ablaze during the war, he took me down to the burning warehouses. We crossed under the snipers' bullets, through the fire. We entered the warehouses and reached for the merchandise, the mountains of boxes and goods waiting to be transported to the Saudis. We shredded through them with our claws and knives. There were boxes of soap, flashlights, perfumes, cloth, boxes of lighters, but we took only the cameras and ran back through whizzing bullets. We sold everything, and Abou-Roro always stiffed me out of my share. He took the biggest piece and threw me the crumbs.

Talking about crumbs, a nice sandwich would do me fine, I thought. Perhaps I could go to a restaurant nearby, enter it, and sweep up the little pieces of bread and other leftovers on the tablecloth, and then follow the trail of crumbs to the counter next to the kitchen and help myself to some of the warmth released from the toaster. But I know how hard it is to steal food in restaurants. Restaurants have many barriers you must cross before reaching the fridge or the salad counter. There is the manager and the maître d', and then the waiter and the cook and his helpers. And let's not forget the variety of knives that can be pulled out and waved around to protect the food from the looting of man, to protect the chicken legs and sizzling, juicy stuffed ducks. Just imagine, I laughed, a stuffed duck à l'orange! And I laughed again as I went downstairs and out onto the street and entered the closest available food source.

I greeted the Korean grocer at the counter and went straight to the beer fridge. I picked up a few bottles and put them on the counter. Then I pointed to a package of cigarettes behind her back and confused the lady by shifting my pointing finger, telling her left, down, and up all at the same time. As she looked for the package like a distracted dog, I leaned on the beer bottles, pushing them together to make loud noises, and simultaneously attacked the chocolate bars below the counter with my other hand. When she finally laid the package of cigarettes on the counter and started to ring the cash machine, I asked her if I could pay tomorrow. She stopped, grabbed the bottles and the cigarettes, and shouted, You pay noweh! You pay noweh! CASHEH! CASHEH! NOWEH. I cursed her and left the store with the chocolate bars in my pocket. I walked around the corner and into a back alley near an Indian restaurant.

It was freezing cold. But chocolate does taste better when it's cold. A chocolate connoisseur knows that chocolate at a certain temperature, exposed to the air to breathe, makes for a refined experience. I peeled the plastic delicately from the top of the bar. Then I opened it completely, threw away the paper, held the bar with two delicate fingers, and watched the freezing air do its work. I shifted my two fingers, making sure that the whole bar was exposed to the cold temperature. I started nibbling the middle, holding the bar like a harmonica. But one must take care to nibble the bar, not blow on it (I let the city wind do that). When I felt that the temperature was getting too low for the ingredients, I moved towards the exhaust of air that was coming out of the back of the Indian restaurant's kitchen. Now the experience would drastically change, not without some risk, of course. I held the open belly of the bar high up towards the steam, like an offering, and counted to ten. A chocolate bar masala, I called it. An exquisite delight direct from the Orient, it was!

No one should suffer in hunger, I thought as I nibbled. Though, to be frank, I only loved those who suffer. I loved Shohreh because she suffered. She had come to see me a couple of times now, and on one of the nights she brought a bottle of wine. She was happy, flirtatious. Short skirt. Low-cut blouse. Pulled-back hair. Red lips. She wanted to drink. She wanted to dance before I laid my hands on her. She asked me to play French songs. I turned the dial on the radio looking for songs. Leave that song on, she ordered me, and pulled my hand, leading me away from the window. Her arms around my waist, she said to me, Relax. I will lead.

I am not used to happy women. I am not used to slow dancing. When I dance, I fly and stomp. I go around in circles; my head rises like that of an ancient fighter. I shake the ground and the underground. In the presence of a sad, slow song I brood and let my long eyelashes reach to the floor. When my sister used to dance she would wrap a scarf around her waist, make me sit on the bed and watch her shaking her hips, barefoot. Once there was a song on the radio that she liked, and she stormed into our room and in the little space that was available between the beds she danced. That was when I realized how grown-up she was, how pretty and how attractive she had become. It saddened me, but also in my confusion and in her presence I felt an embarrassing erection. After that day, and I do not know why, we fought over everything: the bathroom, the water, the radio knob; at night we were quiet, and our fantasies collided on the bedroom wall.

I have had many lovers in my life. But what man has not? Mine all suffered, but what woman has not? Frankly, like I said, I do not feel comfortable with happy women, those who are obsessed with what my shrink calls intimacy. You have an intimacy problem, Genevieve had said, in one of her rare assessments of me.

Intimacy, I exclaimed. What intimacy? I do not understand you.

Like expressing love.

How? For whom?

Like saying something nice to a woman, or bringing her flowers.

So the day before our next meeting I stole some flowers and brought them to her.

She did not know how to react. She was uncomfortable. She laid the flowers on the table, without saying a word.

I stole them, I said.

You stole them?

Yes, I stole them for you.

That is interesting, she said, dismissing the act of theft and changing the subject: Do you want to tell me more about your childhood today? If we do not move forward, if we do not improve, I might have to recommend that you go back to the institution. Frankly, you do not give me much choice with your silence. I have a responsibility towards the taxpayers.

Tax prayers? I asked.

No taxpayers, people who actually pay taxes. Some of us do.

So, I will tell her stories, if that is what she wants. It's better than going back to the madhouse and watching robotic people move between iron beds, pacing the floor, lost between the borders of barbed wired on the windows and the hollow hallways, drooling, laughing, crying, and exchanging life stories with their own private audience. I would look at those people and see them watching their own little stages. Some of the performances, I thought, were genuine, spontaneous, and exquisite. Abstract, even a little esoteric, but nevertheless worth a peek. And frankly, I wouldn't mind seeing again that beautiful lady with green eyes who came for a few days. God, she was so pretty, even when she took off her clothes and ran naked through the room, leaking fluid down to her ankles and through her lovely toes, screaming at the top of her lungs, Freedom! Freedom! I followed her and then I lost her. Like a trapper, I tracked the little patches of urine that had gathered, like islands, on the hospital floor.

What do you want to hear? I asked my shrink.

Let's talk about your mother, she said.

My mother dragged my sister by the hair off our balcony and told her to stop parading her legs in front of the men down the street. Those low-life men leaned on parked cars, smoked, and laughed loudly. They obsessively cleaned and waxed their cars, and like a horny pack of wild dogs they smelled my sister's wetness and pointed at her breasts from behind their erect car hoods.

My sister was beautiful. I used to peek through the bathroom window and watch her in front of the mirror, playing with her wet hair, kissing the towels and brushing them across her face. She would put her hands under her breasts and twirl around. Holding her hairbrush to her face, she would sing to a large audience who came from all over the world to hear her tender voice, oblivious to her topless chest, her naked shoulders, because she, naturally, enchanted them with her graceful moves, her sparkling eyes, and her profound, sentimental voice. She was so enchanting that no clergy cared to object, no man in her presence had indecent thoughts about her, and no woman in the audience was jealous of her firm breasts, her generous, curly pubic hair, her long, wavy locks that covered her buttocks, her radish-coloured nipples. Not even my father cared that his daughter was naked on a stage — he knew that what was important was that she could sing, that she was respected, that she would never be preyed upon by some military man who would deflower her, eject sperm into her belly to inflate her uterus, swell her ankles, fill her bosom with milk.

But one of those men often stood below our balcony, dressed in his military uniform and boots. He carried a gun, and I could see him looking our way, smiling at my sister, stepping on the gas to make his sports car roar and fume. In return, my sister played with her hair, and on her way to the store she swung her hips, stopping in the middle of the street to look back in the direction of our balcony before walking towards the store again. The man with the sports car followed her. In the store he stood close to her and her timid smile, smelling her soapy hands and her hair ointment, examining the lines of the blade on her shaved legs. He pulled some change from his pocket and paid for the bag of goods in her hand. She hesitated and refused at first, but he insisted, calling her *Madame*. So my sister accepted his money, and he followed her home, inside our building and up the stairs, talking to her about beaches and fast cars. He asked her name and offered her a cigarette. She, beaming like headlights, agreed to meet him again, in secret, below the stairs, above the roofs, on a moon with little alleys. And eventually, when she ran out of excuses to go down to the street for fresh air, to meet her girl-friend, to buy sugar, to chase the cats in heat in the middle of the night, she eloped with the military man. He picked her up one night and drove straight to the priest. The priest refused to marry them; the girl is underage, he said. The man pulled out his gun and threatened the priest, made him sign the paper, and drove my sister back to his mother's house. There, after he finished his drink, he deflowered her, and when she asked for money to buy food he beat her.

And how do you feel about that? the shrink interrupted me.

I wanted to kill him, but I was young and he was older and stronger. Once, my mother sent me to my sister's house with some food. When my sister saw me, tears fell onto her cheeks, cheeks that, I noticed, had become round and fat like her belly that was inflated with a child. Her legs to her ankles looked straight as cylinders, she walked slowly with her hand against her back, and she did the dishes as she offered me coffee. Then we sat at the table, and she gazed in my eyes, caressed my hair, cried, and asked me about my father who did not come to see her, my mother who was mad at her, and the neighbours who talked behind her back. I stayed late to scoop her tears and watch her fingers floating towards my face. I closed my eyes and listened to the child in her belly. I was about to leave when we heard a Jeep stop outside, and doors slamming shut, and boots ascending the stairs.

My husband is here, my sister said, and she pulled her hand away from my hair and rolled her eyes. She rushed to set the table, tossing plates like a poker player tosses cards, throwing forks and knives in the air like a circus magician, lighting fires like a primitive in a cave, and sweeping onion-tears from her eyes.

The man was welcoming to me. When he saw me, he shouted, *Ahlan be ibn alaam* (welcome to the brother-in-law). He patted my shoulder and offered me cigarettes. We ate on the balcony and he poured whisky for both of us, and called my sister to bring more ice, cucumbers, and fresh almonds. When my sister told him that she did not have all this, he cursed her. He cursed womankind, and the hour when he had kidnapped her, and the priest who let him marry her.

How did you react? the shrink asked.

I did not say a thing. I kept silent. I should have said something. But I did not.

Why?

Because my sister looked at me. I knew that look: she was telling me not to say a word, not to interfere. I wanted to leave, but the man grabbed me. He persuaded me to stay. He wanted someone to drink with. He insisted. In the end, he even ordered me to stay. He cursed God and swore at the angels. We poured whisky while my sister cooked in the kitchen. Then, after many drinks, he pulled out his gun and started shooting in the air. None of the neighbours complained or stuck their heads out their windows or went into the street in their slippers and cotton pyjamas to look for cadavers or moaning men. There, everyone is used to gunshots. Shooting in the air is a public statement, a celebration of birth, a farewell to the dead, and private words with the gods.

Here, my brother-in-law said. Shoot the fucking passing angels. Here. He changed the gun's magazine and handed it to me. Wait, he said. Let me crank it for you.

I can crank it myself, I said.

Let the boy do it! he shouted with pride, and hugged my shoulders. Here, soon you will be an uncle. And he kissed my sister on the cheek and grabbed her hips. She moved her face away from his whisky breath, his unbalanced feet, his scratchy moustache, and nicotine-stained teeth.

And we will teach this baby boy how to use a gun, right? He caressed my sister's belly.

Our time is up, said the shrink. But I want to hear all about it on our next appointment. How is Thursday for you?

TAXPAYERS, THE SHRINK SAYS. Ha! I thought as I finished my chocolate in the alley. Well yes, yes indeed, I should be grateful for what this nation is giving me. I take more than I give, indeed it is true. But if I had access to some wealth, I would contribute my share. Maybe I should become a good citizen and contemplate ways to collect my debts and increase my wealth. That would be a good start. And who still owes me money but that loud string-plucker with a chicken beak and the fatherless soul of a musician? And then I remembered that every Friday the forty-dollar thief by the name of Reza played at an Iranian restaurant on the west side of the city. He hated it. He thought playing at a restaurant was the worst kind of job for a talented, respected musician like himself. But now I knew how to track him down.

On Friday evening I went to the restaurant. It was a fancy restaurant with all the ornament necessary to transport you to the East. It surrounded you with dunes, lanterns, and hand-made carpets that matched the brown plates flying from the waiter's hands onto woven tablecloths.

I sat at the bar. The owner came over and asked suspiciously, How can I help you?

I am waiting for the musician, Reza, I said. Still the owner looked suspiciously at my clothing that clashed with the fancy surroundings. Reza saw me, but he ignored my presence and continued playing with the other Iranian musicians. When they stopped for a break, he came to me, leaned towards my face, and quietly whispered, You should never come here unless you are going to sit and eat. He said this with aggravation.

Pay me what you owe me, brother, and maybe I will sit and eat.

What I owe you is not enough for you to have a tea here. And you come dressed like that.

Pay me and I will leave.

Okay. I am getting paid at the end of the evening. Do you want to go away and come back around eleven?

No, I have no place to go around here. I am not going to pay bus fare twice, and it is very cold outside.

Okay then, stay here. I'll tell you what: Sit at the end of the bar, and do not look at the women like that. People here do not like it when a bum like you is checking out their wives and daughters like that. I will get you a drink. Just wait and be invisible.

Reza walked towards the owner, bent his large body towards the man's ear, and apologetically rubbed his hands together, explaining everything with a smile. They talked in Persian, both glancing my way from time to time. Finally, the owner approached me and snapped in a dry voice, So, what would you like to drink?

A Coke, I said.

The owner nodded, agreeing that I had made a good choice — the cheap choice and the respectable choice. But what I really wanted was a good glass of whisky on the rocks. And what I really, really wanted was to sit in the middle of the bar and rotate my liquor in time to the soft music, maybe a big fat golden ring on my finger, my chest gleaming under a black shiny shirt, my car keys dangling from a gadget that could open doors and beep and warm the driver's seat despite the cold snow. I wanted a gold chain around my neck and a well-dressed woman with kohl under her eyes, and a late-evening blow job that began in a big fancy car and ended on an imported carpet with a motif of peacock tails fanning shades of purple against my hairy Arab ass.

Instead, the owner went behind the bar and got me my drink himself, calling me over with a nod as if signalling to one of his waiters. You stay here, he muttered.

I sat on a bar stool in the corner, close to the kitchen, and twirled the ice in my drink with a plastic straw. The soft music in the background, the dim lighting, the glowing red from the lanterns, and the gold atmospheric ornaments made me think of the story of the virgins who had lost their lives in the king's castle before Scheherazade distracted him with her tales of jinn and fishermen. I wondered whether, if I had happened to live back then (wearing a different outfit, naturally), I could have saved any of those women. Maybe I could have been the saqi who slipped a few poison drops from my ring into the king's wine. And as I watched him writhe in agony from the spell in his stomach, right before he fumbled another innocent girl, I could have stuck a dagger through his silky purple robe, opened his poisonous entrails, and watched his eyes flicker in awe and disbelief as he anticipated the next and final episode. The smell of food from the kitchen brought me back to the land of forests and snow. And then all I wished was to crawl under the swinging door and hide under the stove, licking the mildew, the dripping juice from the roast lamb, even the hardened yogurt drops on the side of the garbage bin. With my pointy teeth, I thought, I could scrape the white drips all the way under the floor.

When Reza was done playing, he came and sat with me. We were both silent. He leaned on me and said, they are closing in another half-hour. When I get paid, we leave. We watched the employees folding the tablecloths, sweeping up glass, turning the chairs upside down on the tables, sucking the carpets with electric hoses, and mopping the kitchen floor. All the crumbs, all the loose bits of food that had jumped during the evening from the cook's knives and tilted plates — all that had flown and landed on the ground, all that had sizzled and escaped the rims of giant pans, all that had been transported by gravity and chased by giant brooms and battered by wet sweeping, all that had been expelled into the hollow of drains in thin, calm waves of grease and water — now fell into underwaged fists and made me sob.

The owner came out from behind the bar and silently took my glass from me, opened the cash register, called over the musicians, and paid them one by one.

When that was done, I approached the owner with humility, my back hunched, my hand below my chin and close to my chest. I said: Excuse me, sir. May I ask you something?

He barely nodded, not looking at me.

Sir, I am looking for a job.

The owner automatically lifted his head at this, and looked me in the eyes. Do you have any experience? he asked, and then bent his head back towards his money.

Yes, I do. I can work as a waiter, I said.

I have waiters, he replied. Do you speak Farsi? Some of my customers want to be served in Farsi here.

No, but I can work as a busboy. I am very good at it. I

have the experience. Ask my friend Reza here. I worked in a fancy French restaurant here in Montreal, Le Cafard, on Sherbrooke Street.

Reza was annoyed at me for saying that. I could see his raised eyebrows. He stood up, turned his back, and walked towards the door with his instrument case, zipping through the erect upside-down legs of the chairs on the tables.

Come back on Tuesday, said the owner. We can talk.

Thank you, I said, and retreated by walking backwards, my face to his highness, my turban bowing repeatedly, until I reached the royal gates, and opened them from behind my back with an awkward twist of the wrist of my left hand, in the process fumbling against the glass with its Visa card stickers that reminded me of the world outside and the cruelty of the cold.

Outside, Reza was silent and brooding and nervously smoking, and smoke shot out of him like straight arrows, splitting their exit between his nostrils and his tight lips. Finally he couldn't hold in his words any longer. As soon as the last of the smoke had left his chest he ground his voice at me: How could you do that? First you come in just like that, to this respectable place, dressed like a bum. And just look at your shoes. And then, and then — he stuttered with anger — and then you ask the man for a job and you tell him to check with me as a reference. Well, if he had asked me, I would have told him what a deranged, psychotic, spaced-out case of a petty, unsuccessful thief you are.

Give me back my money! I shouted at him. You are the only thief here. How many meals did you get from those Canadian women with your sad stories?

Reza took off his gloves, biting them with his teeth, and dug his fingers into his tight pants and pulled a few dollars from his pocket. He counted his money and gave me a twenty-dollar bill.

Forty, I said, and I was ready to kill for it. You owe me forty. And I was about to pull out my curved dagger, poison his drink, make sure he was dead, and then escape towards the sun on a rug woven by flying camels.

Ah, right. Forty. Relax, here is your money, said Reza. Now I am meeting Shohreh in the Crescent Bar. Are you coming? And by the way, I shouldn't pay you after what you did to that innocent girl.

Who? Who? I said.

You know who. Shohreh! he shouted. You took advantage of her.

Hypocrite! I shouted back. You always wanted her for yourself. Well, too late, musician of doom. She is mine now.

Mine, Reza laughed. No one would keep you, deranged man.

Carpet musician, I retorted.

Fridge thief. Are you coming or not? he asked and walked away.

Yes, I am coming, I said. Because I am sure she wants to see *me* tonight.

WE ENTERED THE BAR and I saw Shohreh sitting at a table with a man, an older man with a moustache and grey hair. Reza looked around for his drug dealer. When he found him, he bought some "baby powder," as he put it, and then he came back my way. Do you want a line? Just to show you what a nice guy I am.

I will consider it interest on my money, I said.

Ungrateful bitch, Reza said, and wobbled his way to the bathroom. I followed him. He pulled out his credit card, sprinkled the powder on top of the counter's white ceramic, and cut it into vertical lines. He pulled out a brand new five-dollar bill, rolled it up tight, and gave it to me. I stuck the money in my nose, and like a rhino I charged and snorted a line before the elephant beside me could change his mind. As I moved to the tip of the second line, Reza leaned his big body over my shoulder, pushed me against the wall, and dove like a kamikaze towards the shiny white counter. He vacuumed up the rest of the white stuff, opened the door, pinched his nostrils, and swayed his way out of the bathroom onto the dance floor.

I walked towards Shohreh's table, very awake, with a numb upper lip that felt as solid and stretched out as an elephant's trunk. As I passed the bar, I picked up a few peanuts and clapped my hands, and continued through the crowd to my love. Before I reached her table, however, Shohreh got up and met me. She took my hand and we started to dance. I danced with confidence, my forehead lifted high towards the sparkling mirror ball that beamed over us with its happy light.

Who is the guy? I asked Shohreh.

A friend.

He looks more like an uncle.

No, he's just a friend.

Well, he just sits there, brooding through the loud boom-booms, smoking like he is about to recite poetry.

Well, actually, he could be a poet.

Ah! So he is a poet.

Do you want to dance or ask questions?

I am dancing.

Good.

While I danced, I looked at the man. Our eyes met. He turned his head, crushed out his cigarette, stood up, and walked towards us. He laid his hand on Shohreh's shoulder and said something in Persian to her. She answered with a brief nod, gave him a kiss on the cheek, and he left.

Reza danced alone. He was happy and energetic, and like a bear his large body secured a void around it. When I squeezed Shohreh towards me and slipped both hands onto her torso, she pushed me away and danced alone. And then slowly she drifted away, and disappeared into the middle of the crowd.

I walked to the bar and bought myself a drink. A hand rested on my shoulder and someone laid a kiss on my cheek.

Farhoud, you man-killer, you should buy me a drink first, I said to him.

He laughed and asked: Is Shohreh here?

Yes — over there. I pointed at the dance floor. Farhoud danced towards Shohreh, and when she saw him she jumped up and down with joy, and moved into his arms.

Though I was filled with energy and the music became even more intense and energizing, I did not dance. Instead I went and sat at Shohreh's table on the same chair the poet had occupied. I smoked and watched the women dancing. Many were young and good-looking. I searched the dance floor until my eyes alighted on a woman dancing barefoot, her shoes swinging in her hand. She laughed and danced in a circle of girlfriends. I watched her and smoked. When she left the dance floor, I stood up, followed her to the bathroom, and waited at the door. When she came out, I faced her with a smile, blocking her way as she tried to squeeze her shoes between my ankle and the wall. She looked at the floor. She pushed her right shoulder against mine. In my high state, with my elephant's head and my ever-growing numb lips, I dipped my arm, swung it like a dangling lasso, and seized her wrists. She stopped pushing and lifted her head. Her face rose from beneath her hair, delicate, cautious, and still.

I like the way you dance barefoot, I said. Excuse me, I did not mean to scare you, but I saw you dancing without your shoes and it reminded me of dancing gypsies.

Do you know any gypsies? she said.

Yes, my sister is one.

Your sister, but not you?

I can't dance like her. So I guess I do not qualify as one.

I dance like a gypsy?

Yes. Will you take off your shoes again?

I will.

I wish I was a gypsy like you or like my sister, I said.

Well, you stole my arm like a gypsy, she said, as she slowly pulled away her arm and walked towards her friends. She must have told them about me because they all looked my way. They formed a shield, a circle of human hair balancing on heels. Some of them were barefoot. In the middle of the circle of sweat and flesh that flashed and disappeared through strobes of light I saw those girls laughing, and I felt ashamed to be a hand-thief and a gypsy-lover.

I looked away, and I saw Shohreh's wide brown eyes watching me. I knew she had seen everything. She turned her head away. I went and sat next to her, and she ignored me. She stood up immediately and went to the bathroom.

Later that night, I walked Shohreh back home. She lived down the hill, towards the train tracks. She told me that she had ambivalent feelings about trains. When a train passed in the evening, she said, it made her sad.

When I asked her why, she held my chin and said, Well, there are some feelings that are only one's own. Then she ran towards a snowbank and threw snowballs at me.

I chased her and we threw snow at each other. I caught her by the coat and wrestled with her in the snow, both of us breathing hard, our eyes locked onto each other's. I crucified her wrists and moved my face towards her lips, but she moved her face away and said, Let go. Let go, she repeated, shaking her neck in the snow, dodging her face away from my lips.

I pressed her some more, and she turned and shook her whole body violently. Let go, you bastard. Now!

I still held her, not letting go. When I tried to hold her face between my palms, she liberated one of her hands and scratched my face, cursed me, and threw ice in my eyes. She pushed me into the snow and shouted, You fucking bastard, you fucking bastard, you let me go when I tell you to! And she ran down the hill and disappeared, cursing me in Persian into the cold night.

THE FOLLOWING THURSDAY morning, the sun shone again and I tossed off my quilt. I watched it suspended in the air for a moment before it fell again and joined its own shadow. I searched for my slippers and hurriedly washed my face, brushed my teeth, and covered myself in layers of underwear, cotton shirt, socks, and jacket. There were no cockroaches to be seen today. The brutal temperature must have driven them down south to the boiler room, looking for warmth and comfort. I searched for my shoes, but could not find them. Only one place left for them to hide: I slipped under the bed and crawled across the floor, but found only one shoe. So I took a deep breath and squeezed myself under the dresser to find the other shoe. I laid the pair out on the cold floor and cleaned off the dust I had collected on my body everywhere — even on my chest and eyelashes.

As I walked towards the clinic for my appointment, I was still picking dust off my clothing and my face. I stood outside the window of a clothing store and looked at my reflection, now appearing like a ghost against layers of displayed and suspended cloth. I turned and shifted against the store window and watched my reflection clad in the latest fashionable cuts and colours. I captured the last dustball and held it in my fingers with a mixture of amusement and cruelty. I let it fret against gusts of wind and then released it, watching it leave confused, pain-struck, and disoriented in the whistling air, which sounded like mournful trains and sirens of war howling at the sight of fighter planes that descend and ascend and tumble in the air and land and freeze on the ground like insects with metal wings, like a child's toys in the bath brought back to the surface by the small hands of an invisible hero or tossed out and hidden under a wooden dresser until they are forgotten and invaded by dustballs, deserted in favour of the call for food and the threats of giant mothers.

When I told the shrink that I had arranged a job interview at a restaurant on Tuesday, she was delighted. She clasped her hands against her chest, her eyes open wide like a mother looking at her child onstage in a kindergarten play, a child dressed as a bee and buzzing around a flower with another child's face, singing springtime songs.

Tell me more, she said, smiling. That is such wonderful news. It will be such a good step for you to reintegrate into society.

Well, nothing is definite yet, but I feel I would like to work in that place. To start, I know that I would have food to eat, and the under-the-table tips would be good, something to add to my welfare cheque.

You must tell me if you get it. This will be a good step, a very good step in your assessment, she added. Now, where were we on our last session? Yes, here, I wrote a few notes after you left. Your sister . . . you were telling me about your sister and her husband, I believe.

Well, I can't really remember exactly where I left off. Could you read the last few lines for me?

Yes, you felt helpless to defend your sister from her husband's aggression. What was the man's name, by the way?

Tony.

Tony, she said. Okay, Tony.

Are you going to write it down, before you forget? I asked.

No, that's okay. Later. So, tell me more.

Well, doctor...

Genevieve. Call me Genevieve.

Yes, Genevieve. I feel as if I do not know you and here you are, asking everything about me. But who are you? I mean, you are silent most of the time. You remind me of priests in the confession booth. Nodding all the time, and then telling us to go kneel and mumble a few prayers for a virgin, and one for a man with a beard. You know?

Did the priests hit you?

Well, of course. Sometimes.

Did they do anything else?

Like what?

Like maybe asking you for something or touching you?

No, not that I remember.

Okay. So, your sister?

Well, my mother went to the hospital for the delivery of my sister's baby. This was the first time my mother met Tony.

Yes, Tony. The shrink wrote the name down this time.

Tony, I said. He was in the room when my mother came in. He was smoking next to the window. And my mother, the first thing she said to him was to go smoke outside.

He hid his cigarette behind his back and extended his arm to my mother, and when she ignored him, he smiled at me to show her what good terms he was on with me. Then he walked outside the room and smoked in the hallway with the rest of the fathers.

Was your father there?

No.

He did not come?

No.

Okay, go on.

Well, my sister had a girl. And Tony wanted a boy to shoot guns with. My sister called her Mona.

What kind of work did Tony do?

I'm not sure, really. He joined the militia at one point and he would disappear for a few days every now and then, and then he'd come back. At first, when he made money, I suspected it was because he was in charge of some kind of racketeering. People feared him because he was allied with the people in power. He always had guns.

How did your sister feel about that, guns with a baby in the house?

With a baby in the house? The baby does not understand about guns. What would the baby care?

Yes, but . . .

Maybe what my sister wanted was a fighter. Maybe she wanted to bring a fighter into this world.

Nietzsche!

What?

Nothing. Go on, please.

Well yes, things are different there. Some people had guns over there at the time.

Did you carry a gun?

Yes, later on I did. And I tell you, if I had a gun with me here, I wouldn't have looked for a rope and a branch.

Why didn't you get one?

I did not know where to get one in this land. And I did not have any money! I raised my voice.

The shrink was silent. I was silent. I looked her in the eye. She looked back at me. Neither of us moved.

She finally blinked and said: You might get a job. Then you could afford one.

I got up, opened the door, and left. The shrink did not follow me. She did not call me back. That woman is living in la-la land, I thought.

I went downstairs and waited at the entrance to the clinic, and as I waited I paced. I smoked and watched the newcomers to this land dragging their frozen selves into the elevator of this poor neighbourhood's clinic, where they would wait in line, open their mouths, stretch out their tongues, inflate their lungs under the doctor's stethoscope, breathe the names of uncles with tubercular chests, eject their legs like pompom girls, say "Ahh" with an accent, expose the whites of their droopy, malarial eyes, chase their running noses, wives, and imaginary chickens . . . I checked my watch. It was around four-thirty. At five, a few employees started to leave the clinic. I imagined the white ghosts of their aprons hung by the neck on the back of their office doors. I positioned myself in a corner close to the elevator and waited for the therapist. For Genevieve.

When she passed, I did not recognize her at first. She had covered herself with a dark coat. But then I recognized her ankles and shoes, and I followed her. She walked from Côte-des-Neiges towards Outremont. I crawled behind her and six legs appeared from my sides like external ribs, and a newly thick carcass made me oblivious to the splashing water from passing cars. No element of nature could stop me now.

It was a long crawl. I noticed that Genevieve did not seem cold. Some creatures are oblivious to the heat and the cold wind, I thought as I crawled behind her toes. She did not stop to buy supper, or even bread and butter. She lived in a rich neighbourhood with shop windows displaying expensive clothing and restaurants that echoed with the sounds of expensive utensils, utensils that dug swiftly into livers and ribs and swept sensually above the surface of yellow butter the colour of a September moon, a cold field of hay, the tint of a temple's stained glass, of brass lamps and altars, of beer jars, wet and full beneath wooden handles that gave me a thirst for an executioner's hands, for basement doors and the downward swing of falling boats, sailor's knots, and ropes stretched around gulping, gorging, foaming throats, sounding calls for the last meal, the last count, the last sip before the return of the sun.

I saw where Genevieve lived, and then I crawled home.

THE NEXT DAY, FRIDAY, I woke up early. I returned to Genevieve's place and watched her leave her house for work. Then I slipped past the building's garage door, went down to the basement, and crawled along the pipes. I sprang from her kitchen's drain, fixed my hair, my clothes, my self, and walked straight to her bedroom. On the bedside table were a few prescription pills, some books and magazines. A painting of a naked lady in an intimate, yet unrevealing, position hung above the bed. She had a large bed, unmade. I crawled up onto it and sniffed her pillow and bathed in the scent of her sheets. I found a spot that was still warm. I measured it, speculating that the weight of her torso gave it that curved shape (I am fond of torsos, the arched ones that stretch like endless valleys between soft green hills). I curled up and rolled like a kid down the hills. I covered myself with a sheet, inhaled, and wept a little under clouds of cotton and the blue sky. Then I made Genevieve's bed and lay on my back and looked around her room. I wanted to see what she saw before taking off her glasses, before she closed her eyes for the day. What if I were to stay here, in her bed? I thought. What if she comes home and sees a considerate stranger who makes the bed and saves the other side for her to slip her toes into as she asks me if I am asleep, if I had a good day, kissing my forehead, hoping that I will wake up, take her in my arms, listen to her story about the man who was caught with a rope on a tree looking for a solid branch, in the park, early on a cold day, on a sunny day, and how he confided that he had had the best cup of coffee that morning, and he insisted that he wanted to escape the sun, and why the sun, what is wrong with the sun, *mon amour?* Can you tell me before you sleep? Can you ignore the desire to stroke my inner thighs, can you please listen to me after my long day in the office nodding to battered wives, impoverished immigrants, depressed teenagers; I need you to listen to me . . .

The stranger stood up and walked to the kitchen, opened the fridge; it was filled with food — French cheeses, ham, and eggs. He made himself some toast, pasted on some ham and tomato slices, dropped a few thin sheets of cheese on top, decorated it all with lettuce, and moved to the living room with a large plate in his hand. As he ate, he examined souvenirs, figurines, pottery, travel books, and coffee-table books. He opened the pages of a large, heavy photography book. Then he picked up a book on Weegee, with its photographic work from the forties and fifties. He ate his ham sandwich and examined Americans dancing the cha-cha, poor people working, kids with hunched shoulders smiling under the fountains of fire hydrants, and then images of murders, people stabbed, shot in the face, men stretched out bleeding, a dead man lying under the shiny shoes of inspectors, and curious hats gathered to watch the dead, many men with round hats, spectators, some even smiling at the camera. He flipped the pages again and again, looking at well-dressed men lying shot, with open arms, as if still calmly breathing through their blood-covered faces. And the stranger laughed at one caption under a photograph that said: "Here he is left in the gutter." "Dead on arrival," another caption said. But the stranger was intrigued most of all by the one that said: "Their first murder." The image showed a crowd of kids and adults, a close-up of their faces. The photographer must have been very close to the crowd, thought the stranger. Some of the kids were even laughing and playing and stretching their heads towards the lens, and in the background a woman, surrounded by the crowd of kids, was crying.

The stranger finished his sandwich, picked up every crumb and put it on the plate, and closed the book. He thought about murders, about how all nations are built in the image of a murder. Then he noticed a pair of slippers faithfully waiting in the middle of the dining room for Genevieve's toes to come back, wiggle inside the slippers' bellies, fuse into one another and slip over the wooden floor in the sequences and stops and waltzes of virgins and princes, to the accompaniment of string quartets (and trays carrying sandwiches of ham, tomatoes, a few thin sheets of cheese, decorated with lettuce) and large fancy chandeliers, and marvellous tables, marble and marvel, darling, and dancing white gowns turning towards bowing men, future officers, who shall bear arms and dance and dance like me... After the cockroach danced, so the tale goes, he lay down on the floor. He closed his eyes and rested his cheek on the slippers and acted dead (without a hat), smiling, then inhaling the faint smell of Genevieve's feet, aware of his own erection, satisfied with his full belly, feeling the soft carpet. With his many feet he caressed the floor beneath him and fell asleep.

When he woke up, he rose and picked up a portrait of Genevieve from when she was younger. She was hugging a handsome man with blond hair and good teeth, both of them smiling back at the intruder in the living room, not seeming to mind his presence, heads leaning in towards each other. In the background there was a blue beach glittering with pools of sunrays, which explained the need for the sunglasses that crowned the lovers' foreheads. The intruder, feeling at home, turned on the TV, put up his feet on the table, and watched the confessions of single ladies, sleazy men, and a talk-show host discussing relationships, sex, and betrayals. A large lady in a jogging suit was pointing her finger at an ex-boyfriend, saying, "He slept with my girlfriend, my mother, and my sister." And before the chairs started to fly on the stage, before the crowd cheered for blood, before there was hair-pulling and disorder, the stranger in the house decided to wear the slippers, go to the sink and clean the dishes, roll back the ham, cover the cheese, and put the lettuce back in the fridge. He opened the fridge again, drank some juice, then turned off the TV, left his tube of stolen lipstick, open and red, on the dining table, took the slippers, and left down the drain, hugging his loot, making sure that his prize did not get wet and was not touched by the mildew on the dripping walls.

ON TUESDAY MORNING, the day of my interview at the restaurant, I was awakened by the noise of my dripping faucet, a noise that persisted in its monotonous, torturous tune until it forced me to drag my feet to the kitchen, put my grip on the faucet's neck, and twist it into a permanent silence, that of a morning lake. And in the same spirit of cruelty, I reached for my slippers and pounded the walls above the sink, flattening a few early risers.

I decided to smoke a cigarette before going to meet the restaurant owner as promised. I also decided to take a shower and walk all the way to my meeting. In the shower, my big toe touched the drain, feeling the stream of water running through it. I also felt a vibration, the sound of the drain gulping like a quenched throat on a hot summer day. I got out of the shower and rubbed my skin with the towel. I walked naked around my bathroom, looking in the mirror behind the door. I combed my hair. Under a certain oblique angle of light I could see the scar on my face. Shohreh had asked me about it once, and touched it with her thumb as if trying to erase it. I told her that I had fallen.

It is a cut, she said.

I fell on something sharp, I answered.

She dropped her hand from my face and said, So, you do not want to talk about it.

Many people in my life had asked me about it, but no one had touched it before, maybe because it looked fragile, as if it was about to burst wide open and spray a fountain of blood.

I looked for my socks, and goddamn it! They were still moist. I usually put them under the bedcovers and slept on top of them to dry them out, but last night I forgot and just tossed them on the floor. Perhaps I was thinking a little fresh air would do them good. I dug around in my laundry and found an older pair that were dry — dirty but dry. I put them on, reminding myself that, no matter what, I should not take off my shoes in the presence of a woman or the restaurant owner. That bastard of an owner has a nose for poverty. He knows well what a threat to his business an impoverished presence might be. The rich hate the poor, and they especially hate those whose odour surfaces like a cloud to overshadow the smell of cigarettes and hot plates or to overwhelm the travelling scent of an expensive perfume. Nothing corporeal, nothing natural, should emanate from a servant. A servant should be visible but undetectable, efficient but unnoticeable, nourishing but malnourished. A servant is to be seen, always, in black and white.

I walked down St-Laurent and approached the Artista Café. Inside it was foggy with smoke and warm breath, and the glass of the window dripped water. I stuck my face close to the glass (so as to see others and not my own ghostly reflection for once), and I moved my eyes left and right, searching to see if any lost immigrants had arrived. No one I knew was there yet, so I continued walking.

A merchant was sprinkling salt on the sidewalk like a prairie farmer. Taxis waited on the corners with their engines idling, precipitating fumes like underground chimneys. A falafel store on the corner sported a sign with neon hands and a swinging moustache, the hands slicing meat with the speed of light. A Portuguese used-clothing store hung churchgoers' dresses in the window, dresses suspended behind glass like condemned medieval witches. A little farther down, the street, gentrified now with a strip of chic Italian restaurants, was getting ready for the lunchtime specials.

I like to pass by fancy stores and restaurants and watch the people behind thick glass, taking themselves seriously, driving forks into their mouths between short conversations and head nods. I also like to watch the young waitresses in their short black dresses and white aprons. Although I no longer stand and stare. The last time I did that it was summer and I was leaning on a parked car, watching a couple eat slowly, neither looking at the other. A man from inside, in a black suit, came out and asked me to leave. When I told him that it is a free country, a public space, he told me to leave now, and to get away from the sports car I was resting against. I moved away from the car but refused to leave. Not even two minutes later, a police car came and two female officers got out, walked towards me, and asked for my papers. When I objected and asked them why, they said it was unlawful to stare at people inside commercial places. I said, Well, I am staring at my own reflection in the glass. The couple in the restaurant seemed entertained by all of this. While one of the officers held my papers and went back to the car to check out my past, I watched the couple watching me, as if finally something exciting was happening in their lives. They watched as if from behind a screen, as if it were live news. Now I was part of their TV dinner, I was spinning in a microwave, stripped of my plastic cover, eaten, and defecated the next morning just as the filtered coffee was brewing in the kitchen and the radio was prophesying the weather, telling them what to wear, what to buy, what to say, whom to watch, and whom to like and hate. The couple enjoyed watching me, as if I were some reality show about police chasing people with food-envy syndrome.

I thought, I will show this happy couple what I am capable of. One of the officers came back from her car, gave me back my papers, and said, You'd better go now if you do not want trouble. So I started to walk. And when I passed the man outside his restaurant, I spat at the ground beneath him and cursed his Italian suit. Then I crossed the street, entered a magazine store, flipped through a few pages, and came out again. I watched that same couple from behind the glass of the entrance to an office building. Now, all of the sudden, they had something to say to each other, so they had started to converse. And I watched the owner come to their table and talk to them as well. Excitement had been injected into their mundane lives. I bet they even got an apologetic complimentary drink on the house at my expense. Bourgeois filth! I thought. I want my share!

Finally the man stepped outside. He buttoned his blazer, put his hand in his pocket, pulled out his keys, and pointed a small electronic device at a blue BMW. The car responded, opened its locks, blinked its lights, and said, I am all yours, master, and all the doors are open for you. The man smoked a cigarette outside while he waited for his woman to exit the restaurant with a fresh-powdered nose. I crawled to the edge of the pavement, rushing with my many feet, my belly just above the ground; I climbed the car wheels, slipped through the back door, and waited on the floor. The man opened the door for his partner and slipped her fur coat in. From below I could see her fixing her hair in the mirror. They both buckled up. The car purred, and neither of them said a word for a while. When we reached the highway, the woman said something about the place, then something about the food. She asked the man if he remembered the owner's name. Alfonso, the man said. I believe I have his card here. He passed it to her. She glanced at it and threw it on the dashboard, and neither of them retrieved it. Then there was silence again. At last the woman said something about the other Italian place, the one they had gone to last time, with Helen and Joe. It is quieter there, she said. St-Laurent Street is becoming too noisy and crowded with all kinds of people.

I knew what the bitch meant by noisy and all kinds of people.

The man must have nodded or not responded.

He was the driver.

She was the driven.

I was the insect beneath them.

At last the car stopped, and the man reached for an electronic device. He pressed it and opened the garage door. I waited until they got out, until the car beeped, blinked, and burped again. Then I dragged myself along the garage floor, avoiding patches of oil from the car, manoeuvred around golf clubs, and slipped under the door and onto the house carpet. When the couple passed me by, I froze in a corner, watching their well-mannered feet.

The woman balanced on one foot and pulled down a stocking, giving her leg a lustier white, silky colour. The man was rotating ice in a whisky glass. He sat on the sofa, untied his tie, and flipped through the TV channels. She went up and then came down the stairs. Now she had on a nightgown, made of a kind of see-through material. And she had plump thighs, ones I had only glimpsed just above the knee at the restaurant. At the time I had been more distracted by the sight of the large plates of food. The woman asked the man if he was coming to bed, and the news anchor was silenced before he had the chance to finish the word "famine." And then both the man and the woman went upstairs and made noises, opening brass faucets and scrabbling toothbrushes against their gums. Their gargles and their spit rushed through the pipes to join the toilet flushes. I sat downstairs on the sofa and finished what was left of the man's drink. Then I went up the stairs, crawled up the bedroom wall, and from above I saw them sleeping, both on their sides. The bed was large and high above the floor, balanced by two small dressers filled with medicine bottles, hardcover books, earrings, and tissues. The woman's thighs were exposed now, and this gave me an uncontrollable urge to fly down and land on the bedsheets and extend my arms like two antennae and extract sweet nectar from between her open legs. She tossed around, exposing different shades of her long thighs. The man, his back to her, snored quietly.

I went and stood at the door of the bedroom. I watched them dream of suvs, cottages, and business deals, comparing dresses and cigars at high-end cocktail parties. I put myself inside the dreams and helped myself to a few shrimp cocktails and picked up a few hors d'oeuvres from the waitresses' drifting trays. I ordered another glass of whisky and rotated the ice inside it counter-clockwise to counter the stuffiness of the room. Then I followed the man with the expensive car to the bathroom at the party. As he knelt to wash his face I passed him, took a leak in a urinal in the wall, jiggled my organ, and made sure the last drop was out before slipping my penis back inside my trousers. I went back towards the hall and, without washing my hands, I pulled up my zipper and closed that dramatic scene.

At the couple's home I stole his gold ring, his cigarettes, a Roman vase, his tie, and his shoes (I took the time to carefully pick clothes that suited my dark complexion). Once I had finished checking myself in the mirror, I slipped under the garage door. And I crawled, glued to the wall, my insect's wings vertical now and parallel to the house's living-room window. Then I walked the dreadful suburbs. Along the beautifully paved roads I made my way through a few dentists' houses, computer programmers' lawns, executives' sailboats

covered in plastic and maple leaves, and all the while I feared
that golf clubs might escape the garages and swing in pairs
and chase me for a raise. But what I feared most of all was the
bark of dogs who smelled my unwashed hands.

As I walked away from the suburb, the dogs' barks went up
like the finale at a high-school concert. Filthy dogs, I will show
you! I said and ground my teeth. I pulled down the zipper on
my pants and crawled on my hands and feet like a skunk,
swaying from side to side and urinating on car wheels and
spraying every fire hydrant with abundance to confuse those
privileged breeds and cause an epidemic of canine constipa-
tion. Down with monotony and the routines of life! I laughed,
knowing full well that some dentist would soon be waiting for
his little bewildered bundle of love to get on with its business.
I laughed and thought: Some dentist will be late for trays of
paralyzing syringes and far from the reach of blinding lights
that hover above mouths like extraterrestrial machines
inspecting the effect of pain on humans trapped in pneumatic
chairs. And I rejoiced and howled (causing more confusion) at
the thought of a salesman stuck like a turtle in traffic, late for
his work, flipping through catalogues, rehearsing apologies,
and mumbling about dogs' damnation.

WHEN I ARRIVED at the Iranian restaurant for my interview, I
humbly knocked on the glass. A teenage girl walked to the
door and said from behind the glass, It is closed. We open only
for dinner.

I told her that I had an appointment with the owner. She

opened the door and let me in, saying that the owner would be back in fifteen minutes.

Can I wait for him at the bar? I asked.

The girl walked to the kitchen and informed the cook of my presence. The man peeped at me from a square opening, nodded to her, then ignored me and returned to his fire.

Are you the daughter of the owner? I asked.

Yes, how did you know? the girl said, and smiled at me.

I just know things.

What else do you know?

That you'd rather be somewhere else today.

Yeah, like where?

In bed, or hanging out.

She giggled.

No school? I asked her.

Not now, she said. In a few days it will start again.

School sucks, I said.

The girl nodded and laughed again.

I used to run away from school, I said.

And where did you go?

I hung out.

Yes, I like to hang out, too, she said.

Maybe we can hang out together, I said.

She smiled and did not answer.

I hang out with my skateboard in Old Montreal all the time, I said. You know, I jump over those stair rails on the government buildings.

No, you don't, she laughed.

Sure I do, I said. I wear baggy pants and my cap in reverse.

No, you don't.

Sure I do. I am only dressed like this today because I am meeting your father for a job.

My father will only hire you if you fear God. He says he only trusts those who fear God.

Do you like God? I asked her.

I don't know.

I do not like him, and I do not fear him.

Well, if you tell that to my father, he will never hire you.

It will be our secret, I said. Our first secret.

What is our second secret?

I will tell you if I am hired.

Okay, she said, and smiled with her head tilted towards the table. I'd better go now. My father will come soon. He does not like it when I talk to strangers.

Oh, is he jealous?

No.

Just afraid that his pretty daughter might run away with a stranger on a skateboard?

The girl laughed and walked away. A few minutes later the owner tapped on the window and the girl rushed to let him in. He entered, his bald head bowed and his hunched posture making him look as if he was about to sniff the floor or fall on his face. He did not say a word. He barely acknowledged the presence of his daughter and ignored me as I stood up to greet his most important presence. I said salaam in a semi-glossy monosyllabic chant.

He replied with a brief dry salaam and went straight to the kitchen. He disappeared for a while and then came back.

Without wasting time, he said: We open from Wednesday to Sunday. You can work as a busboy, Friday to Sunday. I do not need you more for now. You work for part of the tips and three dollars an hour. You stay until the end. At the end of the shift, you vacuum the floor and the carpets, you clean and mop the kitchen and the bathroom. Okay?

Okay, I said, nodding more than once.

Come Friday. Be here at three in the afternoon.

Thank you, I said.

And come dressed in a black suit and a white shirt only. And everything should look clean.

But of course, I said. Clean. Clean like the robe of God.

He gave me a quick look, half pleased, half suspicious.

I immediately put on a semi-fearful face, and a semi-pious one. I nodded only once, because there is only one god left. The rest were all slain while they enjoyed offerings of calves and poultry, while they were drunk on wine in the company of sirens and blind poets. Now everything on earth is mono-chromatic like snow. One, one single nod that goes up and down, like the extended hand of a zealous soldier, is all that we are allowed.

On my way out, I saw the daughter sitting at a table with a big smile. I winked at her. As I walked towards her like a Cyclops, she giggled with joy and fear. I twisted the doorknob, opened the door, and stepped outside into a world that looked flat, square, and one-dimensional.

III

I TOLD GENEVIEVE about my new job. She was happy, even touching my hand. Then she drew back fast, knowing full well that I was willing to take her hand and lead her to a spacious bed where we could always have the session in horizontal.

Why the austerity? I wanted to ask. Why this formality? Maybe all I ever needed to be cured was to be held by warm arms, above silky sheets, and fed by food in a full fridge, and gazed at from pillows, and feel my hair caressed. Maybe all these formalities, these thick clothes, this claustrophobic office, these ever-closed thighs and pulled-back hair are making me reluctant to open my innermost thoughts. I am thinking: Doctor, Genevieve, my luscious healer, my confessor, I confess to you that we should touch. Words have no effect on my skin, will never straighten my hair, won't make my fingers reach out, wet, to explore triangles of pubic hair and soft red cracks, hollows of sensitive secret spots. Words, my love, keep tongues busy with dry air and clacking noise, words are what keep us away from the sources of liquid and life. There must be some branch in therapy where silence is encouraged and touch is the answer.

Tell me more about the job, Genevieve said. Tell me how it happened.

I went inside and waited, I replied. I talked to the daughter of the owner because the owner was not there.

How old is the daughter? Genevieve asked.

Maybe sixteen. I'm not sure.

And what did you talk about?

Skateboarding.

Was she nice?

She giggled.

You made her laugh?

Yes.

Let me look at my notes, Genevieve said, dismissing my attempt at joy and laughter. Okay, so last time when you burst out of the office — do you remember that? You were telling me about your sister and her husband, Tony.

Yes, I was telling you that.

Do you want to go on with that?

I'm not sure where I left off.

Tony had a gun.

Yes, almost everyone did. I mean, many people did.

That is interesting. And how do you feel about guns?

A gun could be useful.

For what?

To get things, accomplish things, defend things.

It will be by means of force — you realize that?

It's not wrong if there are no other options, I said.

You are not a pacifist, I assume?

Pacifism is a luxury, I said.

Can you elaborate?

No, I can't. Well, yes. I mean, you have to be well off to be a pacifist. Rich or secure like you. You can be a pacifist because you have a job and a nice house, a big TV screen, a fridge full of ham and cheese, and a boyfriend who goes with you to nice resorts in sunny places.

How would you know? How do you know I have a boyfriend?

I am just assuming. Just because.

Because of what? Her voice was firm and abrupt, she moved a touch forward, her eyes blinked twice from behind her glasses.

Because you grew up here and you have a job and a house, and you know people.

Not everyone who grew up here has a job or a house. There are many poor people who grew up here. But enough about your assumptions. You were saying about your sister and her husband?

Well, one day my sister came back home to my parents' place, covering her baby in a pink quilt, and her eyes had black rings around them. The bastard had beat her up. My sister cried all the time. She was humiliated. My mother, with her "I knew it" attitude, you should have never married that loser, and my father, with his "women deserve it" attitude, took her and the baby in.

I went looking for the brute. I knocked on the door of his house. He was sitting in a room with two other gangsters, smoking and laughing. When he saw me, he knew I would kill him with my bare hands, with my pierced eyebrows, if I could. His gun was laid out on the table. Everyone became quiet. I stared at the gun, thinking: If I had wings, I could fly over, pick it up, and shoot the three of them from above. Or maybe if I was an insect I could crawl under their doors at night and slay them all in their filthy bedsheets.

What are you looking at, kid? Tony finally shouted. Go back home and bring your sister here. Tell her to come before I have to go drag her back by the hair. He said this not even looking me in the face. Move, he said.

I stood there exhaling my hate, my fists closed, my eyes projecting bullets, flying cigarettes, body holes. And then a kind of elation came over me, I remember.

You still here? Tony said.

And it was as if I was transformed. Maybe I even flew a little. And when I spoke, my voice vibrated loudly.

Tony stood up, grabbed the gun from the table, and walked towards me. One of his men stepped behind me. Tony put the gun in my face and said, You look like a killer. He laughed. The killer is dead, he said. I heard a gunshot. I jerked, thinking, This asshole just shot me! But I did not feel it, not yet. Then Tony and his friends all started to laugh. I can still hear them laugh. Tony's friend had walked behind me and pulled the trigger in the air.

Scared hen. Is that what you want? Tony waved his gun in my face. Is that what you want, kid? He stuck the gun in my stomach. The two other men were amused by it all. They smiled, sat down, and tipped their chairs onto back legs. Tony raised his palm and tapped it gently against my bare neck. He closed his palm on the back of my neck and said again, Go get your sister, pronto, before I drag her here. When I pushed his hand away, bent my body, and liberated my neck from his grip, he boxed me on my shoulder with the back of his gun. He cornered me in his hallway. I could hear the neighbours and their TV — the loud news, the shouts of the woman calling her kids, the clanging of dishes, the smell of warm food. And suddenly I could hear my own mother calling me to her room, telling me to get ice to lay on her black eye. You tell the neighbours that I fell off the stairs, if they ask, you hear? I felt as if I could slip from under Tony's hand and disappear under the neighbour's door. I was sure that I could, if only he would stop chasing me from one corner to another, poking me with the barrel of his gun. His close bad breath, his thick, droopy moustache encircled me, made me crawl against the walls. And, as if I fluttered somehow, I became lighter and more agile. I even slipped under his feet and jumped over his boots. I was so agile and slippery that I almost made him stumble on the stairs. He got mad and said to me: You want to be tough, hen? He slapped me on the head.

I climbed the walls, flew over the ramp, landed on the floor below, and escaped. At that moment, I decided to kill him.

And did you kill him? asked Genevieve.

I was silent.

You do not have to answer that, she said. Even if you do, everything is confidential here.

Is our time up? I asked.

No. Do you have to go?

I did not answer her.

Did you tell your sister what had happened?

What for?

Genevieve was quiet for a moment. Then she asked, Was your mother nice to your sister?

My mother become preoccupied with the baby. My sister cried all the time and lay down on my bed. She slept a great deal and did not want to leave the house.

Depression.

What?

Sleeping and fatigue is a form of depression, explained Genevieve. But we can talk about that later. Go on.

I went straight to Abou-Roro and told him that I needed a gun.

Who is Abou-Roro?

My mentor. A thief in the neighbourhood.

Genevieve nodded. She looked intrigued but held her composure. Her pen made its way inside her lips, and I could see her breathe in a steady, regular motion, in time to her heartbeat. The doctor, like sultans, is fond of stories, I thought.

Maybe we should stop now, you must have a second appointment, I said.

No, no, no. Go on, please.

Well, I said, Abou-Roro said he could do it, but I had to help him in a little operation, if you know what I mean.

Operation? Genevieve asked.

You know, something illegal.

Oh yes, like shoplifting.

Well, maybe a little more than that, I said.

Like what, then?

Well, I am trying to tell you.

Yes, yes, excuse me. I interrupted you. Go on.

Abou-Roro showed me a few blank bank cheques. He could not write or read. Whose cheques are those, I asked him?

The priest's, he said.

A missionary lived across the street from Abou-Roro's house, in the back of the Franciscan convent. One night when the bombing in the city intensified, Father Edmond's room was hit by a bomb. Abou-Roro ran to the priest's room. The priest was wounded but still alive. Abou-Roro took a shattered stone and bashed the priest's head.

He killed the priest? Genevieve asked.

Yes, he made sure Father Edmond was dead, and then he stole what he could find, and ended up with a few blank cheques. He wanted me to fill in the cheques, backdated, so he could quickly cash them before the priest's account was closed. He even had a sample of the man's signature from one of the documents he'd collected.

I looked at the shrink and her eyes were wide open. Horrified. Half the pen was in her mouth. I could tell she didn't believe what I was saying to her.

I said, Madam, if all this bothers you I could stop.

Genevieve pulled the pen from her mouth, fixed her composure, and pasted on a calmer, more stoic face. *Non, non, pas du tout,* she said.

Well, do you need some water?

No, go on, I am fine. Believe me, nothing surprises me in this job. People come with all kinds of stories. Did you help the man?

Well yes, I practised the father's signature. And then I wrote a cheque for a few thousand.

Did the plan work?

Yes, it did.

You were never caught?

No.

So you got your gun?

Yes. I got my gun.

She was quiet, and I knew she wanted to ask me if I had killed Tony once I had the gun. I knew she was hooked, intrigued. Simple woman, I thought. Gentle, educated, but naive, she is sheltered by glaciers and prairies, thick forests, oceans and dancing seals.

Finally, she said: Well, there is something very interesting you said, something I would like to ask you about.

Shoot, doctor.

Genevieve.

Genevieve, I repeated.

You said that when Tony was hitting you, you felt you could slip under the door and disappear, and climb walls, and flutter. Do you still have feelings of slipping or disappearing?

Yes, doctor, Genevieve, I am good at slipping under anything. I told you. I can enter anyone's house.

She nodded. Have you entered anyone's house here in Canada?

Yes.

Did you steal anything?

Yes.

Have you made any break-ins?

Yes.

Genevieve was quiet for a few moments. Then she terminated the session.

A FEW DAYS LATER, I called Farhoud. Farhoud, I said, do you know where Shohreh works?

I can't tell you that. Shohreh would kill me.

Is she upset with me?

I could ask her, he said.

No, don't ask her.

Well, I warned you about falling for Shohreh. Where are you? On the street.

Where? On what street, silly?

Near McGill University. I am standing under those Roman arches at the entrance. Somewhere behind me there is a naked statue.

A man or a woman?

A man, I believe.

Does he look like a naked David? asked Farhoud. I love those naked David statues.

David was a goat-herder, a stinky, bearded boy with dirty nails and worn-out sandals.

That could be all right, he said. Come, I just made some soup. Come over and warm your bones.

Well, Farhoud, I should warn you now, I like my lovers hair-less.

That could be arranged, he said, and laughed. Don't be silly. Come over, silly man, or I am going to start thinking that you are a homophobe.

So was David, probably, I said.

Well, perhaps, but he did fuck the giant.

Myths and lies! I shouted

Anyway, said Farhoud, you are probably a confused

homophobe, afraid of it but secretly craving it. Like the rest of
you men. But come anyway, just because you are such a crazy
character. I will feed you. Come, my pretty boy, come.

So I rang Farhoud's buzzer, and sat at his table. He offered
me soup that released a vapour thick as sweat, and bread
that incited riots, and a little salad that rested on a yellow
plate on an old, squeaky table. Your table is shaky and
squeaky, I said, smiling and winking his way. Maybe I should
eat there, in the living room. Shut up and eat, you nasty boy,
Farhoud said. He had a scarf around his neck and he was
meticulous in arranging the utensils and plates, and he went
in and out of the kitchen with ease, making everything presentable, tasty, and warm.

Stop smiling and stop shaking that table like a kid, said
Farhoud. I invited you to eat, not to judge and speculate.

But, Farhoud, I never judge.

No, but you imagine things.

I deduce.

You assume.

I imagine.

And judge.

No, I just see things.

You presume.

I fancy and create.

You wish, said Farhoud. Now just stand still and eat or I
might send you to your room.

I got a job at the Star of Iran restaurant, I told him.

Well, well, you are going to learn Farsi now. You were hired
as what, a waiter?

No, a busboy, I said.

Well, congratulations. Farhoud went to the kitchen and came back with a bottle of wine. Here, we should celebrate. Another immigrant landing a career!

Shohreh is angry with me, I said.

Well, do not worry about Shohreh. She will come around. She is a little funny with love matters.

I need to see her.

Call her.

She is not answering my calls.

Well, like I said. I warned you not to become attached.

I am not attached.

Wine? Of course you are not, sweetheart. Wine, I asked. Wine? Answer me: wine?

Yes, yes, indeed.

You are attached, my dear, and down to your ears, and around your neck. Face it. You can't even hear me anymore.

We drank the whole bottle. I lay on the couch, and Farhoud lay on the floor across from me.

Look at the snow, Farhoud. It falls without shame. How did we end up here?

I do not know about you, my friend, but I know how I ended up here.

Tell me, Farhoud, how you ended up here.

Let's open another bottle of wine. He swayed into the kitchen and came back with the corkscrew and gave me the bottle. Here, strong man, open it and I will tell you all about me ending up in the snow. After Khomeini won the revolution, we — you know, the gay community — held clandestine parties. Someone must have been an informer who told the regime about us. One of our parties was raided and they took us all to the jail. They separated us and asked us to sign a paper acknowledging that we were homosexuals and that we would never touch another man again. And that our acts were against God and his Prophet, that we would repent and pray every day, five times, and become good, decent believers. But I did not even know how to pray. And I was sick and tired of being pushed around all my life, and imagine me growing a beard, wearing those horrible long robes, and not touching a man anymore? No, baby, no way!

So you refused?

I refused.

Courageous, or fucking crazy. And?

More like crazy. But, oh well, everyone who signed that paper disappeared anyway — probably killed, who knows? No one ever heard from them, and believe me, some of them were loud, darling, very loud. I know. Anyway, all they wanted was a confession from us. The redemption part was bogus. After I refused to sign, they put me in a crowded jail filled with women. It was a statement, you know. When I entered the jail cell I saw a small space packed with women. Some had children, and even a pregnant woman was there. The place was so crowded, no one even noticed me. I even recognized a couple of old girlfriends, who started to cry when they saw me. I spent a few days in that cell until a bearded mullah came, shouted, and asked the guard to remove me. He protested the mixing of men and women, even if I was not a real man, as he put it. So I ended up in a small cell, as big as a box, with no one to talk to, no bed, no chair, and a filthy, disgusting toilet seat, oh my god . . . The next day, I was led by the guard to a shower and asked to make myself clean. While I was in the shower that same bearded mullah passed by me and stood behind me, watching me clean myself. I turned my back to him, but I could feel his looks falling onto my thighs like drops of acid. At night a woman guard came, opened the door of the cell, and led me to an office. That same old man was there, sitting behind a desk. He smiled, and his gold tooth shone. He asked me to close the door and made me sit down across the desk from him; there was a plate of small dried figs between us. He smiled at me and pushed the plate towards me. I did not reach for it. He was insulted. You refused my hospitality, you *kouny* (faggot), he said, and he stood up. A thin cane appeared in his hand from inside the sleeve of his robe and he started to beat me with it. Then he asked me to take off my shirt and to position myself facing the wall. With my arms spread, my legs wide open, he flogged my back. It burned like hell, and then I felt his beard, his lips, and his breath on my wounds, licking my blood and asking me for forgiveness and touching me everywhere. For the next few months he fed me dried figs and raped me. Once I asked him if God approved of his acts. He replied that I was God's gift to him, God loves beauty and rewards believers. And he smiled and touched me.

I played along with the bearded one. I became his concubine. He used to ask me if he was handsome, and I had to answer that he was a gift from above and recite some verses. I never knew if they were poems or prayers, I never asked. But the verses described a garden, flowers, and mountains. I promised the mullah that if he released me, we could still meet on the outside and we could go and walk in gardens above the mountains. Slowly I worked on him, and I was eventually released. He would come every day and pick me up from a corner next to my house and we would drive away to the mountains. He told me that he would always find me, and if I tried to escape he would skin me alive. Eventually, with the help of a few old friends, I dressed as a woman, covered myself, and was driven to the border of Afghanistan, then from there to India. In India I met a Canadian diplomat on the beach. He smiled at me, and I smiled back. We spent a month travelling together. We travelled all over India; we took the train everywhere. We stayed in fancy hotels, smoked dope, and made love in many places. It was the best time of my life! He had money and he was willing to spend it.

Oh, the good days, Farhoud said, and lifted his glass of wine. He looked at the wine from underneath the glass, swirled it gently, then slightly lifted his neck, and his lips opened just when the glass tilted and the liquid rushed towards his mouth. I tell you, I needed it all, after the hell I went through with that mullah. Then I asked my lover if he could bring me to Montreal with him. And I remember we were in the region of Orissa at the time, in an old hotel, both naked on the same bed and smoking, high and happy. Outside there were a few trees rustling, a few bicycles and a few bare feet that passed and brushed the crust of dust under our open window, and we could hear them all. And my lover said, I have something to tell you, Farhoud. And I said, Do not tell me you are gay. And we laughed for a while, and then he said, Well no, actually I have the life of a straight man, with a woman. We laughed some more. Oh my god, we laughed so much. Through a connection of his in Immigration, he got me a visa and bought me a ticket to Montreal. We flew here together. He left me at the airport and I watched him rushing towards a woman.

Did you stay in touch?

Yes, for a while. He calls me Chinita, because I look Chinese. We spent a few nights together when he could get away from his wife. But then he slowly turned into a monster. I even thought he became a little xenophobic over time. Once, he came to my room and we made love. Afterwards he went to the bathroom, wet a towel, and threw it at me. Here, clean yourself, he said. You are not in your own country anymore.

I kept silent. And then I asked him, How come you look Chinese?

Iran is not a homogeneous society, he explained patiently. There are Azerbaijanis, Afghans, Turks, and in the south at the border with Iraq there are Arabs, but I suspect I am the residue of the Mongol invasion of the region. Mongols and their descendants, and also, I believe, Koreans, tend to have some kind of a mark on their buttocks at birth. It is called the Mongolian spot. After a while it goes away, but in some cases it stays for life.

You are lying, I said.

No, even a few East Europeans get it sometimes. Genghis Khan, or Attila the Hun, I am not sure exactly who — but they passed by there.

And what army does not spread semen and blood! I declared.

I would say so.

So, you have that Mongolian spot? I asked.

Yes.

I do not believe you.

Well, if you are nice I might show it to you one day. Farhoud laughed. The diplomat used to be very excited about it.

Excited?

It turned him on, silly. He called it his blue jewel of the east.

What was his name, the diplomat?

Bernard. Why?

Where does he live?

Why?

Is there anything you need me to get from his house?

What are you talking about?

I will pay him a visit. I will break into his house. Just give me his address.

Are you crazy? Why would you do that?

I will break into his house and wet his towel with dog piss.

No. It is done, that relationship is done. Dog piss! You are a bizarre man! I do not know where he is anymore. I don't care anyway. I am here now. And that's what counts. Do you understand? I am alive and here and I don't care. I am here and I have a glass of wine in my hand. I am here now, alive. Farhoud started to cry.

But, Farhoud, my dear friend. I lay my hand on his shoulder. I just want to settle a score for you.

What score? Do you know how many scores there are to settle in my life? Do you? Do you?

And with that, we both fell silent, remembering the red of the wine, the white of the snow, and that night was on its way.

LATER THAT EVENING, the doorbell rang. I woke up and saw Shohreh entering the flat and taking off her shoes.

I came to get soup, and look what I see! she said, pointing her chin at me. You guys are stoned, your eyes are red. Stay where you are. I will help myself to some food.

As Shohreh ate, Farhoud stood up and gave her a shoulder massage. I had a long day, she told him. She ate and talked about her boss. I would kill that man if I could, she said. When she was finished eating, I passed her a joint. She thanked me and smoked, then stretched herself out on her seat.

After a while, she got up to leave and I walked her outside. In the elevator, she looked closely at my face. She caressed the scars carved on my face by her nails and said, Come home with me. I scratched you hard, didn't I? We should put something on these wounds.

So I went back to her home with her and told her that I had got a job at the Star of Iran restaurant.

She laughed loudly. I will come and visit one day, she said. Maybe when Reza is playing. I will listen to Reza and watch you fall with your tray on some customer.

I am there from Friday to Sunday. Come for dinner anytime after four, I said.

I will come with Farhoud, she said, as she patted my face with alcohol. Stop twitching. Come on, be a man and take the pain. This little thing is scaring you?

I am not scared. It just burns.

Well, do not think of it. Let it burn. And she kissed my lips. Then she held my face in her hands and looked me straight in the eye.

Did you call your friend?

Who?

Your friend. The woman who dances with her shoes in her hand.

What are you talking about?

Never mind.

What shoes?

You know what shoes.

No.

The dancing woman with no shoes.

Ah. The gypsy, I said.

She has a nickname now!

No, I did not call her. I did not get her number.

Come, let's go to bed. You smell all smoky. Take off your clothes. Here! She threw a man's shirt at me. Don't ask, just wear it and come to bed.

I did not ask, although I wanted to.

IN BED, AFTER WE CAME, Shohreh was silent. She did not put her head on my shoulder, she did not cover my belly with her thigh, she did not warm up her cold feet between my legs. She smoked and looked at the ceiling, thinking. Then she became worried. She rose, reached for the condom on the floor beside the bed, and checked it.

Do you leave your condoms in your pocket? she asked me.

In my wallet, I said.

That is not good. They could break. She pulled at my condom, tied it at the top, and isolated the liquid in different areas, looking for leaks. When she had finished, she threw it next to the bed. The last thing I want is to bring a baby into this world, she said. She reached for the ashtray, finished the last puff of her cigarette, and said, It is late. I am turning off the light. Tomorrow I am working early.

I opened my eyes in the dark and looked at the ceiling. I amused myself by imagining that I was colouring the flat obscure roof above me with school pencils, making clouds and bright suns. All that is empty in the drawing should be filled in, the teacher said to us kids. First you sharpen the pencil to fill in the thin whiskers, then you use the thick crayon to fill in the wings with brown, meticulously and without letting the crayon leave the page. Six feet can be traced below the soft belly. Now, breathing is hard to detect on paper, the teacher said to me when I asked, but it is easier to feel it in real life. Even insects breathe. So I stretched my fingers from underneath the sheets and lay them on Shohreh's chest. Her half-coloured wings turned and fluttered and she quickly slipped to the other side of the bed. So instead I looked for the thickest pen available, held it, and jerked it until it burst and spilled on my lap, and my teacher came and slapped my hands and sent me to the dark corner of the room.

IN THE MORNING Shohreh cooked me breakfast and got busy brushing her hair, moving from bathroom to closet, from dresser to eyeliner, digging in her bag, changing blouses. Then she stood at the door and said, Are you ready to go? You can take the coffee with you. Here. She poured the coffee into a plastic cup.

I walked her to the metro station and then turned back and walked towards my home. The coffee kept my fingers warm for a while. The steam that escaped the cup danced against the backdrop of the grey roads, the grey buildings, the leafless grey trees, the grey people, the Greyhound buses, and then it lost its energy and turned cold — the fate of everything around me.

I decided to walk all the way home, and on my way I stopped at the Artista Café to get warm. A few North African men surrounded the professor, who sat in his usual chair. He always managed to dazzle those newcomers with his stories and grand theories. For some reason that I do not understand, he always managed to impress his compatriots. But I know the charlatan is in it for the free coffee and to bum cigarettes from those nostalgic souls. He would suddenly, in the middle of a story, ask one of the men to bring him a cup of coffee, and he would take a cigarette from someone else's supply, and then he'd nonchalantly continue his stories about simultaneous escape from the Algerian government and the religious "fundies." He claims that both militant groups wanted his death because he exposed the Algerian dictatorship for what it was, and also exposed the plan of the bearded ones for a theocratic state. He would pull articles from old Algerian newspapers and read them aloud to those naive souls, dipping his finger inside his lip as he flipped through the pages.

That cocky intellect interrupted me all the time. He always dismissed what I had to say. One particular day, when I tried to tell him that a grand change is coming, a fatal one that is brewing from underneath the earth, he chuckled and dismissed me again. He pissed me off so much that day, I decided to follow him and find out where he lived. It turned out that his paranoiac tendencies were more developed than I had thought. Maybe that is how he'd survived the executioner's bullet and the fanatics' knives. How often had he said, Only the paranoid survive, my friend? As I was following him, he looked back and saw me. I pretended to stop and look at a car meter and count my change, but the eccentric professor ran and crossed against the lights, jaywalking the red, the green, the yellow, the purple sky, the blue people, the pink dogs, the squirrels, the wet pavement. He was almost run down by a taxi. He ran like he had never run for his life from dictators or prophets. I was too conspicuous to pursue him further. And really, I just wanted to know more about the suave beggar. I wanted to steal his reading glasses while he was asleep. I tried once to do it at the café, but he hung his glasses around his neck with a rope that dangled below his ever-shifting eyes.

Salaam, I said today, as I pulled a chair from the next table.

The men in the café all nodded briefly and kept on flipping through the newspapers.

I waited a little, and when the waitress came and asked me if I needed anything, I told her I was leaving. And so I did, without saying a word to anyone. On my way out, I looked back and saw the glasses of the professor emerging from beneath the news like a crocodile from a swamp. The bastard watches me all the time. I will get him one day!

AT HOME AS I WASHED, I saw long pieces of Shohreh's deep blue hair swirling in the waters around my feet like eels. And as I was getting out of the bathtub, some force pulled me back. It was as if gravity was magnified; the soles of my feet felt heavy with the weight of iron and chains, my ankles felt anchored in water, I moved sluggishly. I felt heavy, but also a part of me had become light and fleet. I tried to move myself by hanging off the shower curtain, then the towel rack, but instead I became more immobilized. A deep, deep sense of fear and sadness overcame me. I felt I was the last human on the planet. I heard the sound of water, like synchronized drumming, going down the drain — an army on the move with chariot and horses. I saw the mirror shifting and meeting my face, and in the mirror I saw fuzziness and an elongated face that was still mine, but it was as if I had grown whiskers from my forehead. I am going to shave it, I thought. I should shave it. I grabbed the razor and passed it across my forehead. Then the sadness intensified, which made me drop the blade. I wanted to ask for help, but no one, no name, came to mind, and I was certain that no one existed anymore. Perhaps everything had been destroyed by some bright light that had flashed and levelled all that was on the surface of the earth. I reached the door but felt paralyzed, as if some poisonous fang had bitten me. I also felt light, and fragile, so fragile, so weightless that I could be swept up and pulled under by anything. An insect or a shaft of light could carry me; the water could equally sweep me down towards the noise made by armies of galloping horses, flying beneath sabres, helmets, and bright flags held by boys, and villagers turned archers. And I panicked, thinking I was the only naked one in the battle. I somehow managed to partially cover myself with a towel and clung to the bathroom door, but then the door shifted back and forth in front of me. All I wanted was to cross it, to get to the other side and throw my carcass on the sheets of the wounded and the dead. And a part of me felt thin, as if I were on top of a spear and fretting like a banner in the wind. I watched myself, conscious that another me was escaping.

At last I rushed into the bedroom and violently closed the window and pulled myself onto the bed. Maybe I am just hungry, I reassured myself. Maybe I am just tired. A part of me was still thinking clearly, though. I was split between two planes and aware of two existences, and they were both mine. I belong to two spaces, I thought, and I am wrapped in one sheet. I looked at the ceiling. I felt it shifting for a very brief moment, sideways, then down and up. And then that terrible sadness came back into the world like an omnipotent blinding cloud, and tears dropped from my eyes for no reason, as if I was crying for someone else.

IN THE AFTERNOON, Reza knocked at my door. I buzzed him in.

Your building always smells — cooking, curry or meat, or something, man. You look like shit. What were you doing? You cut your forehead? Did you fall?

I went back to bed and covered myself up. Reza, there is tea in the cupboard above the stove, I said. Boil some and bring it here.

I do not want tea.

I do, I said. Could you please make some?

He went to the kitchen. And I could hear him, squeaking complaints. He came back with the teapot. There are no clean cups, he told me. You need to do your dishes, man. It is dirty in there.

I stood up, went to the kitchen, washed two cups, and came back.

Oh, I don't want any, he said.

What do you want?

Money, he said.

You must be kidding, right?

Well, I got you the job at the restaurant, didn't I?

Fucking asshole, I said. Leave my house.

But he stayed and did not move an inch. He had a smirk on his face.

Leave, I said. I am serious. I am not feeling well.

He opened the curtains and said: Why do you live in the dark like that? Open some windows; you need light and fresh air, brother.

Leave, I said, faintly. Leave now.

Reza walked down the stairs, cursing the trapped smells.

I flung the door closed behind him, and drew the curtains.

THE NEXT DAY, I went to the welfare office to fill out some papers — a routine procedure. The bureaucrats want to make sure that you move your ass out of bed once in a while, that you shuffle your feet in the snow to prove that you are alive and willing to lift your legs to the fourth floor of the old monastery-turned-government building. You have to sign here, here, and there before you get your money.

I picked one of the six lines of waiting people, making sure I was behind someone who looked like he had taken a shower. Why should I smell poverty? I live it! In one of the other lines, who should I see but the professor himself. I watched him with a big smirk on my face and waited until he saw me. Of course, the coffee beggar buried his face in a newspaper and pretended not to see me. I told the woman who had lined up behind me that I would be right back and went straight over to the man. I would not have missed such an opportunity for the world.

When he couldn't help but see me, the professor acted surprised.

Hard times, I said.

Well no, no. I am here for a business meeting, a consultation job for the government.

I nodded. I looked at him with that same big smirk. Then I pulled a dollar from my pocket and asked him if he had change.

He pulled out a bunch of coins and started to count.

I said: It is not for a phone call.

He looked up at me and stopped counting his dimes, and his hand was about to close in a fist.

I need a bus ticket, I said, and I am short a dollar and twenty cents. I will pay you right back, when I get the cheque in the mail. And without waiting for an answer, I picked dimes and quarters out of his palm. I wanted something from him. It angered me that the socialist does not want to be identified as poor, a marginal impoverished welfare recipient like me. At least I am not a hypocrite about it. Yes, I am poor, I am vermin, a bug, I am at the bottom of the scale. But I still exist. I look society in the face and say: I am here, I exist. There is existence and there is the void; you are either a one or a zero. Once I was curious about the void. If I had died on that tree branch in the park, I would have experienced the other option. Although . . . experiencing it would have meant that I could see and feel, and that would have thrown me back into existence, which would eliminate the notion of the void. The void cannot be experienced. The void should mean perishing absolutely without any consciousness of it. It is either a perpetual existence or nothingness, my friend.

That bum of a professor often talks about his stay in Paris, and how he saw so-and-so sitting *dans le café*, and how he told her such-and-such and she told him such-and-such. But I'll bet the exile existed in one of those Parisian shitholes, washing his ass and cleaning his dishes in the same tub. I'll bet the asshole sought out a few well-off old ladies and discussed Balzac while he stuffed himself with food and wine. I know his type. He does not fool me.

Of course, now that I have taken his change in such a direct and brilliant, cunning manner, he must declare war between us. The little change I took from him is, I am sure, all he had until the arrival of his cheque. I'll bet he is like me — we watch for the mail delivery and hope for that manila envelope with recyclable paper on the outside and vanishing degradable crumbs on the inside. And the reason he pulled out those fragments of change to show me was because he was seduced by the idea of having a bigger coin — a unified monotheistic empire is better than minuscule slivers that never cease to giggle and laugh in his hollow pockets, constantly reminding him what a destitute financial thinker he is. So I played the oldest trick in the book; I took him by surprise. He must have been disoriented. I caught him on the defensive, when he was busy convincing himself that he really had an appointment with some governmental official. The officials, of course, would love to consult him on the distribution of wealth, equity, and the establishment of an egalitarian society. He is in total denial that he is just like me — the scum of the earth in this capitalist endeavour. I'll bet he thought that, coming from Algeria and having lived and studied in Paris, his *vocabulaire parisien* would open every door for him in this town. Oh yes, baby! Those locals would just empty their desks and give you *le plus grand bureau* to smoke in, and you could gaze from the large window at the falling snow, you could arrive late to work and smile at the security guard, who would greet you with a *Bonjour, Monsieur*, and have a small lunch at the bistro down the street where the chef, Jacques, and everyone else, would recognize you, and naturally, *mon vieux*, everyone would be eager to discuss world politics and women with you, and then you would come back to your mahogany desk and make a few phone calls, *un apéritif* between *séances*, and in the evening you would get your circumcised Muslim dick sucked by those ex-Catholics, and smoke a last cigarette in bed, and in the morning a croissant would hover like a holy crescent at the break of dawn, announcing another day of jubilation and bliss. *Et voilà! La belle vie! La belle province!*

Now I was more determined than ever to find a way to that faux government consultant's shithole of a residence and consult his drawers, his fridge, his glasses, and merge his shoes into one company, and maybe lay off a few excess operatives. The professor got to the welfare window before me, but he was arguing and pulling papers from an envelope. My transaction was straightforward. I handed the man my slips, signed here, here, and there, waited for the sound of the wooden stamp, and left. On my way out, I saw the professor still waiting, pacing back and forth, pretending to be busy, trying to be somewhere between the welfare line and his imaginary appointment. I decided to cross the street, find myself a corner, squeeze myself into it, and wait.

Eventually the professor stood at the door of the welfare office, looked left and right, then walked east. I crouched and put my feet and palms on the ground and let him pass. He walked by in a hurry, and his long coat and his hat gave him the look of an Eastern European spy. I gave him a distance of a few blocks, then followed him. I crawled through and beneath car fenders and hopped above dirty batches of snow and under car tires. At one point the professor stopped and turned back, and I dug into the snow and hid behind a discarded TV on the sidewalk. Its two antennae sprang out of my head like whiskers. One had an advantage being at a low angle like that, close to earth and invisible, I thought; imagine living all your life close to the crust of the ground. When the professor pulled out his long chain of keys, I felt as if I could jump and fly from joy. Just as I thought! He lived in a semi-basement, with a side entrance that led to the kitchen of an old Portuguese lady; he lived in a dark ground-hole. That was all I needed to know. I would take care of him later.

ON FRIDAY, MY FIRST NIGHT of work at the Star of Iran restaurant, I was introduced to Hakim, the head waiter. He was a quiet, gentle-mannered man. He showed me the plastic tray, the dishes, the utensils, the cloths, how to light the candles for the table lanterns. It was all illuminating. Then he introduced me to the cook, Mamnoun, who barely smiled; and to Seydou, the dishwasher, who smiled at me and made his water sparkle in a welcoming manner. Then the owner pulled me towards the vacuum cleaner, pushed me towards the mop, filled my hand with a water bucket, and assigned all of these to me. He led me to the toilets down in the basement and said, This you clean every day, two times, before the customers come and before you leave for home. And then he showed me a little metal closet that held detergent, tablecloths, candles, liquid soap, and napkins.

At around six o'clock, a couple showed up. I rushed to open the lantern on their table and lit the small candle inside it. I ran back to the dishwasher and stacked a few plates, and separated the knives, the forks, and the spoons. By eight the restaurant had six tables full. The owner was calm and quiet.

He stayed behind the bar, watched everything, and gave orders to Hakim, who in turn gave orders to me. I laid out utensils and picked up dirty dishes and laid them on the counter next to Seydou, who asked me to empty the scraps of food into the garbage bin before putting the dishes on the counter. And then he asked me about some Arabic song's title. He tried to sing the tune for me, but it was unrecognizable; it sounded like someone whining with a mixture of anal pain and pleasure. I asked him if it was a recent song.

Yes, he replied.

I haven't heard any recent songs in a while, I said. I've been hanging out with Iranians too much. We both laughed. Seydou smiled again and washed more dishes and sang a few African songs.

A few minutes later, Reza and his band came and the music started. They played their instruments in unison — soft background music. Reza and I did not even glance at each other.

I kept busy, attentive to the bread that had to be sliced, stacking dishes, picking up empty plates from beneath customers' chins. The owner asked me a few times to go down to the big fridge in the basement and bring up limes for the bar and more sodas. The only time I stopped for a moment was when I went to the bathroom in the basement and relieved myself. I washed my hands afterwards: "Employees must wash hands," a sign said. Then I went back upstairs and worked.

Late in the evening, after the customers were gone, Reza got a ride home with the other musicians. He invited me to come, but I declined. I did not feel like sitting on a second-hand sofa in one of those depressing newcomers' homes, filled with smoke and broken alarms. Besides, when Reza and his friends got together they talked in Persian and I could not understand a damn thing.

Shortly after Reza left, the owner's wife and daughter came to pick up the owner. Before they showed up, the owner counted his money behind the bar. Then he waited for his wife and daughter just inside the restaurant door, behind the locked glass. When his wife showed up, he asked everyone else to leave first. When he was alone, he rushed into the car and locked the doors of the vehicle. I watched his daughter leaning against the car-window glass, looking at me. I smiled. She barely nodded, then pulled back her face and disappeared.

I walked home. Late at night in this city, the snow is pasted just above the street like a crunchy white crust that breaks and cracks under your feet. There is a sound to the cold, a constant quiet, a subtle permanent buzzing. It is not the vibration of the long-shadowed fluorescent city lights tracking the trajectory of falling snow, nor is it the wind, nor the people. It is something that comes out from underground and then stays at the surface. After a while stomping through the snow, I could hear the rhythm of my own steps. My breath was smoking like a Bollywood train, my feet were steadily marching; I was all warmed up. I got rid of my scarf first, then unzipped another layer; my hands swung back and forth like those of a soldier. The city was empty and whistling in the wind.

I WENT TO THE RESTAURANT on Saturday and Sunday, and on Monday I was off work. My appointment with my therapist was at three, and I had nothing to do until then. I walked into the kitchen and pretended to be busy washing the dishes. Then, suddenly, I pulled off my slippers, opened the cupboards, and began pounding left and right. Whether they are here or not, I thought, I will keep those insects on their toes! Guilty or not, present or not — this was my new tactic. Well, it was not my own idea, really. I was inspired by the story of a young man I knew who had experienced a totalitarian regime.

I had met this young man on a bus, back where I came from. The bus was crowded and he squeezed in next to me. He asked me for directions, and then he told me his story. He told me that he had been released only a few days ago from detention. The secret service in the small town where he came from made arbitrary arrests to keep the population afraid. For no reason, they would knock on people's doors at night, line up the young men, randomly choose a few, and pack them into a jeep and off to jail. For a week or so the young men were beaten, humiliated, even tortured — all for no reason. Then the young men would be released so that everyone in town could see what was in store for them if they tried anything subversive. The young man on the bus had left his village, he said, and now he was looking for a job in the city. I thought he looked too honest to be hired by my mentor, Abou-Roro. He was either traumatized and couldn't stop speaking or he was naturally too trusting. Either way, I thought, I couldn't help him; he was damaged and he did not fit the profile of a petty thief.

We got off the bus, and the young man said he was hungry. I told him to follow me. I went straight to a grocery store and told him to wait for me outside. I went into the store and came out with a bag of bread, a package of cheese, some fruit, and yogurt. I gave this to him and turned to walk the rest of the way home. But this fellow followed me. He asked me my name, and talked more and more. So at last I asked him what kind of job he was willing to do. He assured me that he was willing to do anything. I looked at his hands and I could see they were rough — banged-up and strong. Had he ever stolen or killed? I asked him.

He stopped eating, bewildered. No, he said.

How far are you willing to go to survive? I asked.

I will steal, but not kill. I am hungry, but I won't kill.

Would you kidnap? I said.

I am hungry, he answered.

Meet me here in two days, I said. Same place. In two days.

I learned that his name was Naim. I watched him eat, and I saw that he was very hungry.

HOW WAS YOUR WEEK? the shrink asked me later that afternoon.

Good, thank you. How was yours? What did you do? Did you watch TV, did you eat a good sandwich, open an interesting book, lie on the floor, walk barefoot, dance a little?

Genevieve smiled at me. How are you feeling?

Fine.

Any dizziness? Do you ever experience episodes?

What do you mean?

As if things around you are shifting or slipping?

No, I said.

You hesitated. You thought about it.

Well, yes. But everything shifts, everything slips.

Like what?

Like, everything around us.

Walls?

Yes, certainly walls.

Beds?

Uh-huh.

Does your bed shift?

The mirror does.

We have medicines now that can help you.

I am fine, I feel fine, I said. And anyhow, a mirror never reflects the same image twice.

Well, we might have to prescribe something for you eventually. But right now I am curious about something you said the last time we met, something about stealing.

I remained quiet.

Any break-ins lately?

No. Well, almost.

Almost?

I volunteered for something, but in the end I didn't do it.

Who did you volunteer for?

For Farhoud, my gay friend.

Why?

To settle a score with someone who abused him.

But did he ask you to do it? Or did you volunteer without him asking?

No. Yes.

Do you like him? Is that why you volunteered?

I like him.

Genevieve was silent.

No, not that way, I added.

Have you ever been attracted to a man? she asked.

Not sexually, I don't think. But my mentor was attracted to a man.

Genevieve flipped through her notes. Abou-Roro, your mentor in theft and crime?

Yes, and it killed him.

What do you mean, it killed him? Do you mean he couldn't come to terms with the fact that he was attracted to men?

No, but because of the attraction he was killed. Shot dead.

Because people where you come from do not accept gays?

Well, yes. But no. It is a long story.

I am listening.

Well, you see, he was approached by a local gangster, a notorious, powerful man, one named Jurdak, to do an operation.

An operation. Like a medical procedure, Genevieve teased me.

No, I said. A kidnapping.

Genevieve lifted her head then, and I could see her ears turning pointy and poking through her glittering straight, long hair. She was struggling to keep her eyes from blinking under the weight of her heavy eyelashes.

I continued: The gangster gave him the name, address, and photo of the son of a millionaire. Abou-Roro was to kidnap the son, and Jurdak would ask for a ransom and deal with the negotiation and money collection, and all the logistics. A pretty straightforward operation. So one night Abou-Roro waited for the boy in the parking lot of a nightclub. He parked his car next to the boy's car. When the son showed up and pulled out his keys to open the car door, Abou-Roro stuck a gun into his ribs from behind. He asked the boy not to turn around and shuffled him into the back seat. Naim, a hungry chap that I had recently met on a bus and introduced to Abou-Roro, covered the boy's face with a hood. He blindfolded the boy and tied his hands, and they all drove outside the city to a house on a beach.

When they arrived, Abou-Roro and Naim led the boy into the house and locked him in a room, and waited for phone calls from Jurdak. There was food and alcohol in the house. Any escape attempt by the boy and they were to shoot him and throw him in the sea. But looking at the kid, both Abou-Roro and Naim knew that they would never do that. The boy had soft, white skin (his mother was Scandinavian), and he had blue eyes and blond hair, and he was very good-looking — kind of frail and soft-spoken. He never once resisted, never complained. Even when his head got banged on the car window and then the door to the house, he never said a thing. Abou-Roro held his hands and guided him everywhere. He would push the boy gently and call him "Beauty." Lower your head, Beauty; lift your head, Beauty; eat, Beauty. Go check on the beauty, he would say to Naim.

One night when Naim went to use the bathroom, he saw Abou-Roro sitting on a chair facing the boy, smoking, with a glass of whisky in his hand and his eyes fixated on the boy's blindfold. Abou-Roro had fallen in love with the boy. He would drink whisky and gaze at the boy for hours. Finally he undid the boy's blindfold, and with a gun in his hand, a cigarette on his lips, whisky in his palm, and the sea at his back, he would look at the boy all night and weep, not knowing what to do, or what to say to him, or how to approach him. But then, one day, Abou-Roro started to cough. The boy in his soft voice said: You should have some tea. I can make you tea.

Hearing the boy's words, Abou-Roro wept again, approached the bed, kissed the boy on the cheek, and released his bonds. He freed the boy's hands and unzipped the boy's pants.

Abou-Roro closed the bedroom door, and he made love to the boy on foreign sheets through a haze of smoke. And then, next thing you know, the boy was riding beside Abou-Roro as they drove along the village streets. They were buying food together, and walking the beaches.

What will I do if Jurdak gives me the order to kill you? Abou-Roro asked the boy one night. What will I do? I can't do it, and if I don't, Jurdak will find us and kill us both.

Finally the boy's father negotiated with Jurdak and paid some of the ransom.

The next morning the phone rang and Abou-Roro picked it up. He said yes a few times, and alright, and then he looked at Naim, nodded at the phone, and hung up. He walked towards Naim and told him that the chief, Jurdak, wanted Naim to leave because someone else was coming to take Naim's place.

But why? Naim asked.

The chief said so. I told you.

When did he say that? Naim asked.

Just now, on the phone, Abou-Roro replied.

Okay, but I will wait until the replacement comes, Naim said.

No, you have to leave now. It's the chief's order. He wants one of his own men to stay here.

When should I be back? Naim asked.

Never.

What?

You are not to come back, said Abou-Roro. He took some money and gave it to Naim. You will get the rest of your share later, he said. Your role in this is over.

I will get my full share, right? asked hungry Naim.

Yes, you will get it all when the operation is done. The father is paying the ransom. Now, start walking.

Naim left that day.

Here I paused in my story.

Is that it? Genevieve said.

No. But do we have time left?

Yes, yes, go on.

Well, Naim left, but he climbed a nearby hill and watched the house. Soon a car came and parked in front of the house. It was full of Jurdak's men, come to pick up the boy. Abou-Roro shot the first man who knocked at the door. He shut the door, ran back to the bedroom, and pushed the boy under the bed, closed all the curtains, and then opened the door again, stepping outside and emptying his gun, shooting with tears in his eyes. Jurdak's men fired back and killed Abou-Roro. And the boy was freed. Abou-Roro was killed because he was in love with the boy's blue eyes, because he wanted to keep the boy and didn't want to hand him over to Jurdak and his men.

And Naim, no one knew about him? Genevieve asked.

No one knew of his involvement except the boy and Abou-Roro, and the boy never told. I saw Naim before I left my country. He told me the story of Abou-Roro's death.

Genevieve sighed. Then she asked: What is your mother's name?

My mother's name? I asked, surprised. You have it — it is in your file.

Well, yes, but I wanted to hear how it is pronounced.

Manduza.

Do you call Manduza now and then?

She is dead.

Genevieve was silent for a minute. Then she asked, How?

She got sick.

When?

Lately.

You were here, in Canada?

Yes.

Tell me more.

I got a phone call.

From who?

My sister.

The one with the baby.

Yes.

Was she crying?

Of course.

What did you say?

Nothing.

Did you cry?

No, I did not.

Do you ever cry?

I can't remember crying. But I must have when I was born and was pulled out of Manduza's thighs.

Do you ever feel sad for other people?

I did not answer this. I did not know what to say. I thought we had gone past this level of intimacy. I noticed that the flowers I had brought Genevieve were dead already, dried out in the blue vase behind her.

What is your sister doing now? Genevieve asked finally.

She works at a store.

Where?

Back home.

What kind of store?

A clothing store. She sells clothes.

And where is Tony?

He left for Brazil.

So you did not manage to kill him?

No.

How did your sister get the job?

It is a long story.

Tell me. I love long stories.

If you insist, doctor.

Genevieve.

Yes, Genevieve. You see, Genevieve, Tony came by my parents' house one Sunday when my father was away. It was summer, and all the neighbours were on their balconies. From our balcony I saw him park his car on the street. We all stood up, and my sister rushed to change her clothes. Tony was all dressed up, sober, and shaven. I ran to my room and got my gun. Then I walked through the living room and met him at the stairs. I let my gun hang low. I asked him where he thought he was going, but he did not answer and kept on marching up the stairs. By this time my sister and my mother had followed me to the door. Before he could cross the threshold, I extended my arm with the gun and put it in front of his face.

Go out of the way, kid, he said.

When the women saw the gun, they screamed, and their screams pealed off the walls and the old wooden doors and brought out the neighbours from down and up the stairs. They watched me curse the bastard, telling him that he couldn't just come and take what he wanted and disgrace our house's honour. He ignored me and told my sister to bring the kid and the suitcase and come back home. My sister was hysterical.

I cranked the gun and took a shot above Tony's head, and all the women in the building shrieked and grabbed their children and ran. The sound of the shot echoed loudly, but Tony did not even blink. The men in the building told me to calm down, to put down the gun. And Tony backed off and said that I would regret what I had done. Then he left.

Joseph Khoury, an older man who had never married and who lived on the top floor, came down and talked to me. He said, This is not the right way to deal with things. Look what you are doing to your mother and sister, look at the children and women around you. They are all scared. Even if you are at war, you should have decency. These days, you young kids think you can do what you please.

And then, seeing that he was having an effect on me, my mother invited Joseph Khoury for a coffee. As the man entered our house, my sister came out of her room in tears. She came out and shouted, Shoot me! Here, shoot everyone! Shoot my baby as well! And she slapped my face.

I pushed her back into her room and slapped her in return, and the baby wailed.

Joseph Khoury separated us and tried to calm everyone down. My mother just stood there watching as the old man asked me for the gun. Give me the gun, my son, he said to me.

I gave it to him. I'm not sure why. He laid the gun on the table and put his arm around my shoulders. He took me to the balcony and said, Listen, you are a man now. I know that you feel you should protect your family, but violence is not the only way.

Did this man know your father? Genevieve asked me.

He knew about my father.

What about your father? What did he know? No, wait, forget it for now; we'll talk about that another time. Tell me what happened.

My sister stayed at home. And Tony did not show up again for a while.

You scared him?

No, he just disappeared. No one knew where or why. Even

when my sister still lived with him, in his house, he used to disappear every once in a while.

One night I came home late, and as I climbed the stairs I saw my sister coming from above our place down the stairs.

Where were you? I asked her.

Upstairs, she said. And I recognized in her face a look filled with dreams of naked men and desperate plans for liberation, for escape to something calmer, richer.

I went straight upstairs and knocked at Joseph's door. He opened it with a big smile, expecting someone else, and then I knew. I knew what was going on because he was startled when he saw me. He looked happy, younger and beloved and bouncy, because that is what a caress can do to the old. I looked him in the eye, and I said, If you do not want to be alone, old man, you take care of those who keep you company.

He nodded. He understood.

A few days after that incident, my sister started to work for Joseph in his clothing store.

So, they slept together? Genevieve asked.

What do you think?

Right. And how did you feel about that?

Nothing. I felt nothing.

Nothing?

How are brothers supposed to feel?

Yes, how?

I am asking you, doctor . . . Genevieve. How are we supposed to feel?

It depends.

On what? I asked.

Well, what do you think?

I think it depends on class, I said.

Class? Yes, the poor are forced to compromise.

We compromise our loved ones.

Genevieve was silent for a moment. Then she said, You will keep me informed of any future break-ins you're planning, won't you?

Why?

Well, it's something we should talk about.

But will this talk still be confidential?

Yes, it will still be confidential, but also something to assess.

Why?

Because talking about it is part of your treatment.

Because it is exciting, maybe? I said.

For whom?

For Genevieve.

You can leave now, the doctor said. I think we are done for today.

ALL WEEK MY APARTMENT was cold. On Wednesday I went downstairs and knocked at the door of my Indian neighbours. A man opened the door. I asked him if he had any heat.

Very low, very low, he said. This landlord is very cheap, very cheap.

Rather be in India? I asked.

Pakistan, he protested. Pakistan.

I went back to my apartment. A little while later, I had an itch on my back. I hunched over and just reached the itch with a long arm. I scratched it, but it still itched. I went to the kitchen, picked up a wooden spoon, and pushed it down my shirt, parallel to my spine. The spoon was too round, too soft. So I laid it over the edge of the counter and pushed down on it. It broke, and now there was a rougher edge to it. I moved the broken spoon up and down my back until I hurt.

I looked out the window. It was still white outside. Patches of sporadic snow covered the mountain in the distance. It is too cold in this dump, I thought. Maybe if I take a walk outside and move my legs I'll be able to heat my bones.

But what stressed me more than the cold was hunger. I went back downstairs and knocked again at my Pakistani neighbour's door. He opened it, and said: May I help you?

I love the smell of your food, I said. I was wondering if you could give me some of your recipes or maybe a little of your food to taste?

Sure, the man said, and smiled. His wife peeked out from the back, covering her head with a silk scarf. And his kids sprang up from the floor and stared at me from behind their mother's long robe.

You have to buy spices, many spices, the man said. But maybe you like it mild? His wife giggled from the back. His kids struggled to escape through the open door and down the stairs but they were caught by the woman and dragged back inside.

I said: Spices are good; they keep you warm.

My neighbour laughed.

I have not tasted your kind of food yet, I said, but the smell is very good.

The wife covered her teeth with her hand and laughed again.

Wait, the man said. He talked to his wife in another language. She disappeared and came back with a big bowl of food.

Oh, I said. All this for me? Very generous, much obliged, very generous. May the moon light your nights.

Yes. Taste it, and if you like it, you come back and I will tell you the names of the spices and how to make the food.

I went upstairs, sat at my table, and started to eat. Then I ran to fill a glass with water from the tap to extinguish my burning tongue. The food was very hot. It burnt in my nostrils, it made me cry. I felt like getting a little jar, collecting my tears, walking to Genevieve's office, opening her door, and showing her the bottle. Here — is this what you want? Here — these are my tears. Does that make me sane, normal, cured?

Suddenly the snow outside my window looked appealing. I could go up the mountain, I thought, and lick the white snow to soothe my burning tongue. And while I was at it, I could sniff the yellow traces on the white snow from obedient dogs that are always well-fed.

The food was too hot for me, but it was food — I couldn't throw it away. I left it on the counter, but not even the roaches, with their massive egalitarian appetites, would approach it. Eventually I thought: What if I dilute it with water and make a soup out of it? Now, there's an idea. I filled a casserole dish with water, let it boil, and splashed the food into it. The mixture boiled for a while. I let it cool down and then tried to eat it. It was better, so long as I didn't drink the liquid.

Damn it! I had forgotten to put the socks in the bed again. Well, I thought, what if I boiled the socks and made soup? After all, they smell like blue cheese. Ha ha ha! I started to laugh and I could not stop — something came over me and tears sprang to my eyes again, this time from laughter. I should gather them in little spice bottles, I thought, and label them: tears from laughter, tears from spicy food, tears from pain, tears from nostalgic memories, tears from broken hearts, tears from poverty. The ancient Phoenicians did it. They gathered their tears and buried them underground. Their whole kingdom floated above small glasses of tears before their boats hit the seas. I wondered why all cultures demand tears. The industry of tears! Tears must be seen then buried. Even Genevieve wanted my tears! When a young unmarried man dies back home, the people dance around the coffin singing wedding songs, and that always seems to bring on a lot of tears. Rasha, the first woman I knew, flooded me with tears the first time we slept together. At the time I didn't know what kind of tears those were. I didn't ask. We met in my building's shelter. I kissed her and moved my hips with a charged rhythm. She clung to my hair, and sobbed. Now I know that those were love tears. And now I know that when Tony came back and dragged my sister down the street by her hair, and she left a trail of tears, those were pain tears.

Later that day, I took the bowl back to my neighbour downstairs. The man was gone, but his wife opened the door. She giggled and avoided looking me in the eyes. I gave the bowl to her and thanked her, bowing, looking at her all the time, and she giggled and shoved her son behind the door. I hope you like?

Yes, yes, I said, it went down smooth as soup.

ON FRIDAY I WALKED to work, and as usual I stopped at the Artista Café to sniff around and see which of the landed refugees had left a yellow trace at the edge of a seat, on the leg of a table, or at the counter, but none of those welfare dogs was there. Maybe when they smell my scent, they disappear. I'm not sure why I still show up where I'm unwelcome, but it has become a habit of mine to choose unwelcoming places. I find it charming, the refugees' confusions and complaints. Their overt pride in spite of their destitution amuses me. I find it endearing. Lost mutts! They don't know what colour they are. They can't decide what breed they belong to. They sit in their own mess, feeling repulsed by their urine. They sprinkle traces of their lives here and there for no reason except to have the illusion of marking territory and holding on to vanishing places. Miserable dogs! All they can do is howl about the past, and their howls are lost between taxi fumes and their own shrinking cigarettes. Which reminds me: I must pay the professor a visit sometime this week.

I continued walking down St-Laurent. I passed the taxi stand at the corner of Prince-Arthur and St-Laurent, right next to a green bank. There I recognized the man who had been sitting at Shohreh's table the night I visited the nightclub. He was smoking in the cold with a few other taxi drivers while their cars idled, little streams of exhaust fuming from their tailpipes. The man did not recognize me, but then again, I had my scarf around my mouth like a thief. I went straight towards the men and asked for the time. One of them slowly pulled his wrist out of his sleeve and said it was two-thirty. I still had a little time before I had to show up at work, so I crossed the street to watch Shohreh's man. After finishing a cigarette, each driver went back to his car. The man's car was third in the taxi line. I knocked at his window and he slowly opened it. I uncovered my face and said: I know you.

The man did not say a word. He looked hard in my eyes, shook his head, and said, I do not know you. Iranian?

No, I am a friend of Shohreh's.

Which Shohreh? he asked. I know a couple.

Shohreh Sherazy.

He nodded.

I saw you at the nightclub last week, I said.

Yes, I was there. Still, I do not remember you.

It was a little dark, a little loud.

Yes, very noisy, he laughed.

Are you a relative of Shohreh's? I asked, blowing breath onto my fingers like a cold God creating the world, rubbing my hands like a happy thief, sticking my neck into my shoulders like a turtle, sniffing like a junkie, shivering like a ghost, inquiring like a Spanish inquisitor dreaming of a flamenco dancer to warm my heart.

Come inside the car if you are cold, the man said.

I hopped into the front seat and introduced myself.

The man nodded his head but did not tell me his name.

Well, I said, I just wanted to meet you, because we did not have the chance to be introduced that night.

He smiled, and said, So, you are a friend of Shohreh's. What kind of friend?

A close friend.

He smiled, and said, Yes, Shohreh has many friends.

You've known her for a long time, I said.

Yes, she was this big. He lowered his hand towards the floor of the car.

In Iran?

Yes. I was a friend of her family. I knew her uncle. We were jailed together.

Mullahs?

No, no, before that. The Shah. The mullahs jailed us afterwards. He laughed. We were tortured by both of them. I survived and . . . He paused.

Her uncle?

Her uncle. He shook his head. Disappeared. What do you do? he asked me.

I am working at a restaurant now. You know how it is, I said.

Oh yes. I was a journalist myself. Now I am a taxi driver. He laughed again.

You can still be a journalist.

No, I do not bother anymore. Now I am a taxi driver. That is what I am. Listen, let me tell you the story of the great Persian poet Farid al-Attar. He was captured by the Mongols. One day someone came and offered to his captors a thousand pieces of silver for Attar. Attar protested and told the Mongol not to sell him for that price since the price was not right. The Mongol was convinced and did not sell him. Later another buyer came along and offered to purchase Attar for a sack of straw. Attar counselled the Mongol to sell him because that is what he was truly worth. The Mongol cut off Attar's head. What do you do at the restaurant?

Busboy. Which reminds me, I am going to be late, I said. What is your name? I asked.

Majeed.

I gave him my hand to shake. Then I continued my walk to work. The ground was frozen bumps of ice. Slippery glass. Thick and transparent. My fucking shoes, however, were totally flat on the bottom. No grip left on the soles, and in any case the soles were smooth to begin with, which made them even more slippery. Walking over the bumps of glassy ice, I extended my arms like an airplane passing above a circus juggler walking a rope in ballerina shoes while below him elephants worked for peanuts and monkeys clapped.

I passed a woman bundled up all the way to her eyes. Only her eyes were showing. I grabbed her hand. She stopped. I said: I recognize you, shifty green eyes!

The woman looked at me. She was cold and shivering and fog fumed from her throat.

We met a while ago, under unfortunate circumstances, I said to her.

The woman pulled her scarf down and when I saw her lips, I knew for sure that she was the woman at the institution. How unusual to see her so willingly bundled up. She had always been so eager to take off her clothes. She had been chased by nurses through corridors and had always ended up in my room, sitting on my bed, buck-naked, her eyes shifting with an empty glaze.

She looked hard at me now, but did not recognize me.

I was in that place with you, I said.

Yes, she said, and I saw that she knew what I was talking about.

You sat on my bed. You would always run away and end up on my bed, I said, and my hand squeezed hers.

She looked in my eyes, not saying anything for a moment, and then she smiled and said, Maybe it was because you had these mischievous beautiful eyes.

Maybe it was because I was the quietest, I said.

Or the sweetest. Where are you going? she asked.

Work. You?

Work.

You are better? I asked.

Yes, with six pills a day and consultations three times a month. She laughed. I have to go. Come by sometime. I work in the clothing store at the corner of St-Laurent and Duluth. Come by and see me sometime, and she held my arm and kissed me on the cheek.

I WORKED THROUGH THE evening as usual, and the morning of the next day I passed by the Artista Café again and peered through its large front window. The professor was there, reading the newspaper. Bouncing with happiness and anticipation, I walked past the café and rushed towards his house. I was so excited that I ran through red lights, was cursed by taxi drivers, and rode the batches of slippery snow like a carefree surfer on a beach.

The professor lived in an even smaller place than mine. Basement houses are easy to break into — a stroll, really. Easy prey. The entrance to the professor's semi-basement apartment was dark and smelly. Inside, his bulky old fridge hummed like a time machine. I did not even need to open it. I know his kind. Even a cow would have stopped and covered her tits if she knew that her most valuable secretions would be forgotten here to stink and grow into a different species. But outside the fridge, everything was perfectly in place. Even the newspapers that the professor usually steals from the café were stacked in chronological order. It was a simple place, with a teapot on the stove of the professor's pseudo-kitchen, a small closet, his two pairs of summer shoes neatly placed side by side, looking like two missing persons beamed up into a spaceship.

I started laughing, and was soon laughing hysterically. I found it funny that the professor's place looked like a neat Oxford student's room. His pencils on his little table were sharpened and aligned. There was no TV. I looked for a radio, and when I found it, I mischievously changed the dial. That would throw off his routine. I imagined him coming home and hanging his coat in his usual place, turning on his radio to hear the news in French, and then mumbling to himself and complaining about the world. But, ha ha! his world was going to change. A new house order, my friend! I chose a hard-rock station and turned on the radio and blasted the volume. His drawers held a bunch of knick-knacks, objects he must have kept from his stay in Paris — a Paris subway map, a few postcards he had received from an old acquaintance, a woman by the name of Lydia, who must have visited Provence and walked through the romantic streets with their old stores, colourful windows, and the wooden doors of French cafés. This must have been the professor's *grand amour.* Then I found a wealth of correspondence. A treasure! I stole some of his letters, thinking that later I would sit on my bed and smoke a joint and read his love life and I would get even higher with the smell of ink and the faint scent of her fingers' residue in every line. In the professor's closet I found an old green suitcase that provoked in me images of departing trains, trench coats, and a beautiful woman in a head scarf and pointy shoes waiting on a platform. I opened it in no time. The locks, almost rusty, sprang upward like eyes opening from a bad dream. Inside, papers and envelopes were organized in bundles, bound tight with thin strings that joined in bows at the top. Under each knot there was a piece of paper with a label. I chose the one on top: "Immigration" said the label. I untied the bundle. The first manila envelope contained the professor's Algerian passport, thick and green. In his photo he looked like an intellectual revolutionary, although his long sideburns also made him look like a sixties-era Third World lady-tourist-chaser.

The second envelope had a word written on it: "Torture." It contained a few X-rays, an official letter of amnesty addressed to the professor, and other documents in Arabic. The other bundles contained photographs and bank documents, and the very last one had newspaper clippings.

I closed the suitcase, put it back on the shelf, and walked into the bedroom. I slipped my hand under his mattress and found a couple of *Playboy* magazines. I opened these, and found some of the pages stuck together like glue. Masturbator! I shouted, and jerked my head boisterously to the music of the rock band on the radio. I put the magazines back and went straight to the professor's bathroom, washed my hands, and looked in his cupboard. I beheld yellow plastic single-blade razors, Aspirin, and a few prescriptions. Then I went back to the bedroom and slipped my hand under the bed again, pulled out the magazines, tore out a few of the clean pages of naked women, folded them into my pocket, and slipped back outside. I walked away, my hand seeking warmth and swirling and fumbling what had happened to fall into my pocket.

THAT NIGHT AFTER WORK I slept with the photographs of naked women, photos that I drew from my pocket like a magician who draws birds from his hat to hand to his beautiful assistant, who, no matter how many times the magician tries to saw her inside his magic box, always comes up intact, in one piece, happily smiling on the stage, under the light. Applause, applause! But I, unlike that sloppy professor, made sure that none of the scum that squirted under my quilt touched the glossiness of the pages or those X-rated bodies.

How crazy it was, I thought, that even when the beautiful lady sat on my bed at the hospital, all I wanted to do was to cover her with my quilt and dry her wet hair with the cotton sheets that softened the harsh metal beds. It must have been the deflated neon light that made everything flat and shadow-less in that lunatics' house. And it must be the harsh lights and dramatic shadows in these photographs that make me agitated, make me rattle and shake with images of slimy snakes wrapped in my hand, and then make me repulsed by what splashes and stains the inside of my bed.

I stood up and walked straight to the bathroom and washed. Then I wrapped myself in a purple towel and faced the day. I pulled open the curtains and waited for the harsh theatre light to blind me onstage while I waved and bowed to the cheers and the applause of the ghosts of an audience, but to my surprise, a soft, even light diffused and flattened the mountains in the distance and the grey streets below my window. There was no shadow to be seen in the world today. I thought, It is the perfect day to go and see that woman from the hospital again. I will ask her to come outside and sit on a bench, and to hum if she doesn't feel like talking, and to sway back and forth if she is cold, and to let her hair get wet from the snow.

The woman smiled when she saw me entering the store. I knew you would come today, she said.

How did you know?

I saw you.

Where?

She pointed at her forehead. And I kind of remembered your bed in the mental hospital. You are the one who thought that you were a bird.

No, I protested, not a bird. I've never flown. I'm always walking on the ground. No illusion of flying. I stick to the ground.

I walked around the store. The woman was alone, and

well-dressed. She followed me. The store had very little merchandise and all of it was expensive. Everything was hung on a few racks and the store had a feeling of emptiness.

You are surrounded by clothing, I said, laughing.

Yes, she said, and she laughed in turn.

I thought you hated clothes.

I do, she said, and we both laughed again.

Heavy and oppressive, isn't it? Tissues and rags?

The woman nodded and looked me straight in the eyes, smiling.

Like gravity, like the sun, I said.

She nodded. Then she held my hand and said, Do not swallow, do not take it.

The sun? I asked.

No, those little colourful things that they will offer you when they come near you wearing white aprons.

The pills?

Yes. Never take them. They will transform you into what you are not. They will make you fat, and sick, and green like vegetables, and yellow like the sun. And if you complain they will just pull something off the rack with a designer's name on it and give you another size, another colour to try, and that will make you happy and slow, and you will believe that you don't exist unless you look at yourself in a mirror. You will disappear, and the only thing you will be able to see is your clothes.

I have to go, I said. The underground is waiting for me.

Come back sometime, in any way or as any creature, she said, as I passed through the door and back into the blue city.

THAT EVENING, MY BOSS asked me to clean his car. Clear out all the papers that are inside, and take a cloth and wipe the dashboard, he said to me. He hates to see an employee standing around doing nothing. He is a real pain in the ass. So now, when the restaurant is not busy, I dry the dishes three times, arrange and rearrange them, mop the clean floor, flush the toilet and clean out its bowl, or hold the broom and swing it across the floor, singing Italian tunes in my head. One night there was blowing snow outside and he came over to me and with his low, menacing voice asked me to clean the windows on the outside. I did not see the point really, in the middle of a storm, but I did it. Then two customers showed up and he left me alone.

Usually his teenage daughter showed up and stayed at the place until around six. Then her mother would come by in the family van and pick her up. When it was safe and no one was looking, I rolled my eyes at her, or even winked, and once I wiggled my backside at her. She loved it. She liked the attention. This evening I was in the basement, arranging the napkins and filling sauce bottles, when I saw her coming down the stairs. She went straight to the bathroom and stayed in there for a while. When she came out of the bathroom, the light from the lamp in the corridor illuminated her face and gave her a dramatic shadow, making her look older. I was on the dark side of the corridor where the dim rays of the flickering fluorescent light were blocked by the metal fridge. She did not notice me. I saw her adjusting her pants, and then she slipped her hand quickly below her blouse to her breasts and adjusted her bra. I froze in the corner, curled up and hunched, and watched. She stopped and stepped back, away from the stairs. Then she quickly turned and went back to the bathroom and locked the door.

I went up the stairs, carrying a box. I made sure the owner saw me, and then I quietly slipped back down to the basement. I knocked at the bathroom door. There was no answer. I knocked again. Is anyone there? I asked. Still there was no answer.

So I waited. And when the owner's daughter came out, I stood where I would be visible, at the edge of the stairs. As she passed, ignoring me, I whispered: Everybody does it.

She stopped, turned abruptly, looked at me, and said, Does what?

You know. Gets a little happy idea once in a while. There is nothing to be ashamed of, or hide. It is nature.

Nature?

Yes, one should never be ashamed of it. Everyone tells us it is bad, but it is all good.

It is good? she whispered back at me. She started to climb the stairs, and on the third step she turned and leaned her upper body towards me. Then, suddenly, she came back downstairs and stood right in front of me and said, If I tell my dad that you are watching me, he will kill you.

Do it, I said. But before you tell him, I want to get my last wish from you.

Our eyes locked.

I want to see, I said. Just see. Then you can tell him anything you want. I am willing to kill and willing to die.

Not here, she said, and she ran back up the stairs.

AT THE END OF THE NIGHT, I pulled out the vacuum, unleashed its cord, and let the machine loose to chase and devour all the crumbs and rice that had fallen over the red carpet. I changed the tablecloths and filled the lanterns on the tables with candles. Then I went to the kitchen and mopped the floor. The tiles in the kitchen were real tiles, thick and square, not the plastic kind found in North American houses. These tiles were the old kind found in marble palaces and grand dancing halls. In the middle of the kitchen, under the cook's counter, there was a drain. I pushed the water towards the drain and it disappeared, eradicating whatever was below the surface. Slices of rejected vegetables, grains of rice, eggshells, and peas swam and rolled on the waves like little boats. I chased the water, surrounded it, at times attacking it from the back, at times confronting it head-on, driving it like a herd of buffalo off a cliff. The drain swallowed everything, nothing was filtered, recycled, tossed away. All was good, all was natural, all was accepted by the underworld.

When I was done, I waited for the owner to finish counting his money. He buried his head behind the bar and licked his thumb as he folded the bills, jingled and tossed the change. Then he said, Come with me. He led me to the door. Do you know how to start a car?

Yes.

Here, this is the key for the car door and this is the engine key. Stay in it, warm it up, and I will be right there. He locked the store door behind me.

I cleared snow from the roof and the front and back windshields and sat inside the car, again rubbing my hands like a happy thief, drawing my neck into my shoulders like a turtle, sniffing like a junkie, shivering like a ghost.

Soft Persian music began to play. I slipped my hand into the glove compartment, quickly searching there. Nothing. I felt in the gap between the two front seats and pulled out a CD case. It showed a group of young men called Boys in Black. I memorized the name and put the CD back.

The owner knocked at the window and I opened the door for him and got out of the car. Without a word, he slipped inside and quickly shoved a plastic bag under the seat.

Amateur, I thought. The money is under the seat.

I waited while the owner pulled away from the curb. His bald head barely rose above his hands at the top of the wheel. He drove away. I stood there, waiting for his taillight to disappear. Then I was alone, and nothing moved around me, and it seemed as if no one else existed. With the cold comes a silence. I zipped up my jacket, put my hands in my pockets, lifted up my collar, and walked. My feet had a different rhythm than usual for them, and I was not sure if this was because the snow was different, the ice less squeaky, or if it was I who was not in harmony. My body passed through different shades of light. When I crossed under the hunched streetlight, I could see my breath leaving my body. In between the streetlights, in the darker places, it seemed as though my breath had ceased. Eventually I started walking to another rhythm. The streetlights must have been well-spaced, at equal intervals, because my breath appeared and disappeared in a regular way, through darkness and light. I forgot about the rhythm of my shoes, and something less noisy, something mute and visual, gave me another kind of rhythm. I tried to pace myself, even while speed-walking, even though I found it hard to stick to a regular rhythm because everything depended upon the obstacles on the ground. Higher snowbanks required more effort and slowed me down, but sometimes I passed in front of well-maintained houses where all the snow on the sidewalk was shovelled and cleaned up, and then I moved faster. Still, I felt that the cleaned-up paths were disruptive, hindering me from creating a perfect harmonious rhythm from my breath and the falling city lights.

I did not know how cold it was. I'm never sure of the temperature, and I never look at the weather forecast. I'm not sure why people in this place always start their conversations with remarks about the weather. Small talk frightens me. I have nothing to say. I do not see the point of communicating just for the sake of saying something. Yes, it is cold. I'll admit it if you want me to, but at least today I was well-fed. Tonight the cook made me a plate before he left. Without calling me over or telling me anything, he shoved a plate in front of me, and then the owner came over and pointed at it and looked at me. I sat at the small table next to the kitchen and ate, really trying not to show how much I was enjoying the food. I know what kind of merchant the owner is. Everything is negotiated. If my boss sensed my dependence on his meals, he might cut money from my pay or ask for more work and give me more orders, and who knows where it would all stop — maybe with cleaning his car, or heating his car, or shovelling his snow, driving his in-laws, cutting the lawn under his suburban plastic chairs, scrubbing his barbecue. Some of these immigrants are still eager to re-enact those lost days of houses with pillars, servants, and thick cigars. Filth! They are the worst — the Third World elite are the filth of the planet and I do not feel any affinity with their jingling-jewellery wives, their arrogance, their large TV screens. Filth! They consider themselves royalty when all they are is the residue of colonial power. They walk like they are aristocrats, owners from the land of spice and honey, yet they are nothing but the descendants of porters, colonial servants, gardeners, and sell-out soldiers for invading empires.

Under the streetlight my breath was fuming like a chimney. I would have liked a cigarette, but what was the point of smoking in the cold? One couldn't even smell the smoke, and a few seconds after being lit the cigarette would turn into a frozen roll of thin paper and damp tobacco. And who dared to pull fingers from a pocket to strike a match in the cold wind? Anyway, at this hour of the night it was better to not draw too much attention to yourself. I did not need to set my face ablaze. What I really needed was to bury my face in a woman's thighs, sweep my forehead across her soft black fur, warm my lips with her first flow. Maybe Shohreh would accept my cold nose. Maybe she would feel generous enough to embrace me in her thighs tonight and block my ears with her soft, tender flesh, and erase the sound of the crunching snow under my shoes. I dug deeper in my pocket, but I did not have any change for a phone call. I even ventured to take my fingers out of my coat pocket and dig into my pants pocket. Nothing! I came to a crossroad. If I went south, I could knock at her door, although at this late hour she wouldn't like it. If I went north, I could walk on St-Laurent Street and pass the bars, and, who knows, maybe I would get some closing arms to embrace me. Instead I chose neither of those directions and ended up in the old port. I did this for no reason, really, except that I was hesitant, hesitant to go home and hesitant to knock at warmth's door. Besides, I doubted if Shohreh would be home. She liked to go out on the weekends. She didn't like her job, and her escape was to wait for the end of the week to dance and dance.

The wind off the water was colder on the bank of the river. I gave it my back and looked at the old city, with all the churches, the old houses, paving the way for high-rises. I wondered how I had ended up here. How absurd. How absurd. The question is, Where to end? All those who leave immigrate to better their lives, but I wanted to better my death. Maybe it is the ending that matters, not the life, I thought. Maybe we, like elephants, walk far towards our chosen burials.

I walked back home.

On the way I passed by the Copa, a dim bar on St-Laurent. I looked through the window and saw Shohreh there with a few other friends of hers. Her girls' night, as she calls it. And no men are allowed to interrupt. I once bought cheap cocaine for Reza there, from Derrick the drug dealer, a brute who hardly said anything. Reza had complained to him about the quality of his product, and the guy had taken back the bag of drugs and told him never to show his face there again. So Reza had to look for another dealer. He begged me to go and ask for Derrick. When they ask, What Derrick? you answer, Big Derrick, he said.

Big Derrick showed up when I asked. Go to the bathroom, I will be there in a minute, he told me. And he found me between the mirror and the pissing walls. Twenty bucks did not impress him. Where had this guy come from? I wondered. You never saw him at the pool table or the bar. It was as if he had some kind of secret room with shelves of white powder and a large scale. In time I learned it was better not to say thank you to the bastard because he would think you were a student, and he might ignore you if he was waiting for an important call. The Big Motherfucker, Reza called him.

I finally made it home, took off my socks and underwear, and washed them in the tub. Then I covered myself and slept.

IV

I SAT ACROSS FROM Genevieve. She smiled at me. She had this caring smile, almost a pious smile, as if she were on the verge of a spiritual orgasm, like that of a nun married to Jesus. Actually, she did remind me of those nuns from my childhood who were married to the rebel from Nazareth. One in particular, Soeur Marie-Josee, passed by every Friday to collect money for the poor at my school. And every time she said the name Jesus, she sighed and that exact same smile appeared on her lips. I could still hear the jingle of her metal can filled with coins. I never gave money. Why should the poor give to the poor? my mother used to say.

Do you still smoke? Genevieve asked me.

Yes, when I can get a cigarette I smoke it, of course.

I was talking about drugs. In your blood test it showed that you smoke drugs. This is confidential information, but I am asking because drugs could be related to the episodes you experience sometimes. Do you smoke drugs?

I do, when I have the money or when someone offers them to me.

What kind?

Hash. The occasional line of coke if I am lucky.

Genevieve buried her notebook in her lap and wrote something. She said, You should be careful with heavy drugs. They might be triggers.

For what?

Episodes of delusion or delirium. Have you experienced those?

I stayed quiet.

You should tell me if you do.

No, I've never had that happen, I said.

You're sure?

Yes.

How is work?

Good.

Busy?

Yes.

You like it.

The food is good. I get fed.

Made any friends?

I'm too busy; I can't really talk. The owner is always there, and very demanding.

Have you seen his daughter again?

Yes.

Is she well?

Very.

You say it in a funny way.

I caught her playing with herself.

What?! Where?

In the basement.

And she saw you?

No, but I let her know that I saw her.

It seems as if you like people to know that you're watching them. Is that true? Or does that only happen when it is a woman?

I'm not sure what you are asking me.

Do you want women to like you?

Do you like me? I asked.

Yes, you are likable.

Why?

I think you are bright.

So you like bright people?

Yes, I am always impressed by them.

So why do you surround yourself with patients? Are patients bright? Or are you trying to make everyone brighter? I asked.

I care for all people, bright or not. And then some I like.

So you like me?

Yes, I do.

Why don't you show it? I brought you flowers. I showed intimacy, like you wanted me to. Now it is your turn.

We are in a professional relationship here. My interest in you is purely professional and it will never transcend that. Listen, I am trying to help you, and I'm doing everything I can to help you. Doesn't that count for something?

That is your job.

Yes, but I wouldn't be so patient with you if I did not see hope for you. Do you understand the magnitude of what you've been doing, breaking into people's houses?

I was silent.

Genevieve changed the subject. Tell me more about your mother's family. What about your mother's father?

He was a bootlegger.

Alcohol?

No, tobacco.

All his life?

No, he worked in a factory as well.

What kind?

A cement factory. He shoved cement into a large industrial oven, very hot.

How many kids did he have?

Many.

How was your mother's relationship with him?

She adored him.

And her mother, your grandmother?

I'm not sure. My mother did not talk a lot about her parents.

Was there violence in the family?

Violence was everywhere.

Right. Well, I'm not interested in the war for now. I am interested in your family's genealogy.

Yes.

Yes what?

Yes to your question about violence.

Who was violent?

My grandfather beat my grandmother when he got drunk.

You saw it?

Yes, once.

And what did you do?

Nothing, I froze. I was a kid. What could I do?

Right. Okay, let's talk some more about Tony. What did finally happen between you and Tony?

He managed to take my sister and her baby back to his house.

You couldn't stop him?

No, he came when I was away at the beach. I used to go with friends to the beach. We used to jump from a high rock.

Was that dangerous?

Yes.

Because the rock was so high?

Well, you had to be careful. You had to land in the water between two other rocks.

And did you land every time in the water?

No.

Ah. So . . . is that how you got the scar on your face?

Yes.

How did all of this make you feel?

Jumping?

No, the fact that your sister went back with Tony.

Well, I'm not sure. I think she wanted to go. But when I heard that he pulled her by the hair, I was determined to kill him.

You kept a gun all that time?

Yes.

Did you have a licence for it?

A licence, doctor? You make me laugh sometimes.

I do? I'm glad I do.

Well, things were different there. There were not so many laws.

Tell me more.

About?

Tony.

Well, I went to Abou-Roro.

Abou-Roro?

The thief.

Oh, yes. Here, I have it here, written down.

I told him that I wanted to kill that bastard and asked him about the best way to do it. He did not answer me. Instead he said, So your sister is working for Joseph Khoury, I heard.

Yes, I said.

I thought he already had two salesgirls in the store.

What are you trying to say? I asked.

Listen, don't take things personally. I am just trying to help.

Help?

Yes, if you think a little, you'll realize that the old man has money. Right? Revenge and honour are good, but if you can get a little money out of it, it is better, no?

What do you have in mind?

I could tell you, but you might get all offended.

Shoot. I won't be offended, I said.

Well, what is my cut?

Forty percent, I said.

Abou-Roro turned and left.

Fifty, I said.

This he accepted. He smiled, came back, put his hand on my shoulder and we walked together while he explained his plan. It is easy, he said, talking with his hands. You let Tony suspect that something is going on between your sister and Joseph Khoury. And I am not saying there is anything going on, please do not misunderstand me. Your sister's honour is safe with me. Still, if you said this, Tony would want to kill the old man. But first you go to Joseph Khoury and tell him that Tony is convinced he is sleeping with your sister, and that Tony promised to put a bullet between Joseph Khoury's eyes. Then tell him how much you hate the guy, how he mistreats your sister, et cetera, and that you have a common interest in getting rid of him. You do not tell him that you will do it. You tell him that you know someone who can do it for, let's say, fifteen thousand lira.

He won't pay it.

He will be scared for his life. He will even put you in his will. Listen. I've changed the plan. You do not say a word to Tony about your sister and Joseph Khoury. I will do it. Let me leak the rumour. That will be my half of the work.

But as soon as Tony knows, I said, he will come and kill the old man. That fucking guy is not going to give the old man a warning. He will just go and do it.

Timing, my friend, timing. It is all in the timing. You warn the old man first. It will give him a chance to leave. He hides, and then we tell Tony. Tony will go to the store looking for the old man, and when he finds Joseph gone, this will confirm everything. I see I still have a few things to teach you.

Then we will have to find out where Joseph Khoury is hiding so we can collect the money from him before we kill Tony.

No, you will drive him to his hideout.

And my sister? You think Tony will save her if he hears something like that?

When you take the old man to his hideout, you take your sister as well. She will be working that day at the store.

She won't come.

You will make her come.

What if the old man wants to leave the country instead of paying the money?

He won't. He is too old for that.

I'm not sure if this will work, I said.

It will. How long have you known me? Things have always worked out, right?

Genevieve listened to my story without saying anything. Now she asked, Did your sister know about your scam?

Of course not.

She was not aware of it at all?

No, she was not.

Someone knocked at the office door and apologized for the interruption. Genevieve stepped out. She came back and said: I'm sorry, but I have to go. There is an emergency at the hospital.

The hospital? I asked.

Yes. You know which one I am talking about?

The one?

Yes.

Give my regards to everyone there, I said.

I am sure the staff remember you.

I meant, give my regards to the patients, whoever, whatever, wherever they are.

Make an appointment at the desk and I will see you next week, said Genevieve. And she ran out of the room and slammed the door.

THE NEXT EVENING, when the girl entered her father's restaurant, we exchanged looks, fast and brief. I quickly buried my head in my work again. As she walked by me, I kept my eyes on the floor and caught a glimpse of her skirt and feet. I heard her father calling her by her name, Sehar. They exchanged a few words in Persian. I tried to think about what I could fetch from the basement, what might need to be fixed, arranged, filled. Then I went to the owner and said, There are boxes of supplies that need to be stacked on the shelves downstairs. Would you like me to empty them?

He nodded. The man barely talked to me. He barely acknowledged my existence. If he agreed with me about something, he would never give me the satisfaction of a Yes! or, What a brilliant idea! And if he objected to something I did, he directed me to do something else.

I waited for his daughter to come out of the kitchen with her daily plate of food. I crossed paths with her, showing her that I was on my way to the basement. Downstairs, I opened boxes with a cutter, took my time placing cans on the shelves, then folded each empty box and tucked it in the corner. I was almost done and Sehar hadn't appeared. She must be eating still, I reasoned. I took the broom and started to sweep the floor.

The boss came halfway down the stairs so that only the

lower part of his body showed. His talking shoes called me back up. He wanted me to help the waiter pull two tables together for a large party with a reservation that evening. Upstairs, Sehar was almost done eating, and I could hear her shouting something to her father. He responded in a full clear sentence, longer than usual. His voice sounded calm. She laughed and kept on telling him something. He ignored her, as if she was taking up too much of his time, and went back to the kitchen, sniffing slowly as he went.

When he was inside the kitchen, I waited until the other waiter went to get more lanterns and then I tried to get Sehar's attention. She noticed me but did not smile. She called me over to her table and said in a loud, bossy voice, Go bring me some sweets and some tea from the kitchen.

Would you like sugar? I asked.

Yes, you should always bring sugar with Iranian tea.

I meant with the sweets, I mumbled, and gave her a large smile.

She laughed and said: Bring me two brown sugar cubes. Brown ones, you hear, brown like my eyes. She smiled mischievously.

And I thought, She shouldn't have said that. Any hint of flirtation and I am out the door. It would take only one encounter like that to make her father realize that his daughter's laugh is accompanied by a sweep of the hair, a slightly longer look than usual, a fluttering of eyelashes, a bend of the neck, and that she even imagines stories that make her touch herself in dark alleys, below the stairs, under pyramid-like quilts. But I lucked out. The owner was still in the kitchen and the dishwasher's water was running, covering up the sound of young, luscious body fluid drizzling above silky plates and silver spoons.

After her afternoon tea and biscuits, Her Highness dipped her toes down the dark stairs. I did not waste time. I followed her right away. While she was in the bathroom down there, I gathered all the empty boxes, piling them in the corner. I cut a piece of rope, made a small knot at the end of it, passed it around the boxes, made another knot around the first knot with the other end, and pulled on the rope until it squeezed the boxes together.

I am good with ropes. It was finding a structure to support the rope and my own weight that had failed me that day in the park. But what if my plan had worked, and my windpipe had snapped with the sound of crunched-together boxes? I would have made a nice sight against the white landscape. I wore my red jacket that day. Just picture, a large red fruit swinging from high up in the tree. Just imagine how it would have looked from afar. No one could have missed it. And from afar the rope wouldn't have been visible at all. All that anyone would have seen was a red dot against the white horizon, suspended above the earth. Maybe that is all that is supposed to be left of our lives: a glimpse of beauty, an offering for those who are still trapped, a last offering to console them in their mundane existence.

The bathroom door opened. Sehar came towards me and asked, What are you doing here?

Working and singing.

I do not hear any singing.

It is in my head.

What are you singing?

A song from the new Boys in Black CD.

Oh my god, you listen to them?

Yes.

I love them. Which song is it?

I can't remember the title, but I have the whole CD at home.

Their last album?

Yes, the whole album. Cool cover and lyrics.

Bring it here next time, she said. I want to see it.

Why don't you come to my place and we can listen to it?

And Sehar put her hands on her waist and said: Wow, the busboy is inviting me to his palace! How exciting. She said this with irony, her body swaying under blue-black shiny hair. And what would we do there? Anything exciting? Like, washing dishes maybe? How fun.

I thought we could listen to the CD and watch what happens.

I think you've watched enough.

Not enough, never enough, I said, and smiled and looked her straight in the eyes, half begging, half suggesting, and fully waiting for a nod from under the stairs despite the risk of expulsion from paradise and the cuts of kitchen knives.

She was silent as she looked straight back at me. Her lashes were long, and her eyes reflected a small rectangular patch from the neon light behind me. It crossed her brown pupil like a streetlight in a store window, or an alien's eyes shining behind a mask. She squinted and said: Where do you live on this earth?

At Pinnacle Street, I said.

That's near my school.

Come after school, then.

Well, maybe. Leave me the address later.

Tuesday?

Sehar did not answer. She ran up the stairs. I opened the freight door, dragged the boxes by the rope up the stairs and through the back alley, and put the whole bundle next to the large metal garbage bin.

ON MONDAY I WENT to the music store on St-Catherine Street. I asked an employee for the latest CD by Boys in Black. I opened the case, slipped the cover booklet into my bag, and on my way out threw the CD in its case into the bag of a woman who was leaving the store. I followed her outside, and continued to trail her all through downtown. She shopped, walking from one window to the next. When she sat in a restaurant, I sat next to her. I ordered coffee, acting as suave and polite as I could, speaking French and rolling my R's. The woman even looked my way and gave me a smile. I smiled back at her. I took off my jacket, and while my hand was still inside my sleeve I slipped that hand into her bag and pulled out the CD case. I actually held it in my hand, making sure she could see what I had pulled out of my pocket, then I got out the CD booklet and read it. After a few minutes I pretended to go to the bathroom and instead walked out of the restaurant.

On Tuesday I got up late and went into my kitchen. Roaches ducked for their lives. I walked back to the bathroom, peed, and returned to the kitchen with a newspaper in my hand. I attacked the invaders on the head with news and head-lines. I spotted a particular one with light-coloured stripes, like an albino roach. It was fairly big and faster than the rest of the herd. It slid, almost gliding above the surface, more than it walked. It was skilful in its manoeuvres, confident. At one point it faced me and stood there, waving its antennae towards me like a TV receptor on a roof on a windy day. When I lifted the newspaper to pound it, it disappeared. I looked into the sink and saw its last white stripe ducking down the drain. I immediately opened the faucet and watched the water run down, imagining it chasing the albino in a gigantic flashing wave, rushing towards the glittering striped creature through the howling abyss. Then I cleaned the dishes and buried the cadavers. I fixed my bed, tucking in my sheet like the flag in a ceremony for dead soldiers. I opened the window to freshen the air and revive the atmosphere. I cleaned the toilet bowl and the sink. I closed the window, took a shower, dressed, and opened the window again. I positioned the Boys in Black CD on the floor below the window, turning the faces on the cover towards the light. The slight shininess of the plastic reflected the light, and I was afraid that the glare would efface the singers' faces. So I played with the angles until I evaded the sun and those smiling boys with the pierced ears and noses became visible again. Then I waited.

Just after 3 p.m., my doorbell rang. I went out into the hall-way and saw a school backpack mounting the stairs.

I am here, I said.

I got lost, Sehar said. This building is confusing.

She entered my apartment. I waited for her to pick up the CD, but she was more interested in the walls and in assessing my few sticks of furniture. She looked at the bed and the desk, and then she glanced out the window. A view, she said sarcastically.

Well, here are the boys, I said, and handed her the CD.

Cool, she said. Can we play it?

My CD player is in the shop, I said. I think I'll get another one soon.

She laughed and threw the CD on the bed.

So, what are we doing here?

Tea, I said.

Tea, she repeated and barely smiled.

I told her to sit, and she looked out the window while I gathered tea from a kitchen drawer. I was out of sugar. I excused myself, took the stairs, and knocked at the door of the Pakistani family downstairs. The wife opened, half veiling herself with the door, peeking out at me like a Bollywood heroine from behind a palace window.

Sugar, please? I asked.

She nodded, closed the door, and wordlessly opened it a moment later, a small bowl of sugar in her hand.

I danced up the stairs. In my kitchen, the water was boiling. Good timing, I thought. Timing is important. I offered Sehar tea.

I do not have much time, she said, and wrapped her fingers around the mug.

Well, then. Have you ever had sex? I asked her.

No. But I've kissed boys.

Did they touch you?

A little.

I do not want to touch you. I just want to watch you touching yourself.

I am not sure if I can do that . . . with you here, looking at me . . .

I won't look at you, I said. We can both face the wall and pretend that neither of us knows what the other is doing.

Sehar stood up, went into my bedroom, and got under the bedcover. I closed the curtains. A feeble light laminated the white wall. I sat on the chair near the bed. We both faced the wall, although first I saw her hand slowly disappear under the bedcover. There was silence. I turned my head and saw that her eyes were closed. Her knees lifted the sheet like a tent. I imagined her fingers steadily rotating and her mind projecting on the wall images of boys and young hairless singers.

I can't do it, she said after a minute. She looked at me. Are you crying? Oh my God, your eyes . . . This is weird! I can't do it. I have to go.

She pulled up her panties, got out of bed, fixed her skirt, opened the door, and ran down the stairs.

AFTER SEHAR LEFT, I took back the sugar bowl to the Pakistani family downstairs. The woman opened the door. This time none of the children stuck their heads into the doorway. When I asked the woman where her husband was, she said, Factory. A baby started to cry from inside. She slowly, apologetically, closed the door. I ran back upstairs. I opened the curtains in my bedroom and for some reason I felt an overwhelming urge to pull out the professor's letters. They all had the same type of envelope, yellow with an aged feel. The paper inside was rough and thin, the handwriting impeccable, large and clear. Each letter started with the words *Mon cher* — no name, just *Mon cher*. In the first one there was a lengthy description of the writer's long walk on the beach, details of the sky, the blue water. She (I determined that the letter writer was a woman when she accused the breeze of lifting her skirt and carrying her away) described an older couple who were walking hand in hand, and how seeing that made her feel happy; *le sable qui se lève avec le vent* reminded her of something, her childhood, her grandmother, a stroll among the flowers. Everything seemed to be about the past, the writer's own past. The letter dripped with Proustian memories: *Le visage mélancolique, les textures, l'innocence, les pas, le vieux monsieur avec un chapeau.* The subject was her feelings or some romantic escapade. The professor was never mentioned, or addressed for that matter; the letter was a monologue about the writer's own emotions, her transcendent state of being, with the professor a receptacle for her *temps perdu.* Poor professor, I thought, how deprived and left out he must have felt, excluded by all these *préoccupations avec la nature, le vent, les hirondelles.* What a lousy lay she must have been, imagining him to be someone else when he was on top, and something else again when he was on the bottom.

In the second letter, the writer seemed to reply to something the professor must have hinted about money, poverty, and their relationship. But everything was dismissed in a smooth, complacent romantic phrase: *Ah, les artistes et l'argent, toujours la souffrance pour l'art et l'amour,* and the letter proceeded to talk about a luscious meal that was presented to the writer by *le chef René lui-même, sur une terrasse sublime avec une vue très agréable. Le poisson frais et la dame au visage ridé.* The professor must have eaten his shoes from envy and hunger. The writer signed only L. at the end, not even a return address. She reminded me of Sylvie, a piano teacher I had met at the gourmet store where I worked before my rope incident. I used to deliver Sylvie's groceries. One time she offered me wine and pâté — or was it foie gras? — and I woke up the next morning in her sensual silk sheets.

Sylvie did not walk, she floated, her expensive silk nightgown trailing behind her as if it came with its own breeze. For her, everything had to be beautiful. She had to live a permanent life of beauty, and everything that surrounded her had to have a nostalgic or poetic meaning to it. Her soft voice, her stylish dresses, her good manners concealed a deep hidden violence and a resentment of nature's indifference to her ephemeral existence. We always met in sophisticated places. There were always dinners, cocktails, theatre. I soon became fed up with her make-believe life. I was bored. I hung around for a while because of the food, the wine and cheese. But any hint of misery from me, of problems or violence, was automatically dismissed and replaced with something happy, light, or pretty. Everything was described as *charmant, intéressant, d'une certaine sensibilité, la texture.* All her friends, too, lived in a state of permanent denial of the bad smells from sewers, infested slums, unheated apartments, single mothers on welfare, worn-out clothing. No, everything had to be perfect, every morsel of food had to be well served — presentation, always presentation, the ultimate mask.

I slept with all of Sylvie's friends. It was easy — all I had to do was call them and ask something about *un regard que j'ai senti de votre part et je voulais savoir si je m'imaginais des choses*. It worked on all of them. Stabbing one another in the back was fine as long as it was for romance, a story — in short, something presentable. One night when we all went for a dinner at a French restaurant, I stole their wallets, walked through the restaurant kitchen, and took off out the back door. I took the cash, tossed the empty wallets in the gutter, and went down to the Copa, sat at the bar, and drank.

Of course, Sylvie and her friends knew that I had done it. They knew perfectly well that it was I who had slipped my hand into their leather bags. None of them said a word; not even their boyfriends dared to confront me. They knew that I would slash their tires, enter their homes, poison their dogs, and break their stereos. They knew because I had showed them my scar. I made up stories about it. The preppie boyfriends felt that they were in the company of a noble savage, and they liked it. One of them, Jean-Mathieu his name was, the son of some big-shot industrialist, invited us once to his apartment in Île Ste-Hélène. He lived in one of those expensive apartments with faux shantytown architecture. While everyone was dancing and sniffing coke downstairs on the kitchen counter, he called me upstairs to his room. He closed the door, went to his closet, and said, *Regarde, mon ami. Ça, mon ami, c'est pour ceux qui* want to mess with me. He pulled out a Magnum, a beauty of an arm, all silver. It must have been worth thousands of dollars. He pointed it at my face and started to laugh. The fucker was high. His hand extended, he was smiling at me, playful.

I smiled back, looked him in the eyes, and faked a loud laugh, leaning my body away from the gun barrel. I pretended to admire the gun and slowly reached for his wrist and pointed the weapon towards the bed. Then I pulled his face towards me and said: Did you ever show that to your mommy? His expression changed as I started to twist his arm slowly. He got confused. I kept my reaction ambiguous, smiling at him, giggling, talking about what a beauty the gun was. Then I said, This beauty, lâche-le, I want to see it. I took it slowly out of his hand. I popped out the magazine quickly and pulled back the top, and the bullet in the firing chamber jumped onto the bed. I pressed the button and the chamber snapped back to its original position. I pointed it at Jean-Mathieu, and said, Now it is safer to put in someone's face, no? He nodded, gazing at me with coke-glazed eyes. I found the bullet on top of the bed and inserted it back in the magazine. Shoved the magazine in. Pushed the security button down. Then I opened the closet, grabbed one of Jean-Mathieu's cotton shirts, wiped the gun with it, and, laughing, I said to him, A baby like that has to be well taken care of, no? We do not want any fingerprints on it. I held on to the gun with the shirt and put it back on the shelf. Then I patted my palm on Jean-Mathieu's face like a godfather, and said, Nice gun. You should always be careful where you aim it. Let's go downstairs before the bowl with the white stuff gets lost in the noses of those brats.

I was the one who provided Sylvie's friends with drugs. I

bought the low-quality stuff from Big Derrick and over-charged the friends for it. They were corrupt, empty, selfish, self-absorbed, capable only of seeing themselves in the reflection from the tinted glass in their fancy cars. The women lived a hedonistic existence, not caring what the boys did as long as their surroundings were fashionable and presentable. I despised them; they admired me.

THERE WAS NOTHING IN the professor's letters but lost, empty lives and illusions of escape from life's ugliness. As I read them, I thought how some people must despise how they look. They must vomit when they see themselves naked, filthy, and wrinkled. They must be horrified to realize that they are made of skin, flesh that can be cut, boiled, and eaten, that they perspire, that fluid runs through them, that always, whatever they eat, no matter how presentable it is, the food that comes on fancy plates, that is savoured as it is illuminated by small candles on red tablecloths, that gives off the aroma of spices, will always, always be transformed into something ugly and repulsive. They are obsessive about masking their humanity, their dung, their droppings, their sweat, their curved toenails that grow and never stop growing. They despise this world and therefore they are engaged in a constant act of covering themselves up — covering up their faces, their feet, their nails, their breath, their decaying bodies. Though I discovered that one of Sylvie's friends, Thierry, the heretic son of a well-known conservative politician, was fed up with it all. He could no longer see beauty in the make-believe. I gave his girlfriend, Linda, a few orgasms between chains and slaps, and she told me about Thierry and his obsession with feces. He eats them, she said. He calls them *mes petits bonbons.* He waits for me every morning outside the bathroom, reminding me not to flush the toilet. He hates it when things disappear down the drain. He scoops out the feces and I have to clean everything afterwards. *C'est horrible!*

Meanwhile, my poor naïf professor was charmed by *le savoir-vivre, le savoir-faire, le savoir* this and that. Peasant! Educated peasant! He must have thought that some of this beloved letter-writer's glamour would spill over onto him and provide an ingenious cover for his deep desire to hide his misery, his provincial childhood. He was waiting for someone else to give him cover. He was too proud to do it himself, and too conscious of his own revulsion at life's raw truth. At least I am not. I see people for what they are. I strip them of everything and see their hollowness. I strip them, and they are relieved of the burden of colour and disguise.

I walked to the kitchen, struck a match, and lit one of the professor's letters. I watched it burn in the sink. A magnificent bonfire rose up and consumed it all: the Mediterranean shores, the fancy resorts, the rolling green landscape that stretched down to southern beaches, the old couples walking hand in hand, and the soft winds that passed by and carried the puffs of smoke out of my window. I looked up at the wall and I saw hundreds of roaches hypnotized, turned towards the light source, waving their whiskers in farewell to the fire.

ON FRIDAY AT WORK, Sehar was absent. I was very curious about her whereabouts, but I knew it was useless to ask the waiter or the cook or the dishwasher. Only her father knew the answer, and I could not ask him. What if she had suddenly grown older, I thought, and could stay home alone? She would walk the streets by herself, straight to her own house, and make her own food, get her own cup of tea and sugar. What if she decided to leave home and find rapture with her own kind and embrace the snow and long roads on her own?

I worked hard that night. I even made sure the owner saw me plunging my feet down the stairs and my hands down the toilet. Whether your daughter is here or not, sir, nothing will change my loyal behaviour and dedication to this God-fearing establishment of yours, I cunningly and implicitly said.

On my way home from the restaurant I turned south and with my cold fist knocked at Shohreh's door. She opened the door and walked back inside without saying a word. I took off my shoes, left them at the entrance to bleed snow, and walked across the hardwood floor to the kitchen, following in my lover's footsteps.

Do you want tea? she said.

Yes, please, I replied.

Are you hungry?

No, I ate at the restaurant.

Shohreh was in her pyjamas and her hair was pulled back and tied with an elastic band. Though her pyjama pants were loose-fitting, when she moved I could see the round curves of her ass. She stood at the sink washing a mug. I approached her and rested my hands on her buttocks. She didn't say a word, and though my hands were cold, she did not protest. I reached for her thighs with one arm and my other arm curved around her waist. I kissed her exposed neck.

I could never predict what Shohreh would do or how she would react to my advances, so when I touched her, my heart sped up. I could never get used to her rejection, but still I always took my chances. This time the water rushed down the sink and a red sponge foamed between her fingers. The mug was in the sink, filling with water. I tried to turn her so that she faced me, but she resisted. She wanted me to hold her like a stranger she couldn't see. Then she reached for the boiling kettle, killed its whistle, cut off its steam. She placed a full teapot on the counter, turned off the faucet, and sat down at the table.

You've been talking to Majeed, she said.

Who?

The taxi driver, Majeed.

Yes. He told you?

Shouldn't he?

Yes, if he wants to. But there's not much to say, really.

You know, you're one nosy and intrusive man.

I saw him by accident. It is not like I went looking for the guy.

Still, you could have walked by. But no, you were curious.

Yes, I could've walked on by, but I thought it was rude that you did not introduce me to him that night at the club.

Do you want sugar with your tea?

No.

How is your work at the restaurant?

Good.

Finish your tea and let's go to bed. You probably need a shower first. There is a towel in the closet. Do you have condoms?

Yes.

Show me.

In my jacket, over there.

Come to bed when you're done in the shower. Shohreh turned off the kitchen light and walked down the hallway. I stayed sitting in the dark and it suited me. I could hear Shohreh enter her bedroom. A small light flashed from her room, passed through the bedroom doorway, and fell into the narrow hallway. I wrapped my fingers around my mug of tea. Then I lifted it up and laid it against my cold cheek. After a moment, I sipped the tea, but I did not finish the cup. I poured most of it in the sink and watched it gladly disappear. I walked to the closet and pulled out a towel. The bathroom floor was cold. I let the water run for a while until it got warm. I stripped off all my clothing and laid it out on the floor. I used Shohreh's soap and shampoo, and her water fell on my face, rushed down my neck, my chest, my legs, and went under, taking with it all the restaurant leftovers, the kitchen smells, and the cold.

WHEN I GOT TO BED, Shohreh had her back turned to me.

Show me the condom, she said.

I gave it to her.

It is wrinkled. It is not good. She threw it on the floor.

But . . . I said.

Forget it. Just hold me.

I held her. She buried her face in my chest. Her hands were folded against her body, not touching me.

What did Majeed tell you?

That he was a journalist.

He was a good poet, too.

Tell me, I said. I am curious.

I know you are. I will tell you, but keep on holding me.

I squeezed her closer.

Majeed was my uncle's best friend, Shohreh said. They started together this underground magazine after the revolution in Iran.

What kind?

A socialist, leftist, intellectual magazine. The mullahs could not pinpoint its source. Finally they found the printer. He was tortured until he told them my uncle's name. They arrested my uncle. They tortured him, but he never gave them the names of any of his friends. Majeed was always grateful to him. My uncle was killed in the end. He was big and handsome, Shohreh said, and smiled. With straight black hair, so black that it almost seemed blue sometimes. He used to come to visit us and my mother would be so happy to see him. When her brother showed up, she would forget us, forget my father, forget the world. I used to watch her looking at him and forgetting herself. She never recovered from her brother's death. They were very close. She changed. A few years later, I had to leave Iran. I came here and got in touch with Majeed. He helped me. He took care of me. He felt responsible and was protective. Until something happened.

She fell silent.

Tell me. I won't settle for half the story, I said.

One curious soul you are, Shohreh sighed. Well, Majeed worked as a taxi driver, thinking it would be temporary until he learned French and found a job as a journalist or a teacher here. At first he kept writing poetry, and he tried to translate it into French, but I guess he did not see the point after a while. Maybe there was no interest in his work. He can recite Hafez. If you only understood Persian poetry and listened to him reciting, you would find it sublime. Anyhow, I was alone when I arrived here. I had no one here but him. He was the only one I could talk to. He cooked for me every day. Shohreh laughed, and said, At first I called him uncle. Then one day I came to visit him. He was on the sofa. He was smoking and drinking that night. He told me that he had always felt guilty about my uncle being dead while he, Majeed, could breathe in and exhale, and he held his cigarette up high. He did not cook and he did not eat that day. I went to the kitchen. He followed me and held my hand. Well, a few weeks after that, I found out that I was pregnant. Leaving a condom in a wallet in your back pocket when you're a taxi driver for ten hours a day is not a good idea. I do not understand men and their pockets. Maybe they should all carry purses. She laughed again.

The baby?

No. Shohreh shook her head. I did not have it. I had an abortion.

And he . . . ?

He knew. I told him. He wanted me to keep the baby. I had the abortion without telling him. I went alone. I walked to the clinic alone, and on the way there I was wondering how my uncle would feel about it. I became a fatalist in that moment. I thought that maybe everything is predetermined, that maybe I should keep the baby. Maybe my uncle had died to save the seed of that man. But still I walked to the clinic. I entered the building. Alone. Every other woman had someone with her. I was alone. Now you know. Satisfied, my curious soul?

Shohreh pulled up the covers and turned off the light. I kept my arms around her.

IN THE MORNING, Shohreh woke me up and offered me coffee. She took a shower. When she left the bathroom with two towels around her body, I followed her wet steps. I stood at the door of her bedroom and watched her drying her hair. Naked, she leaned towards the mirror, her torso arched forward, her ass shining in the soft light that came in from a side window and gave it a three-dimensional, sculpted form. I took a step towards her.

With an eyeliner pencil poised on the lid of her eye, she mumbled: Stay there. I can't. Besides, I am already late. I have no time for that now.

We walked together to the metro, neither of us saying a word. I went with her into the station. She used her pass on the turnstile and entered the tunnel. I watched her going down the escalator, descending towards the underground. I waited, hesitant to go out into the cold again. It was one of

those days that have no mercy on your toes, that are oblivious to the suffering of your ears, that are mean and determined to take a chunk of your nose. It was a day to remind
you that you can shiver all you want, sniff all you want, the
universe is still oblivious. And if you ask why the inhumane
temperature, the universe will answer you with tight lips and
a cold tone and tell you to go back where you came from if
you do not like it here.

Eventually I walked back towards home. Walking made
me warm, but my face and toes were still freezing. I have to
buy some shoes, I thought. The first thing to do when I get
paid is to buy shoes. I arrived at the Artista Café and entered
it without looking through the glass first like I usually do.
Inside I saw Reza sitting alone at a table. He looked like shit.
The professor and his entourage were not there. I sat down at
Reza's table. It took some time for either of us to say anything. Finally Reza lifted his coffee to his mouth, slurped,
held the cup in the air, and with his usual mocking face he
said: Are you going to order anything or will you tell the waitress to bring you water again?

Fuck off, I said.

Be careful. Now they carry bottled water. If you ask for a
freebie you might end up paying for the opened bottle.

I reached for Reza's cigarette box. He snapped it shut and
put it in his pocket.

You look like shit, I said. I see white on the tip of your
nostrils.

Reza stood up and ran to the bathroom. He came back a
moment later and said, Very funny.

Rough night last night?

Yup.

Didn't sleep? But I bet you had a good shit this morning.

Yup. The white stuff is good for your system.

Did you sleep on the couch or on a crowded bed?

On a crowded couch. I'm not too fond of orgies.

Bad experience with that?

Yes, your mother snores, Reza retorted.

Any leftovers from last night?

Yes, and you are not getting any.

I can hook you up with some real upper-crusters. I mean, not the petty dancers and restaurant musicians of your kitsch entourage. Real people. High end, high high end, first fucking class, I said, and joined my fingers together and turned my hand upwards and gestured like a Roman.

What, have you been promoted from kitchen sweeper/busboy in an Iranian restaurant to some kind of event promoter for high society?

Do you want to be hooked up or not?

Sure, show me how.

Where is your instrument? I asked.

At home.

Go and get it and meet me at Bernard and Park in an hour. Can you do that?

This better be good.

You won't regret it, I said.

I went back home. On the way upstairs I passed my neighbour's child screaming his lungs out. His mother was trying to comfort him, speaking to him in Urdu. Then she lost patience, started to scream, and jerked the child back inside the apartment. His cries were muffled, but still I could hear him sobbing through the door, and the stairs cascaded with tears all the way down to the street, and the snow melted with the kid's sadness.

I sat on my bed, pulled out a book, and started to read, but I couldn't concentrate. I read the same paragraph three times. What are the insects in my kitchen up to at this hour? I wondered. I walked to the kitchen, but no one was there. It was time to meet Reza so I went back out to the street and started to walk up towards Park and Bernard.

Reza was waiting inside the drugstore at the corner, waving at me. You are late. Don't you know I can't expose my instrument to this kind of cold? Do you know how old this instrument is? How far are we going?

Two, three blocks west.

He pulled out a scarf and wrapped it around the box he was carrying.

We walked together down the street, then entered a building, and I buzzed Sylvie twice, like I used to do when I delivered her groceries. She buzzed us in without asking who it was. When she saw me, she held the door half open, hesitating, slightly swinging it back and forth. Clearly she could not decide whether to shut it in my face or hear what I had to say.

It is important that we talk, I told her.

She glanced at Reza as if she was thinking about whether to embarrass me in front of a stranger. Then she said: Nothing is important between us anymore.

Her fake Parisian accent made this sound as if she were in a movie trailer for a French film.

I want to introduce you to my friend Reza here, I said, playing my part of the existentialist protagonist in a film noir, although I was missing a cigarette and some plumes of smoke.

I did not think you had any friends left, Sylvie said.

Reza, open your box, I said. Open it now, I snapped. To Sylvie I said, You have to hear Reza playing his Iranian instrument.

I knew Sylvie wouldn't be able to resist anything foreign. The key word was *Iranian*, and so I stressed it when I said it aloud.

Sylvie paused, holding the door steady.

Reza opened his box and laid it on the stairs, pulled out his santour and put it on top of the box, pulled out two little spoons, and started to hit the strings and play.

Sylvie was instantly intrigued, and when she leaned her face against the edge of the door, I knew I had her.

Okay, *ça suffit*, she said. The neighbours will come out now. They are going to think we are crazy, she laughed. She loved being labelled crazy. *La bourgeoise* thinks that she is wild and crazy! She is convinced that she and *la gang*, as she calls her friends, are *dingue*.

Reza and I took off our shoes and entered Sylvie's apartment. Reza walked towards the piano. He recognized the Steinway. He walked around it, passed his palm across its shiny black surface. He and Sylvie chatted about it and then he laid his box on the coffee table. Sylvie was intrigued. On her way to the kitchen, she glanced at me, and said: *Il est charmant, ton copain*. I smiled and followed her to the kitchen, where I remembered the cheeseboard's position, the wine bottle on its belly, the fridge standing upright, the French baguette sticking out from the woven villager's basket. All this brought back the memories of food and good living that I had once experienced.

Sylvie talked to Reza in her broken English with a heavy French accent, apologizing for her poor pronunciation. Reza smiled, assuring her that her English was perfect. He even laid his palm on her arm to reassure her. Their bodies moved closer and Sylvie asked him to play again, and he did. She told him that she loved his music, and that she would introduce him to a composer she had worked with on her own recording. She was very impressed when he told her that the instrument he played was a few hundred years old, that it was handed down from master to student. And that the seventy-two strings stood for the grandson of the Muslim prophet who was killed in battle with his entourage of seventy-two. Reza gave Sylvie the history of the instrument, and she was so intrigued that she asked him if she could touch it. He politely told her that he would rather not allow it, apologizing repeatedly.

Ah, *je comprends, je comprends*, she replied, I understand *ça doit être tellement délicat*.

Spirituel, I shouted from the kitchen, like a salesman closing the deal.

Ah, oui, spirituel. Mais, bien sûr, spirituel. Comment j'ai pas pensé à ça? Then Sylvie sat at the piano. As always, her long, silky robe dangled behind her, falling from the chair and touching the stage like an opera curtain. She played some of her own music for us, and her dramatic facial expressions made me sick. I remembered why I had felt I had to leave her and her lucrative *la gang*. But Reza stood beside the piano with a baby smile on his face, checking out the rich surroundings just like I had once upon a time. As her notes filled the space I went back to the kitchen, opened the fridge, pulled out goat cheese, ham, pâté, lettuce, tomatoes, olives, mustard, and mayonnaise, and made myself a duplex of a sandwich. Sylvie's cat rubbed its whiskers against my feet. I hate pets. I have nightmares about them chasing me, leading me down sewers, into deep gutters, sticking me with their claws and flashing their fangs behind me. Creatures like this only have respect for what is above them.

When I was on my last bite, Sylvie stood in the kitchen doorway. I see you found your way to the food as usual, she said. Eat what you want, but do not steal anything today, please. Your friend looks decent. Do not embarrass him.

Maybe I should be going, I said, still chewing.

Reza didn't want to leave; he gave me a "wait a little" wink. But Sylvie said she had an engagement and that settled it. On the way down the stairs Reza gave me the thumbs-up. We passed the entrance to the building but continued down the stairs, all the way to the laundry room. Reza poured the contents of a minuscule plastic bag onto the laundry counter and cut the powder with his bank card, and we both sucked it up like two loose vacuum cleaners. When we were warm, dry, and fluffy, we went back upstairs and walked the streets without feeling fear or the cold. A kind of grandiose assurance came over me and I felt confident and energetic.

Here is the deal, I said.

What deal? The deal is done. The deal is up your nose, man. The deal has just started. You will make good with her friends. They don't trust me anymore, but you they will trust. You are in. You have skills, you can perform, you do art. You naturally belong with the corrupt rulers, my friend. It must be because you come from a long line of Persian rulers. Six thousand years of civilization is finally paying off.

So, how did you belong? You have nothing to offer, no culture, no shit whatsoever. He laughed.

Do not be so sure about the latter, O grand heir of Xerxes. But okay. Listen. Let's cut the shit. They are loaded. I bluffed my way. You know, I was l'aventurier. I gave them a sense of the real.

Real? You! Reza laughed.

The fuckable, exotic, dangerous foreigner, I said. Play it right and they will toss you from one party to another. I want a cut.

What cut?

I will get you the shit from Big Derrick. You just tell them it is the real stuff. Those guys will snort anything. And we will split the difference. You won't forget your friend who is walking beside you. I know you won't.

How do you know that?

Because. Just like I put you in, I can pull you back out.

Pretty confident, aren't you? Let's see what happens first.

Things will happen, I said. They will.

We separated and I walked back home. As I climbed the stairs to my apartment, I felt the landings getting longer. And when I passed by the windows on the landings, I went faster and faster. The wells of light looked like water that could drench my hair, gush over my shoulder, fall like mop-water out of buckets thrown from balconies by housewives in sunny places, with permanent cigarettes on their lips and aimless twitching eyes. Now I ran up the stairs, looking for my keys, but could not find them. Cursing Reza, I accused him of stealing my keys. Frantic, I took off my jacket and searched it. Then I took off my shoes, my pants, and dug my hands through many pockets. I found the keys at last and somehow managed to open my door. I went inside the apartment and quickly reached for the curtains on the windows and closed them. I had inexplicable energy. I wanted everything to cease moving, but at the same time I knew that nothing was really moving. I went to the kitchen and frantically banged my shoes on the counter, whether the creatures were there or not. I hit my shoes against the sink, the dishes, the fridge. Then I climbed onto the counter and hit the walls, chasing creatures and slapping them flat. I could see myself doing this as if I were someone else's double and could predict every future move. Everything happened within time lapses. And just when I was about to kill a few more creatures, I heard a voice whispering to me: Manipulative, good-for-nothing murderer.

Before it could continue, I scrambled to the floor, lifted my slippers in the air, and said, Stop your insults or I might just slap your face.

Anger, hmmm. I never thought you would act on it again, the voice said.

And when I looked behind me, I saw the gigantic striped

albino cockroach standing on two of its feet, leaning against the kitchen door. It had grown to my size — even bigger, if you were to measure its antennae that touched the ceiling. It had a long thin face, curved like a hunched back, and as it spoke two of its small hands continuously rubbed against each other. Let's see you pounding with your slippers now, it said. Not feeling too big anymore, heh?

I was suddenly convinced that the Last Day the two Jehovah's Witness ladies had told me about had come to pass, and that all the good people had been zipped up to heaven. Only the likes of me had been left to face the creatures, the future rulers of the earth. Judgment Day seems so informal, even personal, I thought. I had always thought there would be collective punishment, an endless line of exhausted people pulling on ropes under the whips of half-naked, leather-bound foremen and slave-drivers. But this seems more personal. A representative of the future ruling race is actually here to escort me.

So, the world finally came to an end, I said to the striped beast.

But *mon cher*. The slimy creature at my door leaned its head sideways. The world ended for you a long time ago. You never participated in it. Look at you, always escaping, slipping, and feeling trapped in everything you do.

It is not escape, I said. I refuse to be a subordinate. It is my voluntary decision.

Yes, yes, the creature said impatiently. Because in your deep arrogance you believe that you belong to something better and higher. You are what I call a vulture, living on the periphery of the kill. Waiting for the kill, but never having the courage to do it yourself.

And what is a cockroach like you to judge? I replied, waving my shoe in his face. Hiding and nibbling on bits and pieces, on crumbs, I shot back at him. I'm not intimidated by your size or your horrific looks.

Yes, we are ugly, but we always know where we are going. We have a project.

An evil, oppressive one, if I may add! I shouted.

A change. A project to change this world, the creature corrected me, and waved his whiskers.

And to subordinate and kill all those who do not conform to your project.

Kill? Did I hear you say kill? Dear child, let's not be judgmental here. Let's not open wounds and recite the past. I have known you since your childhood. I even bit you once. Ah, I am sure you remember that day back home. Imagine: a barefoot child, gliding on those dirty tiles, in a hurry to go outside and play. Without socks, and in a childish hurry, you slipped your little toes inside your little shoes and something soft and tender fretting in there bit you. That was me. When you hid in your mother's closet I was also there, and when you stole candy from the store I was there, and when you collected bullets, and when you followed Abou-Roro down to the place of the massacre and watched him pull golden teeth from cadavers, I was there.

No, you were not! I threw my slipper at the creature's face. Soles will make you shiver, insect! Ha ha ha, no matter how big you get you will always crawl, insect, crawl! I screamed at the monster. I, at least, have no fear of stomping soles, of the sound of earth when it rattles under marching men's boots. I, at least, have the courage to refuse, to confront.

And kill? the insect interrupted me. You are one of us. You are part cockroach. But the worst part of it is that you are also human. Look at you how you strive to be worshipped by women, like those jealous, vain gods. Now go and be human, but remember you are always welcome. You know how to find us. Just keep your eyes on what is going on down in the underground.

V

WHEN I TOLD the therapist about my encounter with the giant cockroach, she was quiet for a moment, and then asked me to tell her more.

It was a big cockroach. And we had a conversation, I repeated.

What did you talk about?

Me.

What about you?

He said that I am part cockroach, part human.

Genevieve was quiet again. She looked me in the eyes. Do you feel part cockroach?

I don't know, but I do not feel fully human.

What does it mean to be human?

I'm not sure. Maybe being human is being trapped.

To be an insect is to be free, then?

In a sense. Maybe.

Tell me how.

You are more invisible.

To whom, to what?

To everything, to the light.

How long ago did this happen?

What?

The encounter with the cockroach.

Five days ago. On Saturday.

And since that time, what happened? Did it visit you again? Or did anything else appear to you?

No. Nothing happened. Or everything happened as usual. I went to work the next day, everything was normal.

Did you take something that day you saw the cockroach?

Like what?

Like drugs.

I kept my silence.

If you still do drugs, I can't help you, Genevieve said. But I am glad you shared that with me. It could be a reaction to something you took. If this happens more often, and especially when you are not on drugs — because you will not take drugs again, right? — you will tell me, right? I won't ask more questions now, but you are lucky that you got out of the hallucination. Some people never recover from episodes. Drugs are usually not the only cause of hallucinations, but in your case they make you more vulnerable. What are we going to do about it?

About what?

About taking drugs! Genevieve's voice became higher and she looked more irritated, more disappointed. I am here to assess your situation, she said, and to monitor your progress. Yes, I am here to help you, but you know what? In the end I am an employee of the government. People are paying taxes for you to be here. Do you understand my responsibilities? I really want to help, but you have to meet me halfway.

Somehow, despite her anger, I was waiting for her to touch my arm as she sometimes had in the past. But with time she had become more cautious. She could tell that I wanted to bring her hand into my lap, to hold on to her fingers. I hate to admit it, but the big roach knows me well. I want to be worshipped and admired.

THE NEXT DAY at noon, a soft, light cascade of snow fell. I could see it through my window. It was the kind of wet snow that hits the glass and immediately turns to water. I opened the window, stuck my hand outside, touched the outer side of the glass, and waited until a falling flake hit my open palm. I pulled back my hand, closed the window, and licked the drop in my palm. I had always wanted to capture one of those flakes before it settled and took over the ground, the cars, and the city roofs. Little creatures that seem insignificant and small are murderous in their sheer vast numbers, their conformity, their repetitiveness, their steady army-like movements, their soundless invasions. They terrify me.

My grandmother told me about the famine days, when zillions of grasshoppers came and invaded the countryside and ate all the grain, all the fruit, all the vegetables. Her family survived only because they had a few chickens and they dug up roots. But the famine took the lives of half the population, and then the Turkish army came and confiscated the stores of grain and food. There was a boy, she remembered, who was her own age and who came every day and asked my grandmother's mother for food. All he said was, Aunty, I am hungry. But her mother chased him away. And then my grandmother chased him away. And then one day he didn't show up. My grandmother cried as she told this story. She watched those insects settle like clouds on fields and turn them bare and plain. I see people that way, I see snow that way, I see wind, cars, the words that fly from people's teeth, the white dust that I channel through my nostrils, the flowing water that way. Everything is made of little particles that gather in groups and invade. All nature gathers and invades.

How can I explain all of this to Genevieve? How can I tell her that I do not want to be part of anything because I am afraid I will become an invader who would make little boys hunger, who would watch them die with an empty stomach. I am part roach now, and what if my instincts make the best of me and lead me to those armies of antennae, hunched backs, and devouring teeth that are preparing from the underground to surface and invade? Could it be that the cockroach saw me throwing my rope over the tree in the park, and rushed to cut that branch above me? Yes, that is what must have happened. I had thought that branch was sturdy. I must go and take a look. I must walk back to the mountain and see if there are traces of nibbling teeth on the tree. I must walk up and look again. I must see it now. I will stand in front of the tree and imagine how I would have looked, hanging by a thread, with only a thin link to existence. But how, how to exist and not to belong?

A little while later, I walked to the park on the mountain, passing through a graveyard of marble angels and words carved in stone. I passed the man-made lake, the few bare maple trees. It is funny, I thought. What I remembered most was these trees. That day, I must have examined them all closely. Now I found the particular tree. I also saw a few horse droppings underneath it, which reminded me of the mounted-police post nearby. I looked up, trying to see the branch, but it was hard to see from the ground. I thought of climbing the tree, but was afraid that if I was seen again and captured by those modern horse-riders, they might think I was contemplating another attempt at my life. I walked around the tree for a little while, pretending that I was looking for squirrels to feed — or at least that would be the official story if I were asked. Then I decided to walk back home because I was getting late for work, that place where humans and insects are equally fed.

I ENTERED THE RESTAURANT. Sehar was there, earlier than her usual time. These days she treated me like an employee, and she hardly ever went down to the basement anymore. If I followed her even accidentally, she looked at me with squinty eyes and said, What are you doing down here? Go up to your work. And she said this with defiance, with the abuse reserved for retards, for the sick-minded, the impolite, the hypocrites, the subversive.

After her meal she called out to me loudly, as one calls ancient servants, and asked me to bring her tea and sweets.

Somehow I found her treatment reassuring, because it meant her father would never suspect anything. His perception was that no princess would ever sleep with her inferior.

But now that I had turned into a eunuch in her palace, a slave to bring her food and fill the pool with warm water for her bath, I knew that she might wait for the king to be away fighting dragons and slaying peasants, and then she might pretend that I was a gladiator, and touch my muscles, and have her orgasm before dropping me into a circle of lions.

I brought Sehar her tea and looked her in the eyes. She shifted her gaze immediately. Then as soon as I turned my back, she called to me and said: This tea is too strong. Go bring me another one.

Shall I put that one in a doggy bag, My Highness? I inquired politely.

I could tell she wanted to laugh, but she kept a serious face. Then she barely smiled and said, Just get me another one, and pushed the cup towards me.

A little later, the owner called me over. He asked me to get my coat from downstairs, and when I did, he said, Come. I followed him out of the restaurant.

Stay outside here, the owner told me, and if anyone comes to the restaurant you say, We are closed until seven for a private party. Understand?

Yes.

What will you say?

Sorry, we are closed for a private party.

Until what time?

Seven.

The owner nodded and went back inside.

After a few minutes, a limousine stopped in front of the restaurant and two large men got out. One walked towards me and stood next to me. The other went into the restaurant. The owner came outside and said to the man beside me, Yes, he works here. He motioned for me to come back inside.

The man walked back to the car, opened a door, and a short Middle Eastern man got out holding his hat, and went inside the restaurant. The owner ran to meet the short man at the door, greeting him and taking his coat. He bowed his head like I had never seen him do before, and extended his arm and showed the short man the way inside. The two big men looked around, protecting the short man like body-guards do, while the owner showered the short man with welcomes, bowing like a servant. One of the large men — the driver — left after looking around. The other sat at the bar with his shaded glasses and big biceps. The short man sat down at a table in the corner. When I went to light the candle on his table, the owner stopped me and ordered me to go to the kitchen and do some work and not come too close. The owner served the short man himself, smiling and rubbing his hands together like the meek merchant that he was. The cook was ordered to start working on the order right away, then called over to the table by the owner. The owner intro-duced the cook to the short man, and the cook leaned towards the man's menu and explained something to him in Farsi, pointing his index finger at the menu. The short man nodded. The cook took back the menu and smiled politely and went back to the kitchen. I watched their gestures; the short man was important.

Sehar was still in the restaurant, looking bored and neg-lected. She went behind the bar and picked up the phone and started to chat and play with her hair. Her father took the phone out of her hand and gave her a severe look that was followed by an order. She went back and sat at the table next to the kitchen door. She looked my way and then went down the stairs, glancing at me again. I continued mopping the floor. The cook was busy, concentrating on the stove. He looked preoccupied, as if he had thirty orders. The owner went in and out of the kitchen, restlessly arranging small plates and distracting the cook with his nervous body gestures and questions. Meanwhile, I pictured his daughter-deity's fingers roaming the underground. They must have reached beautiful Venice and its tight watercourses by now. I swabbed the floor and swung the mop like a gondolier, wishing I could be singing to the drifting tide beneath her thighs.

A few minutes later, Reza showed up with his musicians. Shohreh and Farhoud had also come with Reza. The bodyguard made them all open their bags, including Reza's instrument case. The owner walked to the door to talk to Shohreh and Farhoud. His manner seemed apologetic, as if he were telling them that it was a private party. But Shohreh would not take no for an answer. She continued to talk with the owner, pointing at Reza, who stood by, hesitant. Then the owner bowed his head and went to the short man to ask his permission. The man glanced up quickly at the owner and nodded. The owner turned and snapped his fingers at me. I left Venice and its waters and walked across the floor. You help them, the owner said in his usual laconic manner.

When Shohreh and Farhoud saw me, they both smiled. Shohreh was amused to see me with the white apron around my waist. Farhoud said, Okay, where is the menu, mister waiter? He snapped his fingers and they both giggled.

As they checked the menu, I waited above their heads with a little book and a pencil in my palm, making maps of Venice, drawing old Italian houses and long, wet canals, and the ink flooded across the pages like murky water. Shohreh asked me a complicated question, sometimes talking to me in Farsi, knowing well that I did not understand it. In the background I could hear Reza and his band tuning their instruments, the cook banging on his pots, the rice steaming, the snow falling, and the daughter's heavy breathing sounding like foreign languages on a shortwave radio. Finally they ordered and I went back to the cook, who was not happy to receive my incoherent orders, my mispronunciation of the dishes' names, my slow instructions. He corrected me with curt mumbles that sounded like spitting fire, that hit me in the face like splashes of boiling oil. The whole place was at the service of the short man at the table in the corner. The waiter waited, standing like a guard; the owner buzzed and kneeled and danced and whispered and ordered us around. He looked so pathetic in front of this mysterious man.

A few minutes later I served my friends rice and saffron, lamb in pomegranate sauce, and mast-o-khiar. Shohreh was dressed up and she looked like a lady, with her little black leather purse, her makeup, her high heels, her see-through silk shawl covering her shoulders, twisting around her elbow, and bending down to lick her knees. Farhoud wore a black suit and bowtie, and he had combed his hair to the side and pasted gel to hold it. He looked like a tough gangster from an old

American movie. They were dressed up, playful, exaggerating the elegance of their movements, graceful without shame, assertive, chic, defiant, confident, and they giggled the whole time, not taking anything seriously, not the owner, not the little candles that emitted heat, flickered red, and directed the oval plates in my hands. Shohreh sent me kisses, flirted with me, winked at me, and when I approached the table she took off a shoe and touched my leg with her toes. I imagined pulling the tablecloth swiftly from under the dishes, the candle, and her elbow, just like a magician. I would dangle that tablecloth from the ceiling and annex a part of the room. I would hang it like a veil and strip Shohreh naked, pour yogurt on her breast, and lick it off with my lips and tongue. I would trip the bodyguard, seize a gun, shoot the owner, the cook, and the dead chicken above the stove, pull a red Persian carpet from the wall, flip it twice in the air, and fly with my lover above this white city, through the chilling wind, and land on a warm beach where I would walk with her along the shore, shoes in our hands and the sun in our eyes.

I watched Shohreh and saw that she talked like a star, smoked like a star, drank like a star. Both my friends ate slowly and delicately. Shohreh made sure none of the food touched her red lipstick, and Farhoud served her like she was a queen. They toasted each other, and turned to toast me as well. Sehar watched all of this from behind the counter. She seemed fascinated with Shohreh. When Shohreh got up and walked to the bathroom, Sehar's eyes opened wide. My lover came towards me, and in a seductive melodic tone (just as Reza's santour reverberated to a high note) she whispered: Where is the bathroom, please? I showed her the way. She fluttered her eyelashes and swung her shawl and went slowly down the stairs swinging her hips, carefully depositing every step on the stairs. Near the bottom she looked back at me, and smiled and winked and blew me a kiss. And I wondered if I should unwrap my apron, throw away my latex gloves, make sure the kids were asleep, fix my hair, close the bedroom door, and change into something more comfortable.

When Shohreh came back up the stairs, Sehar stood in her way. Shohreh smiled and tried to pass around her, but the owner's daughter still stood in the way, mesmerized. She wanted to look at Shohreh up close. Shohreh smiled, excused herself, and walked by, swaying her upper body in quarter-notes. And then, as she crossed the floor, she stopped. She looked at the short man. Her hands dropped, her walk changed. She walked fast, back to the table. There she drank and looked agitated. She moved her head left and right, glancing again and again at the short man's back. Then she stood up and walked back towards the bathroom, bumping into a few chairs as she hurtled down to the basement. Sehar followed her. I followed them both. I found Shohreh in the corridor, nauseous, leaning her arm against the wall, her head towards the floor, holding her stomach.

Are you okay, Madame? Sehar asked.

Shohreh released a feeble nod, then rushed to the bathroom. Her face suspended in front of her body, she spilled part of her vomit on the bathroom floor and splashed the rest of it into the toilet bowl. I rushed upstairs to get water while Sehar held her arm. Then Shohreh grabbed the edge of the door frame and leaned on it, unsure whether she wanted to go back upstairs or stay. She barely drank from the glass of water I offered her. I rushed back to the closet and got her some napkins.

I must go, she mumbled.

I helped Shohreh up the stairs. As she crossed the floor, she held the napkins to her mouth, covering her face. The owner saw me holding her arm and became even more distressed. Farhoud stood up, surprised, and the bodyguard too stood up from his stool, facing us and keeping an eye on us. Shohreh went over and talked to the owner in Farsi. He was quiet and kept glancing towards the short man, wondering if any of this was disrupting his important guest's meal. Farhoud pulled out his wallet to pay, but the owner laid his hand on the wallet and refused to take the money. Instead he rushed them both out the door, eager to get rid of them.

I followed my friends outside. They were walking slowly, shuffling their feet on the sidewalk. Then they stopped and faced each other. I rushed towards them and saw Shohreh in tears. She and Farhoud were speaking in Farsi and I could not understand them. Then Shohreh's demeanour suddenly changed and her face looked angry. She appeared to want to go back to the restaurant, but Farhoud grabbed her by the arm and held her back, gesturing with his hands, talking to her in a soft voice. Then Shohreh turned to me, and said, Do you know who the man is? Do you know? Do you know the man?

I was confused, and before I could answer, Farhoud pushed her back, talked to her, tried to calm her down, and dragged her towards the bus station. Then he looked my way and said,

Go back. You will catch a cold without your jacket on. Go back. She is okay with me.

I went back. As soon as I entered the door of the restaurant, the owner rushed over to me and said in a low voice, Come.

I followed him to the kitchen.

He walked all the way to the back. Then he asked me, What happened to that girl?

I am not sure.

My food is all clean. If she said that she had food poisoning, it is not true. She ate the same food as everyone else. What did she say?

I cannot understand Farsi, sir, but she seemed upset. Maybe she had a fight with her friend.

The owner went to the door of the kitchen and called Reza. Reza gave a sign to the rest of the musicians and followed the owner. I saw him bowing his head and shaking it in denial, quietly gesturing with his hands.

The owner come back to me, irritated, and said: Take the mop and clean downstairs. Use soap.

I took the bucket and the mop, and filled the bucket with soap and water. I put everything down at the door to the bathroom, fetched a roll of paper towels from the closet, rolled it around my palm, tore it, and walked back towards my lover's remains. I swept it all up, until the last bit, the last grain of rice, the last fluid, had disappeared into the bucket, and as I swept I wondered if any of my saliva from last night had been rejected today by her body. I dipped the mop into the bucket, squeezed it, and started to move my gondolier's pole through all the sewers that run beneath the earth. Then I poured the bucket into the toilet bowl, and all that Shohreh had eaten was gone, feeding the city gutters honey and jasmine. I thought how the long, hollow tunnels must be happy, echoing with the joy of packs of rodents, insects, pet alligators, thirsty vampires, and blind bats. All shall feast on what her teeth ground, her eyes imagined, her fingers ordered, and her lips have touched.

AT THE END of the evening Reza waited for me at the door, standing there with his instrument box wrapped up in a thick quilt. Let's talk, he said. What happened with Shohreh?

You were there, I answered.

I couldn't see or hear anything. The owner asked me if Shohreh and Farhoud were my friends. I've got to stop bringing people I know to this place. First you — the owner thinks he did me a favour by hiring you. Now if I want to ask for a raise he will mention you, just to make me feel like he did me a great favour. And then, this tonight! Shohreh acting like a drama queen. What the fuck! I am making a living here. What's with you people? You come here and get me in trouble. So, tell me what was wrong with the diva?

I don't know, I said. I just don't know. She kept on asking me if I knew that man.

What man?

I don't know. Call and ask her.

Which way are you going? Reza asked me.

Home.

Come over to my place.

No, I am going back home, I said.

Reza turned and left me and walked towards the subway, and I watched his big body hugging his instrument case as if it were a permanent companion. I kept walking, and when I had gone a block, a taxi pulled up beside me. The window rolled down and I saw Majeed. He gestured to me to get in. I opened the door and sat in the passenger seat.

Did you see where that man who was in the restaurant went? Majeed asked me. Did you see what direction?

What man?

The man in the restaurant — a short, bald Iranian man.

The owner?

No.

The customer?

Yes.

He left a while ago, with his bodyguard. His limousine driver picked him up. So that's what Shohreh was upset about? She asked me about the man as well. Did she send you here?

Majeed did not answer me.

What is going on? I persisted.

It's not important. Where do you live?

Pinnacle Street.

I will drive you home.

In the car there was silence between Majeed and me. Only the radio dispatcher spoke, calling out car numbers, giving addresses, making the car sound like a spaceship travelling past houses of humans and nests of squirrels. Majeed looked pensive, perhaps a little stressed. After a while I tried to make a conversation with him, but it seemed as if he was in a rush to drop me off. He offered me a cigarette. I took one. He partially opened his window and drove with one hand on the wheel while he smoked with the other. I cracked my window and smoked too, puffing at the passing buildings, the passing signs, the passing lives, the wind, the cold, and the deep, dark sky.

You must meet a lot of different people in this job, I said at last.

He nodded, then smiled, and then he said, Yes, all kinds. In this job you meet all kinds. He was taken with his thought, swallowing the cigarette's fumes, holding every inhalation, making sure every ounce of nicotine touched his heart, stained his lungs, rushed through two cycles of his blood, yellowed his teeth, and was finally released to face the trembling cold air that rushed through the open car windows, smashed against the windshield, ricocheted off dizzying wipers that swung back and forth like a man caught between many thoughts, streets, languages, lovers, backseat conversations, red lights, traffic, metal bars, a few women, and a storm.

Yesterday these two kids got in the car, Majeed said. They wanted to go to a strip joint on St-Catherine. But they said they wanted to stop at a bank on the way. So I stopped at the bank. I watched them in the rear-view mirror. The girl was maybe sixteen. She had high heels and a very short skirt and only a small jacket. She must have been very cold. The boy was drunk. When they reached the bank, the girl took the boy's hand and they both started to run. I made a U-turn in the middle of the street and chased them with my car. They went into the back alley beside the bank building. You should have seen the girl running with those high heels and her underwear almost showing. The boy was so drunk she had to hold his hand and pull him. I caught up with them. I made them come back inside the car. She said to me, I was looking for the manager but the bank was closed.

I said: I am getting paid or I will take you to the police.

Then the guy said, Take me to a depanneur.

I said, Okay, but only one of you goes into the store. The other stays in the car.

When I stopped at a depanneur, the girl said, I will get the money. She got out and then she ran, leaving her boyfriend in the car.

I said to the boy, Your friend left and you have to pay me or I will take you to the police.

He was scared. He got out the money and gave me twenty dollars. I said, You are not getting change back. Go now. He left. There are all kinds of stories, my friend. This business is just crazy. Then Majeed asked me: How long have you been here?

Seven years, I said.

Your family is here?

No.

I haven't seen my parents in twenty years, he said.

Shohreh is your family, I said.

Majeed looked at me, smoked, and kept quiet. Then, for no apparent reason, he said: You know, we come to these countries for refuge and to find better lives, but it is these countries that made us leave our homes in the first place.

What do you mean?

You know, these countries we live in talk about democracy,

but they do not want democracy. They want only dictators. It is easier for them to deal with dictators than to have democracy in the countries we come from. I fought for democracy. I was tortured for democracy, by both the Shah and the mullahs, on two separate occasions. Both regimes are the same. And you know what I do now because of democracy? I drive a car for twelve hours a day, he said, and laughed. Do you think if the mullahs go away there will be democracy in my country? No! They will put back somebody else who is a dictator. Maybe not a religious one, but it will be the same. Do you understand?

Yes, I do.

Does that bald man come often to the restaurant?

Maybe you should ask Reza. He has been working there for a long time, I said.

That musician will not tell me anything. He just wants to play. I will not ask him anything. He does not care about anything. He does not want to talk about politics. He belongs to that new, hedonistic generation. So, you had never seen this man before?

No, I said.

Majeed stopped in front of my home. He pulled out a business card, wrote a number on the back, and said to me, Here. This is my number. If that man comes again to the restaurant, could you call me?

What about that man? I asked. Who is he?

Let's just say he is an old acquaintance of ours.

Who is "us"?

Us! Exiles! He left me on the sidewalk and his car lights

trailed away, bouncing off the reflections of neon signs on the wet ground. I watched him disappear.

I pulled off a glove and dug with my hand in my pocket. I felt the bills the restaurant owner had given me and remembered that I had been paid today. I felt a sense of pride, and also a desire for revenge. Revenge for past hunger, cold, and those days when the sun chased me from one room to another, making me sweat and making me blind. I pulled out my house keys and shifted them from one pocket to another. I pulled down my woollen hat over my forehead. Then I turned and walked around the corner.

There was a bar there called Greeny, one of the few rundown bars that had not been given a facelift in my slowly gentrifying neighbourhood. I entered it. Perfect! Dark, just as I liked it. I entered like a panther, and I could hear the wooden floor creaking under my paws. I ordered a mug of beer, some fries, and a large, fat hamburger that came to me in a basket (brought to me by the granddaughter of Québécois villagers who, one hundred years ago, were ordered by the priest to get pregnant and to kneel beside church benches every Sunday). I gave the waitress the wrong change, and asked for her forgiveness, and to reassure her that I was not trying to stiff her out of the money, I threw her a big fat tip. This made her change her tone, and she called me *Monsieur* as I bit through the bun and the meat. I drank ferociously and looked at her in her apron, nodding as I chewed. I gulped and wiped my mouth with a white disposable napkin.

I have ambivalent feelings about these places. To tell the truth, they kind of repulse me, but I always end up coming back to them. I am drawn to dark places like a suicidal moth to artificial lights. I certainly avoid any contact with the other customers. I keep it simple: I order, I drink, and I eat. I keep to myself. I have no interest in sports or small talk, but I like watching the other men, leaning forward on high stools, gazing through the liquid in their glasses. I also like the reflections of the TV screens that splash over these men's faces with buckets of light, making them change colours like chameleons. I like the waitresses. I like how strong and assertive they are. They are immune to all pickup lines, and their asses, with time, have developed shields, like those of cartoon heroes. The dirty looks of men bounce off those shields and are splashed back in the villains' faces with a ZAP! BANG! and TAKE THAT!

But I know, I know how to disarm those shields, and it is not by using kryptonite; it is not through the power of my penguin suit or my flying umbrella or the big tip or the smile. It is done with politeness and also, even more important, gratitude. On my days of pay I am grateful, I am grateful for everything, and it shows. I am grateful for the good food, the warmth, the service, the forgotten ketchup that is relocated from a nearby table by the waitress's own hand and offered to me. I am grateful for the waitress's thumbs that grasp the edges of the food plates, and their palms and their wrists that juggle them all my way. And at the first sip of beer, the first fries, I forget and forgive humanity for its stupidity, its foulness, its pride, its avarice and greed, envy, lust, gluttony, sloth, wrath, and anger. I forgive it for its contaminated spit, its valued feces, its rivers of piss, its bombs, all its bad dancing. I forgive it for not taking off its shoes before entering homes, before stepping on the carpets of places of worship. I also forget about the bonny infants with the African flies clustering on their noses, the marching drunk soldiers on their way to whorehouses. I forget about my mother, my father, the lightless nights I spent with my sister playing cards, dressing up toy soldiers, undressing dolls by candlelight, reading comics. And as soon as my eyes become accustomed to the dim light of these places, and just when people start to become more visible, more shiny, their shapes as humans more defined, it is then that I realize how exposed I must look to all these creatures who arrived before me. They must have seen everything. They must have seen my gluttony, my conspicuous tendencies, my aloofness. I feel X-rayed, as if every bite of the fries that went down my stomach was anticipated, watched, analyzed, and bet upon. It is then that I start rushing, frantically waving my skeleton-like index finger at the waitress, and with my clacking jaws insisting on the calculation of the bill, the check, the record of the meal, its price, its nutritional value, the list of ingredients sugar to sulphites, everything that keeps food conserved like Egyptian mummies, and it is then that I demand to see the little squares in the waitress's book, squares that graded me an average, satisfactory, good, or very good customer.

Finally I managed to rush out into the street. I was stunned to realize how the change of scenery felt suddenly burdensome in the aftermath of my consumption of dead animals, alcohol, scratchy soggy lettuce, and tomatoes. And I was overwhelmed with the particular guilt of the impulsive poor who, in a moment of grandiose self-delusion, self-indulgence, and greed, want to have it all. The poor one is greedy. Greedy! Greed is the biggest stupidity. But I was filled with greed.

I stood on the street corner, undecided, satisfied but undecided. Then I thought: I deserve another drink. I deserve to spend. I deserve every drop of substance, every drip of intoxication. I deserve not only to forgive but also to forget. I walked down St-Laurent to the Copa and entered the bar. The Anglos of this city love this place — unpretentious, with an air of the pseudo-working class, it even has a fake plastic coconut tree that sways only for those customers who have drunk a great deal. All those McGill University graduates love to hide their degrees, their old money, their future corporate jobs by coming here dressed up like beggars, hoodlums, dangerous degenerate minorities. They sit, drink, and shoot pool. The few old-timers have their stools reserved like Portuguese monarchy. They have blended in with the old wooden bar to become part of the retro decor. And after a certain hour, they sway with the coconut tree.

I have never understood those Anglos, never trusted their camouflage. Some of them are the sons and daughters of the wealthy. The very wealthy! They live in fine old Québécois houses, complain about money, and work small jobs. I have never understood their fathers and why they hold money over their children. My father was a generous man. When he had money he showered us with it. Once he bet on a horse called Antar. No one else had bet on it. The horse crossed the line first and my father came back with cigars, two bottles of arak, five pounds of kebbeh, a row of livers, Arabic sweets, six

pounds of fresh almonds, and five of his gambler friends.
They ate and drank all night. They sang, repeating the same
chorus for hours. My father called our names, chased us, and
asked my sister for kisses as he spilled tears and drooled words
of love and regret at her. He handed us money, large bills, left
and right. He called my sister by his mother's name and kissed
her on the mouth. My sister did not blink, did not move, when
he caressed her hair. My mother stood there silent, watching
the men getting drunk. She even filled their tiny glasses. They
all toasted her health, and she nodded and waited. Then, when
they all started to wobble towards the bathroom and aim their
urine at the floor, she pulled them aside one by one and
pushed them down the stairs. And when my father fell asleep
on the table, she asked me to help her, and we carried him to
the bedroom. I watched her remove his shoes as she muttered
and cursed. She stripped off his pants and dug her hands in his
pockets. She pulled out the rest of the money and closed the
door; that night she slept on the couch. She turned to my sister and said: How much did he give you?

My sister jeered, climbed outside the window onto the balcony, pulled out the money, and balanced on the edge of the
rail. Behind her the moon looked large and full. She looked
like a bat-woman about to fly into the city's lights. This is what
my father gave me, evil one, the bat-woman said. You take one
more step and I will release the bills against the full moon and
fly after them.

I sat under the coconut tree. I ordered the special: two beers
for the price of one. The tree gave me shade from the spotlights. I drank. I ordered some more beer and finished it all.

After that, I went outside. Somehow the cold weather felt irrelevant. I strolled, and my breath smoked against the freezing city walls. I broke into a run and cut across streets and slipped down the slope towards St-Catherine, all the while looking behind me. I had that strange feeling of being chased. So I ran as if I was being hunted by giants who could pick me up and ponder me, then drop me and make my blood splatter like roadkill, like an insect splashing on a car windshield. I zig-zagged, frantic, scanning the sky for any shadow of a giant's shoes or rolled-up newspapers that would suddenly land on my head like a collapsed roof, like ten layers of sky falling to earth. I sucked in the coldest winds, the cruellest air, and jumped like a storm in front of car tires cutting the wet asphalt, the red light, the brick houses, the curling spiral Montreal stairs that might well lead you up, if it was your lucky day, to a winter party where you would surround yourself with rings of smoke, curved toes, rolling French R's, knives carving triangles of brie in front of Eurotrash with foreign beers in hand and wearing Italian leather shoes. I reached Chinatown, passed through its arches, and asked the dragon that guarded the gate to spit fire on me, to warm my chilled face, my wet toes.

Hélas, the dragon replied with a heavy accent, all my fire was exhausted last night on grilled ducks that now hang in the steamy windows of restaurants with dirty floors, hot woks, and solemn, quiet faces slurping whatever is fished out of bowls with chopsticks.

I reached Notre-Dame Church, and then walked down to the old terrain of the circus. I looked at the ships docked at the city port. The long promenade was empty, no American tourists strolling with sugar cones, looking like moving icebergs, no five-handed jugglers, no lovers locked together by their fingers, no eternally smiling clowns, no bicycles, unicycles, or tricycles, no caricatured faces drawn with charcoal on ten-dollar canvases. The tourists were away, the sailors were away, and there was only one crazy creature to be seen crossing through the cold night.

I DRAGGED MYSELF to see Genevieve again. I did not feel like seeing her. Talking about your mother when she is gone is not a decent thing to do.

I entered the health centre and informed the elderly lady at the desk of my presence. I picked up a magazine and looked around at the posters on the wall. One good thing about waiting in these health-care places is watching the nurses, therapists, psychopaths, cleaners, and secretaries that pass by. They all look equally preoccupied, some rushing, some even brooding. I could never figure out who was who. Who was hearing voices and who was making them, who was trying to stop them and who was suppressing them? But when you sit and wait, everyone knows what you are here for. Everyone knows that you are going to confess something — something evil that was done to you, something evil that you did. Still, the past is all in the past. If you sit, wait, behave, confess, and show maybe some forgiveness and remorse, you, my boy, you could be saved. Jesus shall appear from behind one of those office doors in a skirt and stockings, holding a file of lives in his hand. Jesus will lead you, walk in front of you, swinging his ass up the hallway. And you, my boy, you must not even dare to wonder how Jesus will look naked on top of the desk. Do not wonder what he thinks of you. Jesus is very sensitive to men's looks. He can detect your innermost thoughts by the twitch in your eye, by the slightest wink and stare. And Jesus will tell you straight up, Son, if your right eye is causing your downfall, pluck it out and throw it away; it is better for you to enter the kingdom of God with one eye than to have two eyes and be thrown into hell. Jesus, unlike working-class waitresses, does not need a shield. Jesus knows every thought in your head; he knows well that you, my boy, want to make him confess as well. But Jesus is strong-willed and is on his way towards you, smiling at you, leading you to that familiar chair, that small table, and he will be asking you how your days were, and your nights, starting with the bad weather and finishing with your cold mother.

Have we met any more giant insects? Genevieve asked me. What was it again — a spider?

No, no visits from the cockroach.

That is good. No? Don't you think it is good?

What is good?

That you did not have any more visitors, Genevieve said, and made quotation marks with her fingers. Let's go back to your family.

Where did we stop last time?

You were plotting to extract money from the old man who was involved with your sister.

Yes, Joseph Khoury.

Yes, go on.

Well, I visited my sister at the store. It was the lunch hour and I asked her if I could take her for a falafel sandwich at the corner. She was very happy. She rushed to the back and got her purse, fixed her hair in the mirror; she even pulled out some lipstick and covered her lips with red. She held my arm and we walked to the store at the corner. She talked to me about work. When I asked her if the old man was treating her well, she nodded and said that he had a big heart. Then she said that the two other girls who worked at the store were nice to her as well. She was in charge of making coffee in the back room. We offer coffee to all the good customers, she told me. In the afternoon, there are these older men who come and sit around Joseph's desk and talk and smoke cigars. One of them does not take sugar, because he has diabetes, the other likes it sweet, and Joseph and the girls like it medium. I make three different kinds, she smiled.

When we sat down, I said to her, Have you thought about leaving your husband?

He is the father of my child, she answered, and her smile disappeared. Her bubbly face changed.

You should leave him, I said to her.

She shook her head, slapped her hand on the table, and said, To go where? To live where? I can't stay in our parents' house. It is too small . . . with the baby. And I can't stand our mother and father fighting all the time. Our father, the other day when I was staying there for the night, he came back at one in the morning. I had to pick him up off the floor and throw him on the sofa, he was so drunk. If I left Tony, where would I go?

If he hits you one more time, I said, I am going to kill him.

Would you kill the father of my child? My sister raised her voice. Would you? Great. And when my daughter Mona grows up and asks me where her father is, I will tell her, Your uncle put a bullet in his head. Is that why you invited me to lunch?

She was about to stand up, so I grabbed her arm and asked her to stay. She sat still. She cried. Then her hand reached across to touch my arm.

My little brother, you are my little brother, she said.

I stood up and got the food. I put the tray on the table and put her share in front of her.

We ate, then she smiled and said: Rima, one of the girls at the store, asked about you.

Which one?

The one with the long dress.

I did not notice her.

Come back with me. I will show her to you.

And what am I supposed to do with her?

Do whatever you like.

Right, and then what will you do when she starts crying and blaming you?

You are planning on making all the girls cry for the rest of your life?

Only those that like me.

Yes, only those that like you, she said, and she pulled a Kleenex from her purse and blew her nose. Maybe there are no good men in this world, and us women have to endure it.

If he touches you, I said, I will beat him up. Do you understand?

You can't beat him up. He is too strong for you. He will hurt you. You do not even know what he is capable of.

What does he do all day, anyway? Just tell me. You do not even know what your husband does.

He works for the militia, my sister said. That is all I have to know. He brings food.

You are working now. You do not need him. I will give you money, I said.

Let it go, please. Let it go.

You love that brute.

Look, you are not so different, my father is not so different. I am surrounded by men that come from the same mould. Look around. The only decent man I know is Joseph Khoury.

Marry him, then.

What? You little cockroach, how could you say that?

I walked my sister back to the store. Are you working tomorrow? I asked her.

Yes. But don't visit me. Look, come now and I will show Rima to you. Just look through the window. She is the one with the red long dress. She is nice, a very nice girl.

What is her name?

I told you: Rima. You know what? She is too nice for you. Go, my little brother, go away. She kissed me on the cheek and I walked away from the store. I passed the pharmacy, the church, and the parking lot, and arrived at Abou-Roro's back alley.

The man was in his yard, surrounded by his junk — old stereos and machinery. His radio was playing loud. Come on in, he said to me. Come on in. When are we cashing in on the old man?

We aren't.

Changed your mind? he said.

Yes, forget it. I am not killing the father of my niece.

Abou-Roro had a smirk on his face. He stood up, went back inside, and brought out some fresh almonds and two bottles of Almaza beer. You know where you can find Tony every morning, right? he asked me.

No, I do not know much about that man.

Every day he is in Abou-Fares's joint. He spends hours on those gambling machines. The man must be making money somehow.

You followed him, I said.

I know everything.

What else do you know?

He works for the Special Forces. The man is connected. The man is dangerous.

If he hits my sister one more time I will break his bones, I said. I do not care how dangerous or connected he is.

There is some action coming, Abou-Roro said. Are you in?

Talk.

Wait. He turned up the volume on the radio and the entire neighbourhood was now listening to the hourly news. You know the Armenian who does money exchanges on the corner, not too far from the Jesuit garden?

I'm listening.

He is a sitting duck. You know he has a booth there?

Yes, I have seen it.

He does not keep money on him. When he has a customer, he asks the person to wait, and he calls his son, and his son brings him the money from his home. The house is two minutes away.

Okay, I said. So who gets the son?

I get the son. If I go for the exchange, the Armenian will be careful. People know me in this neighbourhood.

Don't you think he will be suspicious of me if I ask for the exchange?

Yes, he will probably be suspicious of you as well.

We need someone else with us. Give me two days, I said. I have someone in mind.

The next day I made some sandwiches and went back to my sister's store. She was surprised, but I told her that my mother had sent me with food. And then I walked over to the girl my sister had told me about and said, You must be Rima.

The girl smiled and said, You must be the brother.

My sister told me that you like your coffee in the afternoon to be medium strength.

Your sister is right, Rima said.

My sister is always right, I said. She thinks that you are very beautiful. And like I said, my sister is always right.

The girl laughed.

I smiled back at her and left the store.

That evening I waited across the street from the store. I watched the old man pulling down the metal door while the girls stood chatting in front of it. Joseph said good night to them, and they all went their separate ways. I followed Rima. Then I darted down a side street and cut across it. I came out

just as Rima was right at the corner across from me. I called
her by name. She turned, surprised.

I said, We meet again.

Yes, we meet again.

I chatted her up, and then I told her that I had been thinking
about her.

Rima blushed.

I told her that tomorrow I would be at the falafel store at
lunchtime.

She nodded, and blushed again.

I walked back to Abou-Roro's alley that same night. I
turned up the volume on his radio. And I said in his ear,
Tomorrow at noon. How much should we stiff him for?

A thousand dollars is good.

Do you have it?

I will get it tomorrow morning, he said.

The next morning, Abou-Roro whistled from below my
balcony. I put on my shoes and walked downtairs. He handed
me a big bundle of lira.

At noon, come to the falafel store, I told him. The girl sitting with me will be the one doing the transaction. When I
give you the sign, rush back to the corner and wait for the
Armenian's son.

At noon I met Rima. I paid for lunch. She was self-conscious
and wore heavy makeup that day.

Abou-Roro came in and sat at the table behind me.

I talked to Rima and told her that I was leaving on a trip to
Cyprus for a few days. And I needed to exchange some money
with the Armenian. But, I said, he and I have had a quarrel. I

explained to Rima that the Armenian's rate was better than the bank's. I could ask my sister to do the exchange, I said, but the Armenian knew her, and he would know that I had sent her. I asked Rima if she could do the exchange for me. She agreed; she was very willing. I pulled out the bundle and said, Just tell him that you need a thousand U.S. But Rima, I added as I laid my hand over her hand, with the money between our palms, please do not give him the money before you make sure you see the dollars in his hand first.

She agreed.

I gave Abou-Roro the signal and he zoomed away.

I waited. I smoked. Fifteen minutes passed, and Rima came back. She was agitated and confused, and told me that someone had mugged the Armenian's son. The kid had come back bleeding from his nose. She pulled out the bundle of lira from her purse and gave it back to me, apologizing.

I assured her that it was okay, and I apologized for putting her in such a situation. I walked her back to the store. She pushed open the door, smiled at me, and thanked me for the lunch.

When I came to this point in my story, I looked at Genevieve. She had a completely blank expression on her face.

Doctor, I said, is our time up yet?

She thought a little before she answered me. And then she said: No, we still have time. I have no other appointments until four. Why don't you finish the story for me?

It might take a while, I said.

Yes, that's okay. I want you to finish it for me.

I can see that you're thinking, doctor. I am curious to know what you are thinking. You are probably thinking about how I used that innocent girl, right, doctor?

Go on with the story for now.

No, I want to know what you are thinking.

It is not important.

Yes, it is. It seems like you are judging me.

What I think is not important.

Then why are we having this conversation, doctor?

I will tell you what I am thinking after you tell me the whole story.

I am not sure I want to, I said, stubbornly.

Fine, Genevieve replied. You can leave, then.

But I stayed. No, I said. I will tell you the whole story. And if you have nothing to say about it I will never come back here.

Finish the story, and we'll see.

Fine, I will show you who I really am. And it is not pretty, doctor. It is not.

And who do you think you are?

You tell me, doctor. But first, here is the rest of the story, since you insist.

Genevieve. You can still call me by my name.

Two weeks passed, doctor, and then one day when I came into my parents' home, I heard the cries of my sister's baby. My sister saw me and quickly went into the bedroom and shut the door. But I had seen her clothes on the sofa. I pushed at the bedroom door and she tried to stop me from coming in, telling me that she was not decent, telling me not to come in. But I pushed open the door, and then I saw her bruised face. I pulled out my gun from under the mattress. She screamed and stood at the door, blocking my way. She screamed and followed me in her nightgown down the stairs, barefoot, begging behind me all the way down our street. Wailing, calling people to stop me. But I left her behind and I walked with the purposeful walk of an executioner, the walk of the vengeful. I walked, doctor, like a prince going to battle.

The first place I went to was the gambling joint. But Tony was not there. I walked to his home. I knocked at the door, but no one answered. For hours I paced up and down at the entrance to his building. Finally I went up to the roof to scout for his droopy moustache and his Jeep. Then I went back to the gambling joint. There I walked back and forth again. I smoked and held on to my gun in the empty hallway between the dirty stairs. Then I left and banged on Abou-Roro's door. I told him, I want you to find him.

Calm down, Abou-Roro said. Calm down. That is not the way to do it. I will find out where he is for you. But do not do anything today. Just promise me. We'll do him and get something out of it. Let's go back to our plan, he said.

I walked back to my parents' home. When my sister saw me she attacked me with her fists and nails, she shouted and cried, she called me crazy, murderer. She took the baby and walked back to her home.

The next morning, Abou-Roro whistled below my balcony and I went down to meet him. The man is at the gambling joint, he told me.

When I tried to rush back up to get my gun, he grabbed me. Stop and listen to me. You kill him in front of everyone, his men will never forgive you. They will hunt you down like a dog. Think. He held my shoulders and shook me. Think. Just be calm. And be smart, like I always taught you. We can get some money. You can do what you have to do and go away.

Go where?

The world is big. You can't just leave without money. I will get you a ticket and a fake visa, and then you can split. Just be smart. Is your sister working today?

She is.

Good. I will go to the joint and tell Tony that your girl at the store told me that she saw your sister with the old man. Just go quickly and get a car. Where is the baby?

She left Mona this morning with my mother. My sister won't go anywhere with us without her baby.

Can you get it?

Yes, I will tell my mother I am taking it for a stroll.

Do that. I will wait for you to come down, and then I will leave. Take a taxi from here to the store to get your sister. I will walk back to the gambling joint to talk to Tony.

I went upstairs. My mother insisted on dressing Mona first. I did not protest because I did not want to seem like I was in too much of a hurry. But I managed to get the baby, and then I took the taxi. I asked the driver to wait. I went inside the store. Joseph Khoury was there, but when I asked Rima where my sister was, she told me my sister had had to go back home. Her husband had called her. I handed Rima the baby and ran through the streets. I went up the stairs to my sister's home. The door to the apartment was open. When I entered, the first thing I saw was the broken mirror, then the brute's eyes, red, and then I heard him breathing heavily, his hand on the dining table, his eyes looking at the floor. I recognized the shoes, then the open palm, then the exposed thighs.

She is dead, he said.

I pulled out my gun and stretched out my arm.

Do it, he said, calmly breathing.

I couldn't pull the trigger. I couldn't.

I stopped speaking. At first Genevieve said nothing. Then she said, Did you regret it?

Not pulling the trigger?

Yes, she said.

Not anymore.

Do you regret anything?

My greed. Greed, doctor. It is my greed that I regret. Humans are creatures of greed.

Aren't all creatures greedy? she said gently.

No, doctor. Other creatures only take what they need. That is not greed.

I stood up. I did not and could not cry. I walked out of Genevieve's office without looking at her.

LATER, I THOUGHT ABOUT how strange it was that a few years had passed since my sister's death, and how strange it was to be lying in a distant land, half covered, half clothed, on familiar sheets and between dim walls. A hand stretched out and touched my shoulder and Shohreh asked me if I had ever killed someone.

No, I said.

Did you ever want to?

Yes, but I hesitated when I had the chance.

Tell me about it. But wait, let me turn off the light first.

And the closet looked like the bogeyman, the dresser talked to me, a coat hanger waved its short arms when I said, I never killed anyone. But I did cause the death of my sister.

Shohreh lifted her head, and despite the dark shapes in the room I saw her eyes blink at me.

How?

I told her the full story. I told her about Abou-Roro. About Tony. About my sister's death.

And the baby? she asked. What happened to the baby?

First she moved between my mother's house and Tony's parents' house. Then I heard that Tony got married again and took her away from us.

And he got away with it, just like that?

Yes, all he had to say was that my sister had had an affair. It was the war and he knew all the militiamen.

People should pay the price for their crimes.

Sometimes they don't, I said. They just don't.

People should pay the price, just pay the price, Shohreh said, and dropped her head on her pillow, and the bed bounced, and the bogeyman moved and the dresser sailed away like a gondola pushed by the coat hanger, singing through arches over the sewage.

Why were you so upset at the restaurant last week? I asked Shohreh. And who is the man who upset you?

It is someone who should also pay the price for his crimes.

To whom? Why?

To society, to individuals, for chance, for revenge. What does it matter?

And the individual is you?

I need some water, she said. Do you want a glass of water?

No.

Shohreh went to fetch the water, but she took so long that I got out of bed and followed her to the kitchen. The house was cold and I was half-naked. She was smoking, and she gave me a puff from her cigarette. She crushed it before it was done. Then she held my hand for the first time and walked me back to bed. Come, she said, it is cold. What was your sister's name?

Souad, I said.

Was she pretty?

Yes, very.

Older?

Yes.

For a long time after . . . after what happened to me, said Shohreh, I did not think that I would be able to touch another man. In Iran I got myself a woman as a lover, an older woman. After I was jailed and tortured, men all looked like beasts to me. Are you shocked?

No, not at all. Nothing about humans shocks me. But then, I am only half human, I said.

Half human. She laughed. What is your other half? She burst into a louder laugh. A fish? Are you a fish?

No. A cockroach.

Cockroach, she laughed again, and jumped up and put the lights on. She flipped back the bedcover and ran her hands over my thighs, my chest, all the way up my head, caressing my hair.

I do not see anything unusual about you, she said. You look perfectly human to me. Do me a favour next time you choose to be something. Be a tiger, or a pony. Why do you choose to be such a despicable creature?

I never wanted to, it just happened. I think the species chose me, I said.

Freak. You are a silly freak. Okay, cockroach, I need a favour from you. She turned serious. When that man comes again to the restaurant, I want you to call me. Actually, could you find out where he lives?

No. I am not doing anything unless you tell me why.

She paused, and then she stood up and went to the bathroom. I waited for her in bed. I heard her pulling down her underwear, crouching like a female cat, spraying like water guns. I imagined the little pool of water slowly turning yellow. She did not flush. She shut the lid on the seat because at this hour, in this stretch of wooden houses, everything can be heard. Wood is a conductor of voices and steps; wood is hospitable and considerate to insects, oblivious to water, and a support for mattresses.

Shohreh returned to bed, drank from her glass, offered me some water, then lit another cigarette, blew smoke in the air, and said: He was my jailer in Iran. I took part in the student movement during the early days of the revolution and got arrested. This man you saw eating at the restaurant, he raped me, many times. He was my jailer. I was put in a small room. I was alone for months and months. I was barely eighteen when they came to our house and said to my mother that they needed me to go with them for questioning. Just normal procedure, they assured her. They even told her that they would bring me back in a few hours. Three years passed and I was still there, in a cell as big as a coffin. I was not allowed to speak, to cry, or even to breathe. And then they tried to indoctrinate me into their fanatic religious world. A TV played twenty-four hours a day behind the backs of all of us in our little cells. We could not see it, we could only hear the voice talking about God all day and all night. I blocked it out during the first few months. Then the words started to ring in my ears like noises or music. At times I wanted to laugh at how certain words were pronounced, how the voices thickened to give listeners a clue that an important person or figure was being mentioned. Then I started to escape into my head, and my mind drifted and I recalled the faces of my family — my little brother, my mother, my cousins. Sometimes I struggled to remember their names. Then I started to look at my space like a universe — every detail of the walls, my feet, my arms. Once a fly landed on my hand, and I sat and watched it sucking my blood, I watched it gorging on my vein and its belly inflating like a balloon. I did not stop it. This is life, I thought to myself, spilling blood is part of it, and just before it flew, I hit it, I crushed it, and watched the blood, my blood, splatter on my hand.

Shohreh paused. Then she asked, Would you kill your brother-in-law if you had the chance to do it again?

I stayed silent. I did not know. What if I could not pull the trigger again? What if I turned and left again? What if I walked away and grew a beard and stayed silent for years and disappeared, took a plane, left and never came back?

Shohreh said, You understand why I think about killing?

Yes.

Why do you say yes?

I just understand because I wanted to kill someone myself.

My torturer and your brother-in-law are the same kind.

You and my sister are the same kind.

Will you help me? Shohreh asked again.

Yes.

Majeed is useless, she said. He gives up on everything. He is content with so little of life. He wants to expose that man to the media, he said. How naive! Bring him to justice. Can you imagine? What would that do? How could we prove what he did after all these years? And did you see his big car and all those men around him? He obviously has money. He has power. He probably has some kind of diplomatic immunity. He is connected here. I saw the car plate. I need a gun. Can you get me a gun?

Yes.

When?

Soon.

How much? I will pay for it.

No need. I will get it, I said.

Shohreh smiled, kissed my forehead, took a long look at me. Then we lay on our backs and we both looked up and pretended to fall sleep under the wooden ceiling and above the mattress, enveloped by smoke and the haze of our breathing.

AROUND FOUR IN THE MORNING, Shohreh woke me up. Could you take a taxi back home? I need to be alone, she said. I will pay for it. I am sorry, I am so sorry. I need to be alone, she whispered, and she cried and turned her head away because she couldn't face my sleepy eyes, my thick eyebrows, my flat nose, my uncombed hair, my sealed lips, my interrupted nightmares.

I went to the bathroom. In the bowl there was one small piece of toilet paper that had floated and marinated all night in Shohreh's yellow piss. I stood above it and aimed at it. I made holes in its middle and drove it down to drown, and then I flushed, making sure that the whole building would hear it in their dreams like apocalyptic rain.

I put on my clothes. Shohreh kept apologizing. She gave me my woollen hat and helped me with my jacket and walked me to the door, touching my back. I walked home. I wanted to walk. I refused to take a cab. I wanted to walk and hear crushing sounds under my feet again. Night is the only time when one can impose one's own sound on the world. In the absence of wolves' howls, hyenas' laughs, nightbirds' songs, and a full moon, it was up to a human to make noises, to fill the void.

But the snow was soft. My steps were muffled. It was quiet, so quiet that I felt as if I did not walk but instead crawled in silence. The snow covered everything and I walked above cotton, on silent carpets, on beach sand. Softness is temporary and deceiving. It gently receives you and gently expels you. I saw no one, no one. No being at all, not even a rabbit, not even the trace of a cougar, crow, or deer, nothing in this northern terrain. I thought: I will tell every tourist I encounter, every sister who has ever received a postcard, that nothing here exists; there is no queen, there are no seals, no dancing bears, moose, cabins, high trees, bonfires. Descriptions of these are all a ploy, an illusion, a conspiracy. There is nothing but that which freezes, and the only way to escape it is to dig deep holes, dig and sail under it. There, my friend, you can encounter rivers of steam, tropical paradises with noisy crickets, crocodiles, muddy rivers, green fungus arching like wallpaper over trees, and expert scuba-diving rats, and troops of roaches receiving signals, conspiring to take over the world. All that exists, all that will ever exist, shall pass through this passageway under the ice, the dead corpses when they turn to dust, the big happy meals, the wine, the tears, the dead plants, the quiet settling storms, the ink of written words, all that falls from above, all that ascends, all that is killed, beaten, misused, abused, all that have legs, all that crawl, all that is erected, all that climbs, flies, sits, wears glasses, laughs, dances, and smokes, all shall disappear into the underground like a broken cloud.

My fingers were frozen, my house keys cold and painful to touch. The lock on the front door of my building was cold, too, and the keys would not twist in the door. I walked back to the street and tied a knot in the key chain. Like a spider, a fisher with a rope, I pulled a thin thread from my sweater and dangled the key down into the sewer, where the temperature was reasonable. I let the metal warm up from the underground steam, then I brought it back up and put it in my mouth, and it quivered like a fish. I ran back to the lock before the key slipped through my lips, before I lifted my neck and swallowed it like a fresh cod in a seal's throat. I opened the door and took the stairs up to my home. There I took off my shoes, lay down in bed, covered myself, and slept with my clothes on, wishing I was a pony or a tiger.

THE NEXT DAY, the janitor's wife, the Russian lady from the basement, came up to my door and knocked. She is asleep, she told me. The old lady is asleep. We can take the trunk now.

I rushed to the corner of my bedroom, looking for my socks. I found them. They were damp in the toes, but not wet. I put them on. Then the shoes, which I found under the bed. I pulled the laces and felt pressure on the arches of my feet. I made delicate, perfect knots on both shoes. If I can't wear a bowtie for a Victorian encounter like this, I thought, a bowtie knot on both feet might compensate. And tidiness, for the occasion. When in Rome do as the Romans, et cetera. And now a light jacket, and I am ready for counter-imperial looting. Excitement was lingering in the corridors, excitement manifested by the rushing of our feet and the smirks on our faces.

We entered the old lady's apartment. Many of her photographs had turned yellow, and the sepia faces of colonels and waves of desert dunes covered the walls.

Aha! Here it is. The infamous trunk. Yes here, here! The janitor's wife pointed her finger.

A small dog came up to me and started to sniff around me. Then he started to growl at me.

Give him your hand, the janitor's wife hissed at me. Give him your hand to sniff.

But before I had the chance, the dog started to bark, calling me names such as "pest" and "intruder" and "thief."

The lady will wake up, the janitor's wife said. Hurry up.

The dog was yelping and twisting and blocking the way.

We carried the trunk and started to move towards the door, but at that moment the lady shouted from her bed, Natasha, is that you?

Yes, yes, I am here to take Elvis for a walk. Stay asleep.

Is my husband back? the old lady asked.

He is feeding the horses. Go back to sleep, Natasha said.

But the dog kept on yelping. Put the trunk down. Put it down, Natasha said.

We laid the trunk on the floor. Natasha opened it, grabbed the dog and threw him in, and closed the lid. The barking was now muffled, but the dog must have gone crazy banging his head against the wood inside.

We took the stairs down to the basement. When we arrived at the janitor's apartment, Natasha opened the trunk. She grabbed the dog, who was whimpering by now, and let him loose in the apartment.

The dog was partly blinded by the sudden light. He sniffed the carpet and the legs of the coffee table. Nothing like darkness to calm an animal down, I said with a wise glance at the creature.

Okay, Natasha said. What do you want to take? You can take only one thing.

There were books and clothes, including a military jacket, letters, and thick leather boots. I tried on the boots. They were a little loose, but that could be fixed with thicker socks, I thought. I flipped through the trunk again and found two pairs of thick socks.

One thing only, Natasha repeated.

Two things, I said. Or shoes and socks count as one thing.

Okay, you take them and go. Before my husband comes home.

I took my loot and crawled back upstairs. On the landing between two floors I sat and took off my shoes and my socks, and wiggled my toes. Making sure that my bare feet didn't touch the cement, I slipped on the new thick wool socks and the boots. Then I ran down the stairs and out of the building and walked above the earth and its cold white crust, feeling warm and stable.

VI

I WALKED TO Genevieve's office. The grip of my boots' soles anchored me more firmly than ever in the soil hidden beneath the street's white surface.

Genevieve and I sat as usual, facing each other. There were a few seconds of silence between us. I put each of my hands on a chair arm. I crossed my legs and moved my feet in my boots, bending them forwards, backwards, and twirling them a bit, thinking of the old lady's husband marching to confront his enemies beyond the trenches and muddy battlefields. Now that I had laced my feet into boots, blood, and mud, this health clinic had started to feel homier. The door was open to the hallway and Genevieve sat across from me, looking into my eyes. She always started with an assessment: you look tired, happy, sad, or good. And I knew her words had no relevance, no connection to how I looked; they were always just an excuse to start the conversation. I usually nodded and I always agreed, but I also knew I could look like all of the above at the same time, as if I were a cocktail of emotion that was not defined, that had no scientific term, that needed a new space to exist in, a kind of a purgatory that no medical paper had ever described.

257

Do you lie to me? Genevieve asked.

Why do you think I lie to you?

You told me that you talked to your sister on the phone once, when your mother died, and now you tell me that she was dead long before then.

She is dead.

So you lied.

Maybe. I imagine things.

You imagined that she was alive?

You know that I imagine things. I even imagine you sometimes.

Stop that. It is predictable, what you are trying to do. I am not even curious about what you imagine about me.

I got up to leave.

Do not leave, Genevieve said. Sit down. Listen to me. Sit down. Listen. Dealing with death is a hard thing. You have anger, you have guilt, and you have to deal with your loss. Are you willing to work with me? Good. Fine. Let's go back to your sister's death. Perhaps you think by committing suicide you can rectify what you did.

You do not understand anything, I said.

Well, help me to understand. Is that why you wanted to hang yourself?

No.

I think it is.

No.

What did you do after your sister's death? Why did you leave your country? You do not want to talk? All right, you can leave if you like.

I will.

Good, go. Here is the door.

I will.

What are you waiting for?

I stood up, took my jacket from the back of the chair, and walked towards the door. I am not coming back, I said.

Fine. Quit. Go.

I left. I took the fire exit. On the way down, I buttoned my inner jacket and zipped my outer jacket. I searched for my woollen hat. I couldn't find it.

I went back upstairs. Genevieve was standing at the door of her office with my hat in her hand.

I walked up to her, snatched it, and turned away.

Somehow I knew you would be back, she said.

For the last time, I said. For the last time. Now, doctor, go home and relax, sleep on your silk sheets, turn on your giant TV, open your fridge and put your slippers on, if you ever find them.

Stop, Genevieve said. What did you say?

I said slippers. You lost your slippers. You can't find your old slippers.

It is grave, very grave, if you are implying what I think you are implying. Very grave.

There is nothing wrong with offering some hospitality, I said.

I never invited you into my personal life.

No, but I went anyway.

This therapy is over, she said. She looked deeply sad and alarmed.

You tolerated me breaking into other people's places, I said, but now that it is your own place . . .

Genevieve turned and went back into her office, and before she closed the door she said, I can't help you anymore.

I WENT OUT onto the street and I walked fast, disoriented and alone. I stopped a man and asked him for a cigarette, but he didn't answer me; he kept on walking, ignoring me. I cursed him and called him cheap. I went to the Artista Café and walked straight up to the professor. I looked him in the eyes and said, I want back the cigarette I gave you. He was startled. He must have seen how my eyes shone. He put his hand in a pocket and started to search. He pulled out a packet of cigarettes and handed it to me. I took the whole thing and started to walk away. When one of the guys sitting at the table protested, I walked back to him and asked him if he had a problem. If he did, I said, he could step outside. On my way out I heard the professor saying, *Il est fou, il est fou.*

I had no fire. I stopped people and asked for a light, but none of them wanted to light my cigarette for me. Even before they heard what I had to say they sped up their steps, protected their change, their hidden wealth. To get a fire you have to have a suit and tie these days. Filth! They are all filth, these people, walking above the earth. I entered a restaurant and walked to the counter, grabbed a bunch of toothpicks and three packs of matches, and walked out. I went around the corner, and at the side of an old building I surrounded a match with my palms and tried to light my cigarette. Filthy wind, it wouldn't let me have my fire. Every time I tried to light a single match, the wind stood right beside me, blew on my face, laughed and mocked me. I threw the cigarette on the ground and started to crush it, cursing it, threatening it, and reminding it that there was no fresh air anymore, there was no pure breeze, there was only filthy gas filled with smog and diseased coughs. I walked away from the cigarette, but it chased me; I could feel it breathing down my neck. Then I remembered the Russian restaurant nearby, and its basement entrance. I found it and dodged below the surface of the street. I lit my cigarette and walked up again in triumph, laughing at the wind, showing off my burning tobacco leaves to every passerby, every human with a dog and a leash. I felt no shame parading my triumph. I blew my smoke with the air of an aristocrat. I stood in the middle of the sidewalk with a sardonic smile on my face, my neck outstretched beside citizens' hats, and I blew thick, dark clouds in their faces.

AT THE RESTAURANT the next evening, I broke three plates. The owner came squeaking over to me like a mouse. He stood above me while I picked up the shattered pieces and gathered the crumbs and scooped up the stew from the floor. Then I fetched the mop and pushed the dirty water towards the hole in the floor. When I was finished, the owner asked me to warm up his car. He left the kitchen without saying a word.

After I came back from heating the car, the owner's daughter snapped her fingers at me. I moved my feet towards her.

Who is the lady that was here last week? Sehar asked me.

Her name is Shohreh, I said. Why?

I ask you a question and you answer. That's all. Is she coming back here?

If I ask her to, she will.

Is she your girlfriend?

Maybe, I said. Do you like her?

She is very pretty, Sehar said.

Yes, I said. I only know pretty girls. Would you like to meet her?

Maybe. I want to ask her where she buys her clothes. I like her hair.

I like her hair, too, I said, but I do not care about her clothes. Actually, I prefer her without clothes.

Bring me tea, quickly! Sehar snapped at me.

I brought her tea with two brown sugar cubes.

You can meet Shohreh if you like, I mumbled. Maybe you two can go shopping one day.

Sehar poured the tea. Okay, she said.

But I also have a favour to ask, I said.

Oh, now the busboy wants to bargain?

Well, this is just a question that the busboy has.

Okay, let the busboy ask it.

Who is that man who came here with a bodyguard the night Shohreh was here?

Oh, Mr. Shaheed? You are asking about Mr. Shaheed.

Yes, the short, bald man, the one who sat over there.

He is a very rich man and he works for the government.

The Canadian government?

No, silly, the Iranian government.

He seems very important.

Yes, he is. He gives my father money.

Have you been to his house?

No. But he came to our house once.

For a visit?

On some import business, my father said. Why you are asking?

Because I like to know how important men become rich and powerful. I wish I were rich.

You will never be rich.

Why do you say that?

Because. Just because, Sehar answered with a snotty smile. She waved the back of her hand at me, telling me to go back to work as the poor should.

The owner came back from whatever he had been doing in his warmed-up car. He'd probably stuffed another plastic bag under the seat like some old villager. The habit of sticking silver coins stamped with the emperor's head under a mattress never goes out of style, I thought. It just gets transformed and adapted. I don't know why the owner uses such thick, long, wide bags and then wraps the money inside a hundred times. I often see his eyes shifting as he sits at the wheel while his hand fumbles the buttock of the seat, stuffing it with that big ugly bag with Arabic lettering. He always uses the same bag. Well, at least he recycles. I know that cunning owner wanted to test me the first time he slipped his bag under the car seat. Filth! So suspicious of servants and cooks alike. I'll bet he got that old feudal habit of spying on the help from his father, who walked the village streets with pride, twirling his long moustache, a thin stick in his hand.

The restaurant got busy. I carried many empty plates, swept many tables, and went up and down the stairs. I pulled out chairs, hung coats, and lit candles, and at the end of the night I returned to my dark home.

THE NEXT EVENING, Mr. Shaheed came to the restaurant again with his bodyguard. He was accompanied by another man, who wore an impeccable suit and tie and carried a briefcase in his hand. They entered to the bows and royal fawning of my boss, the meek, the degenerate, the transformed small merchant and pitiful tyrant. The man with Shaheed had blond hair and he held his briefcase straight in front of him so that it pointed the way and led him through the rows of tables and chairs. The bodyguard sat on his usual seat at the bar.

The owner, my boss, that little food trader, snapped his fingers at me. I put down the boxes I was carrying and walked towards him. Without a word he pointed at the blond man's chair. Despite all the hideous, monstrous organs my boss possesses, like a prehistoric turtle he only uses his neck to point. I pulled out the chair for the large blond man and, in turn, my boss pulled out the chair for Shaheed. And then, agitated, my boss chased me away with a fanning motion of the backs of his hands. He leaned over Shaheed, nodded as if to say he should and would, and then turned around, smiling. He was actually smiling — that austere food purveyor was capable of a mouth crack! He leaned over the blond man with a menu in his hand, explaining it in a drooling accent, his syrupy lips, bent knees, hunched torso, and shiny, unappetizing pate sweating under a beam of light. Then he rushed to the kitchen, briskly transformed into an erect Napoleon.

The cook, who was the only one who could treat the owner like an equal, listened and nodded and turned his back to him. But the little Napoleon went around the island and whispered some more requests and instructions.

While I rushed around with the breadbaskets and the pickles and up and down the stairs to the basement, I was thinking of a way to call Shohreh to tell her that her torturer was here again, eating and merry. But it was too complicated. The owner's phone was inside the dining room, facing the cash machine. To cross the line under the bald man's gaze would require an even more experienced cockroach than myself. And what if I managed to pick up the phone? What would I say? Under the circumstances, Shohreh would never understand or detect my ultrasonic insect sounds. I could rub my feet for hours, send loud signals and wave my whiskers, she would still never understand. Besides, no one is allowed into this place, not before the bald man eats, receives bows and compliments, and leaves. After what had happened with Shohreh last time, the owner was strict about not letting anyone else in while the bald man ate. He kept repeating to the rest of us, My food is clean, my food is clean.

Reza arrived, and when he entered the dining room he went out of his way to bow to Shaheed. Shaheed barely nodded. Then Reza turned and bowed to the blond man. The blond man asked about his box and quilt. Shaheed waved his hand to Reza and Reza laid his box on the table opposite and pulled out his santour. Shaheed was proud, smiling as the blond man asked questions. Meanwhile I tuned my mop, ready for a swing above the waters.

The food came and both men ate. The bodyguard went to the kitchen and asked for a steak. I looked at the dishwasher and we winked at each other. The dishwasher laughed and rushed to the back, opened a closet, and handed the bodyguard a ketchup bottle. Then we all laughed, which alarmed the owner. He came into the kitchen and towards us with his wide eyes, thick-knit eyebrows, and neck that turned left and right, sniffing for subversion or any sign of rebellion.

As the men in the dining room ate, Shaheed leaned in and talked and explained and laughed. Soon the blond man pulled out his briefcase and opened it. He extracted a few papers and put them to the side of his plate. He read from the papers and explained, and Shaheed, oblivious to numbers and charts, ate and nodded, glancing from time to time at the papers. When his plate was empty and he had ordered tea for the table, Shaheed started to talk again. Now the blond man listened.

Sehar entered and twirled around the kitchen, hungry but not knowing what to eat. She opened the fridge and leaned over the cook's shoulder. And then she settled for a piece of Afghani bread. She held it and started to snatch little bites with her teeth, humming a feeble tune of boredom. She walked around, swinging her shoulders while eating.

Ketchup with that? the dishwasher ventured to ask, and laughed.

Sehar turned to him and said, with excitement and anticipation: Why, do we have hamburgers today?

Everyone in the kitchen chuckled, and we looked at one
another with fraternity, equality, and bold freedom in our eyes.

In the dining room Reza played a soft, calm tune. The
blond man glanced at Reza from time to time and smiled. He
was interested in the music, as a refined, well-travelled man
would be, I thought, and I wondered about the artifacts he
would have in his house, all the maps and objects, the large
library of books and records. He seemed to me like a gentle,
well-mannered man. He was even thankful and a little apologetic for the tea I brought him.

After a while, the bodyguard stood up and walked towards
the coats. That was the sign for departure. The owner rushed
over to help.

Shaheed asked the blond man if he needed a ride.

I will walk, the man said.

Walk! Shaheed laughed. Why walk? It is so cold. We have a
big car. We can drive you anywhere.

I like the fresh air and I do not live far. Walking is fine.

Sure, walking is good, but it is cold outside, Shaheed persisted.

I know it is cold, the man said, slightly closing his eyes and
giving Shaheed a small smile, but I will walk. I don't mind the
cold. I like it.

Shaheed laughed upon hearing these incredible words.

In any case, said the blond man, I will send you the docu-
ment and we shall meet again soon. Is your stay here okay? Is
the place to your taste?

Yes, very good, Shaheed said, and thanked him again.

Then the blond man told Shaheed that he would like to talk to Reza and see the musical instrument once more.

Yes, yes, this is the most famous and oldest instrument in Iran; it is beautiful, beautiful, art ... Shaheed tried to explain.

Reza stood up and bowed goodbye to Shaheed from afar.

I watched the blond man smile and walk toward Reza's music box. Reza welcomed the man with a smile and the man started his questions, and a long conversation ensued that went longer than our closing rituals of sweeping, toilet cleaning, dish drying, and oven scrubbing.

When closing time came I left the restaurant with a general goodnight that was ignored like a flat note. I went outside, crossed the street, and waited. I stood in the bus-stop shelter. There was some graffiti on the glass. I angled my face between a red circle and a bit of the graffiti and I kept a watch on the restaurant door.

The blond man left and Reza followed him, and they talked some more on the sidewalk.

Then they shook hands and separated. I waited until Reza turned the corner and started my pursuit of the man. He walked briskly, his briefcase brushing against his long coat. At the collar of his coat bulged a burgundy scarf that gave him the air of a tall, well-dressed bird. I followed him, wondering if he had lied to Shaheed about the restaurant's close proximity to his house. I was hoping he had not lied because the streets were wide and empty, and the sidewalk made noises like the insides of wooden houses, and our breaths left vaporous trails that could be detected from distant mountaintops, read, and decoded by red coyotes, crazy horses, and pipe-smoking chiefs. We breathed against the cold wind in the manner of chimneys and coal trains crossing between Indians' mountains. And I pursued the blond man, hoping he was someone who never looked back, never remembered he had forgotten a glove, an umbrella, or a paper on the floor. If he did remember, I thought, and if he went back to the restaurant and crossed my path, I would walk straight past him. I would not give him even a nod or a smile.

But one day, I knew, I would be intimate with him. One day I would get to know him well. And I wouldn't forget where he lived.

TWO DAYS LATER I was up before dawn. Through a small crack in the curtains I could see a blue-grey sky reflecting little waves of colour on the glass. I alternated opening one eye and then the other. One eye at a time. One streak of light at a time. And I stayed in bed to see the sky's progression, the slow approach of the light, and I watched the wall get slowly, gradually brighter. Some objects on the floor couldn't be fully seen, but I knew what they were: shoes, a dirty plate, an ashtray, and a chair. When the room was light I stood up, washed my face, and decided to walk down my street in the hour before the newspaper gets thrown on doorsteps and the squirrels dig up underground roots for their morning meals. I got dressed and went outdoors. It was a bearable day. The cold had mellowed, the wind was in retreat, the wet asphalt held streaks of neon light, reflections from shop signs that skimmed its surface in the shape of unreadable letters and words that lost their meanings when flattened and splattered on the ground. But then, who wants to know the meanings of words at this hour? Everything has turned into shapes and forms that confine you and guide you, between the city streets and building walls, to your final, inescapable destination.

I arrived at the blond man's house. I stood across the street and waited for a minute. The cold didn't bother me. I knew my reward would be grand: food and a morning glass of milk. Of course, the blond man would have milk. What well-established man does not own that exquisite liquid? But I couldn't just stand there on the street for too long, not working, not moving. I would raise the neighbours' suspicions. Everything on this street had to have a purpose. Stillness and piercing foreign eyes would soon be questioned by uniforms under whirling police-car lights. As I was drooling over my future looting, I saw the blond man's door open. A large dog and the blond man, bundled and ready to jog, left the house. They reached the sidewalk and both started jogging, the dog trailing behind. That dog, it seemed, loved the colour red. There was no red-painted hydrant that didn't interest him. The dog was also fascinated by upright, refined three-dimensional shapes. A true art connoisseur.

I turned and walked in the opposite direction. When I arrived at the street corner, I grew wings and I hurried back to the soil below the blond man's garden, seeking pipes and the road to warmth. Inside, I ate my breakfast first and then went to the living room. It was a modest house for a man with such a respectable exterior and manners. There were books, of course, many on war and politics. No TV, believe it or not, not even in the bedroom. And no wife or kids. That is good, I thought. Why have the extra expense? It is enough that one has to pay lavishly for handsome clothing and over-sized hardcover books. With bread and a glass of milk in hand, I went over to his desk. Sure enough, there was that leather briefcase he happily swung in the cold the other night when I followed him home. I finished my food, went back to the kitchen, and rinsed out the glass of milk. I opened the cupboard, looked for the hot sauce, and put a few drops in the dog's bowl. Have some spicy food, and welcome to a new world, my dear friend. Bland food is passé. Curry and exotic food are in style. I picked up the briefcase and walked out of the house, calm as if everything were routine. I walked with my head down to work, to the office in the high building, in that morning hour when the trains clear the way so the bureaucrats can be on time.

LATER IN THE DAY I went down to the Café Artista. I looked for the professor. He was not in his usual seat. I asked the waitress where he was, and she pointed to the bathroom.

Indeed, his coat was on the chair. I sat in the chair and slipped my hand into his coat pockets. Nothing was there, nothing, not even a piece of a crumb.

When the professor saw me on his seat, he rushed towards me, rubbing his wet hands against the sides of his trousers. What are you doing in my chair?

Oh, I didn't realize it was yours, I said.

Well, it is someone's. There is a coat on it. It is reserved.

I stood up and pulled the blond man's briefcase out of my bag. Twenty dollars, I said, showing it to him. Leather. Real leather. I swung the zipper back and forth and rattled the buckles up and down, opening and closing the little golden locks. Solid and light, I said, thinking that it was a good thing I had emptied the files and the pens and everything the brief-case had contained. It is light, I said. Light is in, light is a bril-liant marketing tool, light meals, light women, everything is valued by its lightness these days.

The professor forgot about our territorial dispute. He picked up a napkin from the table and passed it around and between his fingers, looking at the briefcase.

Fifteen, I said, and pushed it towards his chest.

He held the briefcase. He flipped it over. He couldn't help but take a peek inside. Is it yours? he asked me.

It is yours, I said, for ten dollars.

I do not buy stolen goods, he said.

Well, professor, I said, what land is not stolen, what seat is not claimed, what container is not the product of theft and destruction? We are all coyotes in this land.

Non, je ne peux pas faire ça. You should take it back to whomever you took it from. But the professor held the case tighter and closer as he said this.

Fine, I said. Just buy me lunch and a coffee to go, then.

I took the food and went to the back alley. I couldn't eat in the presence of that dishonest hypocrite. I vowed I would never share a meal with him. Hypocrite. I knew he would soon walk the streets like a lawyer to an office. It is with objects and false acquisitions that he thinks he can assert his

ideas and gain respect. Filth. Charlatan. Just like his new briefcase, he is an empty container made of skin-deep materials.

AT HOME I LEAFED through the files from the briefcase. One of
the files had papers with a mix of Persian and English, and
charts and tables, and what looked like a list of products for
sale. I could pronounce the Persian words in the papers but I
did not understand their meaning. So I read a few pages aloud,
listening to my own voice uttering Persian without having a
clue what it meant. I chanted the words like some kind of
scripture. Ah ha! I thought. This is what it must be like for the
faithful who repeat holy scripture in foreign languages without understanding a word.

Later I went downstairs and walked over to the taxi stand. I
asked for Majeed, but no one had seen him. I was about to
leave when a cab driver called me back and pointed to the end
of the line. I saw Majeed lining up his car.

I walked over to him, opened the taxi door, got in, and
slammed the door shut. I handed him the file and asked him,
Can you read this? He flipped through the file, smiled, and
nodded quietly. He read with attention and silence. Then he
looked at me and said, Where did you get this?

Someone's home, I said.

You stole this?

No, I found it, I said.

Can I keep it? I will read it carefully later and bring it back
to you.

Yes, do that. I just want to know what they are selling in

these papers. See? Look at this chart here. Allow me, please. You see? Here, starting from this page.

Do you want to go somewhere? Majeed asked me. I can drive you.

No, I live nearby.

Thank you for this, he said. I will look at these papers.

WHEN I TOLD SHOHREH about the file she asked me why I had not told her about it immediately, and why I had given the file to Majeed and not to her.

I told her how the lists looked like products for sale. I said: I thought maybe I could bring the taxi driver into the deal for whatever was being sold. Maybe we could do business together somehow. You know, find out where the merchandise is being stored, and acquire it using his car . . . I didn't think that you would be interested in such things, I said to Shohreh.

To change the subject, I told her about my conversation with Sehar, and how the restaurant owner's daughter wanted to meet her. Shohreh said: Arrange it! Arrange it right away. And next time, you must tell me when the bald man arrives. Does he come in on a regular schedule?

No. And I will tell you when I find out what the files say. His name is Shaheed, by the way.

Shaheed, she nodded. Shaheed, and *shaheed* (martyred) he is. He tortured me and humiliated me and I never knew his name. Shaheed, she said, and laughed and stopped and hesitated and thought and laughed again, and shook her head.

A FEW DAYS LATER, Shohreh took Sehar shopping. I arranged the encounter between the two. Shohreh met Sehar after school. After shopping, she took Sehar home and put up her hair, painted her eyelashes, and powdered her cheeks, and they both tried on dresses and changed their hairstyles.

Sehar came to her father's restaurant walking like a diva and talking like a diva. When she asked me to bring her food and tea, she did so with sophistication, politeness, and theatricality. She even used the word "fabulous."

Later she called me over while her father was in the kitchen. She handed me a few dollars and asked me to go across the street and buy her cigarettes. When I told her that I couldn't leave the restaurant without her father's permission, she stood up and walked over to her father and told him to order me to go and buy her chewing gum. The man nodded my way and I took off and got her a pack. We met in the basement, where she was waiting for me. She leaned against the wall like a young high-end prostitute and opened the new handbag she had been carrying since her encounter with Shohreh. I dropped the pack inside. She closed her bag, said, Thank you, darling, and slowly danced her hips up the stairs.

NOROUZ IS COMING, Shohreh said to me that night. You know, when we Iranians celebrate the coming of spring. I am thinking of throwing a party. In Iran we stay up all night, eat, and celebrate. So, next week let's invite people to my home. Here, you roll it.

I am not good at rolling, I said. My fingers shake.

Give it to me. I will do it. Invite Reza and his band. Let him play some traditional tunes.

Yes, okay, I will, I said.

I saw Reza at the end of my shift at the restaurant the next day. I told him about Shohreh's party. He was reluctant and noncommittal, as usual. He said that he had not been getting along with Shohreh lately. He felt that she was snubbing him.

It might be a good idea to invite Sylvie and her friends to watch you perform in an informal setting, I suggested.

Reza was intrigued by this idea.

It is always good to be around those people and keep up the contact, I reminded him. Besides, it will be good to show your traditions around those rich folk. Shohreh and Farhoud will dance, and you will play. It will be perfect. You should entertain and extract, my friend. You should put some culture to it if you want to live and shit.

Reza promised to call Sylvie.

THE NEXT DAY, I paid my rent with my money from the restaurant and even bought some groceries, bread and cheese. While I ate, I realized how loud the fridge was. I could unplug it, I thought. It is almost empty anyway. But the cheese would go bad. So I decided to eat all the cheese without any bread and then unplug the fridge.

I lay on my bed and looked at the ceiling. I contemplated and strategized. The idea of conspiring with Shohreh intrigued me. I would help her. And I decided that I loved her. I would give her whatever she wanted. Lately I had an even bigger desire than before to be with her.

I napped, then woke up and took the stairs down to the street. I was tempted to just walk somewhere, anywhere, but I hesitated. I felt indecisive and frozen. I am not hungry, I thought, I am not sleepy, I am neither sad nor curious. I just want the time to pass before I see Shohreh again and my plan springs into action. I just need to decide what to do with myself. Luckily, it was cold, and before too long I had no choice but to move on. I contemplated going to the Artista Café, but I felt disgusted with that crowd — especially the professor, who had tolerated that woman of his from the letters. How petty, how spineless of him to tolerate her neglect, her narcissism, her stupid letters. She had obviously used him for her own escapism.

I could smoke, I thought. I could climb up to some roof and watch the neighbourhood from above. But the last time I had tried this, it took two minutes for the police to come and ask me why I was on the roof. Some lady had complained that I was looking into her bedchamber and called them. It was summer and all I had wanted was to hang out on the roof like millions of people on countless planets do in this universe. Billions of farmers, forgers, waitresses, and housewives stand on roofs and look around and smoke, hang laundry, and contemplate. When I told the policemen that I had always done this, all my life, he replied: Well, here people do not look at each other from their roofs.

I will only look at the stars then, I said.

He forbade me from looking at the stars, and threatened

me with jail. Where all you would be looking at is walls and men in the shower, he said, and his partner laughed.

So I walked up and down my street, and finally I went to the café. I saw the professor and a few of his friends. When they saw me come over, all puffed up and angry, they stood up and surrounded the professor. One of them even attempted to push me.

I told the man not to touch me. He was bigger than I was, but still I knew that I could take him. The professor tried to calm everyone down. But I wouldn't back off. I asked the professor for some money that he supposedly owed me. The waiter came over and told us that he would call the police. Take it outside, he said.

Fine, I said, let's go outside.

We all went towards the door to the back alley, me in the lead. Just before I got to the door, I stopped and looked behind me and called out to the waiter, telling him that I would see him afterwards. As everyone looked back to see the waiter's reaction, I grabbed an empty coffee mug from a deserted table. As soon as I reached the back alley, I swung around, jumped forward, and hit the big man on his forehead with the mug. He collapsed. Everyone ran to his rescue, and then some of the men came towards me. I put my hand behind my back, pretending I was holding something dangerous. The professor, trembling, stood between me and the others and shouted, waving his hands in the air: Stay away! He has something, maybe a knife. They all stopped in their tracks. I walked away. When I reached the end of the little alley I started to run. Then I stopped. I felt a bit of coffee liquid sticky between my fingers. It smelled like sour milk, and the idea that it had touched some human's lips repulsed me. I buried my hand in a snowbank and started to clean it. A dog and his owner passed me by. The dog stopped and licked itself. Filthy dog, I thought.

I walked. I walked all evening. I could have picked three more fights. I did not feel the cold anymore. I felt the warmth of violence. I thought: All one has to do is substitute one sensation for another. Changes. Life is all about changes.

THE NIGHT OF THE PARTY, I stood in the hallway outside Shohreh's apartment and watched Sylvie's bracelets. Her painted nails grabbed the stair rail, and I heard her laugh ascending towards Shohreh's door. I leaned over the landing and thought how much I had come to despise that woman. I could not stand her or her friends. I was worried that her friend the politician's son would breathe processed food in my face. But even more than that, I was worried that the industrialist's son wouldn't show up. At last his head came into view, and I was relieved. I saw his straight yellow hair and I went back inside to Shohreh and said to her, They are here.

Majeed will give you a lift, she said.

Sylvie and her friends entered, loud and happy. They were already drunk and high. Reza was laughing among them, hugging his santour and his quilt. Inside there was plenty of food displayed on the table in the middle of the kitchen, where everyone would end up smoking and drinking.

Majeed entered the apartment and walked straight towards me.

Give me a minute, he said. He went to the bathroom.

I found Shohreh. I stood beside her and said, I am off. She squeezed my hand. I leaned my lips towards her ear and told her that I wanted her to hold my hand forever. She smiled, and squeezed my hand again.

Majeed came out of the bathroom. I followed him out of the apartment and down the stairs. He walked slowly. He even opened his car door slowly. We drove across town, down towards the bridge. We took the casino exit and arrived at the place where the son of the industrialist lived. I told Majeed to stop just before we reached the entrance. I asked him to park and wait across the street from the building. Then I hurried towards the entrance. I crawled against the walls and under the glass door of the lobby entrance. The doorman was sitting at his desk. I looked up at him and passed right under his nose, and made my way into the apartment. I rushed straight to the bedroom. I dug into the son of the industrialist's drawers. One of his drawers was filled with medicine. I cursed him: weapon-loving hypochondriac, son of the manufacturer of filth. I turned to the closet where I knew he kept his gun. It was still in the towel I had used to wrap it all that time ago. I pulled out the magazine and saw that it was still full of bullets. I passed my hand over the shelf in the closet and found a small box with bullets in it. This I took. And then I went downstairs looking for money, gold, anything small I could carry. I found nothing. I slipped down the stairs to the basement, exited, and walked around the building.

I climbed back into the car with Majeed. He did not say a word to me at first. Then he broke the silence and asked: Did you get what you need?

Yes, I said.

He nodded and drove back towards the city.

Majeed, what is in the file I gave you? I said.

Information about weapons. Canada is selling weapon parts to Iran. Does the man who comes to the restaurant have an Iranian or a Canadian bodyguard?

Canadian.

Yes, of course. The Canadian government assigned him protection. They want to make sure he stays well and that the deal goes through.

But Canada . . .

Of course, Canada! Montreal, this happy, romantic city, has an ugly side, my friend. One of the largest military-industrial complexes in North America is right here in this town. What do you think? That the West prospers on manufacturing cars, computers, and Ski-Doos?

Do you still have the file? I asked him.

No. I gave it to Shohreh. She asked me for it, he said. I thought she would have told you. There are these charts in English . . . Did you read it before you gave it to me? Oh, right. You can't read Persian . . .

Well, I can, but I don't understand what I read.

Right, of course. We use Arabic letters in Persian.

What else does it say? I asked.

Well, some local weapon manufacturer is in the process of producing lighter weapons. And Iran wants the light weapons.

Light, I said. Everybody wants things to be light.

Yes, agreed Majeed. Light arms for boy soldiers so they can use and handle these weapons better. The old machinery is too heavy for those kids who are forced to join the armies. The light weapons could be easily managed. So they are manufacturing them light.

I am always suspicious of the light, I mumbled.

This should be stopped, Majeed said.

Yes, I said. Let's drive back to Shohreh's place. The music must have started.

I ENTERED SHOHREH'S bedroom and slipped the gun under her mattress. Then I went back to the living room. Reza was tuning his instrument and everyone was quiet, waiting for the music to start. Finally Reza and his band played. Sylvie and her friends applauded. They were impressed, of course. But they were a little aloof towards me, and they avoided me all evening. They feared me still, but no longer admired me. The phase of the foreign savage was gone. Now was the time of the monkey with the music box.

Later, Shohreh danced with Farhoud. They pulled me onto the floor and all three of us put our hands on one another's shoulders and danced in a small circle together.

A last dance, Shohreh whispered, weeping and kissing us on both cheeks. And then everyone started to dance. I left the crowd, fetched my jacket, went back to the bedroom, pulled out the gun from under the mattress, hid it under my jacket, and walked out. I saw the industrialist's son coming my way, and he was high and swaying and mumbling. He approached me with open arms, wanting to hug me with his family rings and arms. As soon as he got close to me I grabbed him by his collar. I made sure he never touched my jacket or the gun underneath it, and I pushed him away hard, cursing his father and mine. I took the stairs down to the streets and walked back to my home.

THE NEXT AFTERNOON when I arrived at work, the owner asked me to pick up a sealed envelope from his lawyer downtown. On the way to the metro I saw a man dressed in a new suit, a handsome fellow in his forties, hair neatly combed. He was standing with two magazines in his hand, smiling with confidence and leaning towards waiting commuters, offering them the word of God.

I approached the man. He smiled.

I am lost, I said. I need direction.

Where do you want to go?

No, I am lost in general, I said.

He smiled again. The Lord can guide you to the right place.

And where is that, you filth? I asked between grinding teeth.

God's kingdom is the right place, he said. You will never be lost again.

I see you are all ready and well dressed to meet him.

His face became larger with pride and exuberance. He leaned towards me. Yes, he said, it is like meeting an important person. You have to look your best.

Like a lawyer? I asked.

Lawyer?

Or a good citizen, I finished. And do you need to dress up to be a good citizen?

Well...

Well what, you charlatan? I said. Look at you, all dressed up to seduce, charm, and bring these poor citizens into your fantastical imaginary world. To make them kneel on hard benches, repeating redemption chants inside the same walls, through the same burning suns of their hard-working days. And then you take their money, breed their daughters with other sheep from the same flock, promise them heaven full of incestuous clouds. Filth. You are a charlatan, standing there with your magazines full of promising images like opium. Look at you, human, all dressed up. Look at you, son of man, dressed in silk. You can't be handsome without weaving the saliva of worms around you, without stealing the wool from the backs of sheep, without making the poor work like mules in long factories with cruel whistles and punch-in cards. I, at least, do not need any of your ornaments. Look at me! Look at my wings straight and hard, look at the shine of their brown colour, look at my long whiskers and my thin face, look at all my beauty. All of it is natural. I have never needed rags or jewels. I have an all-natural shine, well brewed and aged like distilled wine.

And then I extended one of my many arms and snatched the man's magazine. I turned my back to him, pretending to read, and quickly I nibbled on every word that looked like God. I gave the magazine back to him and said: Now look, read, and tell me what happened to your God. Is he still coming? Is he still here? Cannibals! Cannibals!

And I walked away and went down the stairs into the tunnel. As I went down I noticed the low beams that hung above the staircase. I bent my long whiskers and thought how self-absorbed these humans are. All they ever build is for their own kind and their own height.

I WORKED ALL EVENING, went home and slept soundly, and the next morning I walked down St-Laurent Street. I avoided the café. I was not in need of confrontation that morning because somehow my head felt clear. A euphoric sense of existence had come over me, maybe because the weather was getting warmer, and soon, in a few weeks perhaps, these streets would be filled with shirtless young men and half-naked women, and bicycles and flowers and gardens. A rare mood I was in, indeed. I took arbitrary turns. I stopped at shop windows and looked at merchandise and displays. When I reached a quieter street, I saw a woman coming towards me with a hesitant smile on her face. I recognized Genevieve only when she was close to me. I had almost passed her without stopping. She stood in front of me and it took both of us a few seconds to say something.

Nice day, she said, and followed this with, How are you feeling?

Great, I said. I am very happy today. I do not know where this source of happiness is coming from.

Maybe it is the weather, she said. The sun. You are still without a phone, eh?

No phone, I agreed.

I tried to call you. I wanted to talk to you.

About what?

I filled out a report on you.

Did you?

She nodded and quietly said, You will be contacted soon by someone from the hospital.

They won't find me, I said.

Where are you going?

Underground, I said.

You can't live like a runaway. It is best if you go and get some treatment.

No, I am going underground, I said.

I recommended that you see a psychiatrist and stay in the hospital ward for a short while.

And what would a psychiatrist do for me?

It is more of a medical approach. You might be put on pills.

Pills? What for?

They might want to monitor your behaviour at the hospital.

I am not going back there. They won't find me.

Well, they just might. They might do you some good.

I just wanted to know you, I said. I just wanted to be invited in.

I have to go, she said. Take care of yourself.

It is a nice day, I said.

Genevieve glanced back once as she continued her walk.

AS I STROLLED, a few clouds moved over the sky and covered the sun. All of a sudden things started to turn grey and damp, and the darker side of nature appeared on people's faces. I saw some looking up at the sky and muttering to themselves. Then, a few streets later, drops of water fell. You could see the drops dotting the pavement. At first they were distinct and visible because there were only a few of them, but then the whole city was taken over by thunder and a homogeneous wetness that swallowed everything and changed the city's colour and odour. Tin roofs sounded like snapping lashes across a monster's back. Car windows looked like cascading water. A few human silhouettes with invisible heads hurried down cobblestone streets. The edges of the sidewalks harboured little streams that soon became swollen and fast. I followed them, oblivious to the water falling from above. I am interested in water's flight, not its source. Everything became wet, the walls, my hair and clothing, even the gun beneath my jacket was wet. My pants stuck to my legs. My socks made squelching noises. Then the rain stopped, suddenly. And I walked back home to the tempo of my wet feet.

At home, I took off all my clothing and piled it on my chair. I found an old T-shirt and used it as a towel, brushing it all over my body. Then I took another T-shirt and dried the gun with it. I snapped the chamber back and checked it. It did not seem wet. A good gun does not leak. Bullets are waterproof. My mood, like the weather, suddenly changed, and I felt the need for darkness again. I rushed to the window and closed the curtains. Then I sat on my chair facing the gun. I held it; I looked at it from many angles. I pointed it and walked around

with it, scaring all the creatures that inhabited my place. I
went to the mirror and aimed it at the mirror. I saw the large
cockroach facing me, wings and jacket and all. I pointed it at
his chest and spoke to him. I told him to go away. Shoot, he
said to me. You know what they say: When you pull out a gun,
you shoot. If you have no intention of shooting, never pull it
out in the first place. A hand went up to my face, and I could
see that sardonic smile of his. I did not blink. I wouldn't give
him that satisfaction. I looked straight at him. Shoot, coward!
we both said. We lowered our hands and cocked the gun at the
same time. He laughed, and I could almost feel his index finger
pushing the trigger ahead of mine.

The doorbell rang.

We both laughed. He shouted towards the door, One
minute, please!

I wrapped a towel around my waist and opened the door.

The Pakistani woman from downstairs stood in front of me
with a plate of food in her hand. She smiled when she saw my
bare chest. I asked her to come in. She shook her head and
pushed the plate towards me.

Come in, I said. Please.

She looked behind her, then entered.

I held the towel with one hand and took the plate in the
other. She turned around, and I could see she had decided to
leave right away when she saw my bare wings. I put down the
plate, held her hand, laid it on my chest.

No, she said. No, too much problem.

She quickly drew away her hand and walked out my door. I
closed the door and went back to the mirror. The gun was on

the sink. I took it and walked to my bed, pushed it under the pillow, and, exhausted, fell asleep.

THAT EVENING THE OWNER of the restaurant rushed into the kitchen. He called me over and sent me to make sure the bathroom was clean and that there was an empty bottle of water above the sink. Between his and his daughter's flamboyant demands I was kept busy running around. The cook was carving a lamb thigh with his large kitchen knife. The dishwasher was carrying plates. The waiter was standing at the door. Then the door opened and the bodyguard from the other night stepped inside, followed by the bald, short man. Shaheed took off his coat and the owner whisked it away from him and snapped his fingers, and I ran over and hung it in the back closet. The coat was wet and heavy, and from this I knew it was still raining in the outside world.

LATER THAT NIGHT, after my shift was over, I went to Shohreh's place and told her that the man had been at the restaurant again that night. She became agitated and asked me why I had not called her right away.

I told her that the phone was behind the bar and protected. And besides, I told her, the time was not right yet. But soon, I said. You will face him soon.

Couldn't you go outside and call me?

Next time, when we are all ready, I will do that, but the owner and his daughter are demanding.

She paced and smoked and went to her bedroom and closed the door. I could hear that she had picked up the phone and was talking loudly in Farsi. I decided to leave, but before I had put my jacket on, she called me back and made me some tea in the kitchen. She held my hand and asked me again about the bald man and the owner. She made me repeat every detail of the evening. What did the owner ask you to do? What kind of car did the man arrive in? What did he order?

I told her that the owner had asked me to make sure the bathroom was clean. And to make sure there was an empty bottle above the sink.

Yes! Shohreh snapped, to clean himself, that religious hypocrite, after he takes a piss. He never cleaned himself before he made me spread my legs. It was lucky I did not get pregnant. The women who did get pregnant were killed.

She took a sip of tea. Then she said: Can I see the gun? Who did it belong to?

The industrialist's son.

Which one was he?

The one with the flowery shirt.

They are all so artificial and flowery. Where did you meet those buffoons? And Reza was kissing their asses all evening.

Have you handled a gun before? I asked.

The guards in the jail used to walk with guns hanging off their belts. I did not know how gunfire sounded until one night we heard trucks coming and going, and for a week every night we heard shots coming from the backyard. They brought people every night and shot them against the wall. They must have killed thousands of men and women. How quiet they were.

None of those prisoners complained, none of them objected or said anything. They must have known that they were about to die. Maybe they were too scared, too tortured, too weak, or maybe they were just happy to die. At times I wanted to be there, I wanted to be against that wall, I thought they were the lucky ones. One night, just before the shooting, I heard one man scream: For Iran! And the rest of the prisoners started to shout, For Iran! And then there were many shots and a long silence. Can I see it?

What?

The gun!

I do not have it on me.

Can you teach me how to use it? Shohreh asked.

Yes.

When?

Wednesday. We will go far north and into the woods.

Good. I will rent a car. It will be only the two of us. We can go far and away from this city.

AT ELEVEN IN THE MORNING on Wednesday, Shohreh knocked at my door.

I opened it, and saw that she was wearing sunglasses and had a backpack over her shoulder. She entered. I slipped under the bed, crawled over to the middle of the mattress, and pulled out the gun.

We took Highway 15 north. At the beginning of our drive we passed many cars, houses, gas stations, and generic restaurants with large signs that stood like faux totems. The farther north we went, the fewer cars we encountered and the more hills appeared, the more curved roads, more trees, more wind, more sky, and more horizon.

In September, Shohreh said, the leaves are orange and gold. It is so beautiful. Just beautiful. Everything turns to gold here.

We stopped at a diner. The waitress, who was old and talked in a jolly tone, who smiled in spite of the absence of teeth, handed us menus. We both had eggs, toast, and coffee. Then Shohreh disappeared into the bathroom. The waitress smoked at the counter. A couple of truckers watched TV, hunched over white oval plates. I could hear noise coming from the kitchen, sizzling sounds and drumming on pots. The cook, a Native Indian, came out of the kitchen, went downstairs, and reappeared with a cart in his hands. He stopped and looked me in the eyes, and before I had the chance to bow my head, to thank him for the food, for the trees, the mountains, and the rivers, he disappeared again.

I followed him to the kitchen entrance. I stood there and asked if he had seen any cockroaches. Before he could be alarmed, I said: I am interested in these creatures and their history.

Come. Follow me, he said. I will tell you all about them.

We stood outside the kitchen's back door and smoked peacefully. Listen, he said. After the Creator made the mountains and the sea and everything, he left behind a huge drum made from a white buffalo skin. He had used the drum when he was creating the world, but he warned all the creatures not to play the drum, or the sun would come closer to listen, and never go back to sleep, and melt all the snow. At this time the birds had never flown and they ate bugs from the ground.

Cockroaches, too, I asked?

Yes, those too. The birds didn't need wings, because everything was available — fish in the sea and bugs on the land. The bugs were kept in good numbers, because the birds ate them every day for a long time. Then, one day, the coyote came to this land on a large ship. The coyote was curious and hungry from his lengthy travel. He was looking for food and anything that he could steal and take back with him to the other side of the sea. When he saw the large drum made from the white buffalo skin, he wanted to steal it. But the bugs were always crawling around the drum, protecting it. So the coyote trotted over to the birds and told them that the bugs around the drum were sweeter and tasted better than any other bugs. The birds were excited by this news, and they rushed over and ate all the bugs around the drum. The coyote stole the drum and took it onto his ship and sailed away with it. On his ship he played the drum, and this woke up the sun and made it shine. When the birds saw the sun they grew wings and flew towards it and left the earth. There was no one left to eat the bugs anymore. And the land was covered with bugs, and the bugs grew more and more numerous. They covered the land and ate everything.

I thanked the cook for his story, and when Shohreh came back, we paid and left. We drove for hours, and the farther north we drove the colder it got. The snow still covered the landscape in patches that were reluctant to melt into streams and slip under the rocks and the trees to form pools and lakes and sweeten the seas. The trees were bare. The sky looked bigger, endless, and Shohreh had a smile on her face. She was filled with joy, she was so happy to be behind the wheel. She gazed through the windshield at the flying-by landscape of trees, wolves, hills, and deer. After a while she flipped through the radio stations. She asked me what kind of music I liked, and before I answered she found a song that she liked. She told me how much she loved that song. It was a French song and she sang it in her heavy French accent. Suddenly she turned right and took an exit. She stopped the car on a little deserted and unpaved road, unbuckled her seatbelt, moved her palm to my hair, pulled my head towards her, and kissed me. We kissed for a long time. When I touched her breast, she pulled back and put her seatbelt back on and we drove north again.

Do you have a place in mind? I asked her.

Yes, she said. It's a little place that I know, a faraway place with a cabin. I was there once before. I spent a week there with an ex-lover. We came in the summer and we decided to live like two wild women in the woods, without anything. It was fun. She grew up in nature and loved nature. We fished and ate wild berries, we jumped naked in the river. We hiked and climbed. You should try dangling above a cliff with only a rope to hold you.

Oh, I might fall, I said. I have an attachment to ropes and dangling, but the cockroaches always cut it for me. I was silent for a moment. Then I said, I often think of you. Do you think of me?

Shohreh smiled, reach her hand over, caressed my hair,

and didn't answer. Then she smiled and said, You and your cockroach!

WE WALKED TOWARDS the cabin. Shohreh entered it and called me in. Look, she said. It is still the way we left it. We used to sleep on the floor and we made a fire over there.

Later I pulled out the gun, cranked it, and aimed it at a tree. I fired, and the echo of the shot rose from the other side of the mountain. The tree trunk released a little air from the spot the bullet hit.

Okay, Shohreh said, blowing warmth into the joints of her fingers. My turn.

I pulled the magazine out. I show her how to insert the bullets, how to push the magazine inside the gun's butt. I showed her slowly how to crank it, cock it, lift it. I told her never to point it in someone's face, always to point it to the floor or up to the sky. I showed her how to make an imaginary line that starts at the end of the gun and goes to the end of the barrel and extends to the target.

She grabbed the gun and stretched her arms.

Where are you aiming at? I asked her.

The stone, she said. The big stone at the edge of the water.

She fired and her hands swung a little. The bullet was far from the target.

I told her to hold her hand steady, and before she shot to hold her breath, focus, and then not to hesitate.

Once you decide to shoot, just do it. Do not think, and never hesitate.

The second shot was closer. Shohreh kept on shooting until she emptied the magazine. She hit the stone once and then she turned, bouncing, and asked me if I had seen the shot.

It was getting cold. Shohreh suggested we make a fire and stay inside the cabin for a while. But nature horrifies me and open spaces make me feel vulnerable. I wanted to leave and go back to the city before night came and the deer howled, and the wolves twittered, and the bears danced, and the moose and the beaver wrestled down by the river, and the trees bent down to watch me sleep. And what if early in the morning birds came and laid their giant claws on me, held me to the ground and dug their beaks into my chest and tore my flesh, threw me on my back and devoured me alive, with my feet dancing in the air under their big, monstrous eyes.

I need to go back, I told Shohreh.

Too soon, she said. Let's stay a little longer. See how quiet it is? Smell the forest. Look, look there are birds in the sky.

I looked up and saw two black dots suspended in the air, floating under a blue sea. I rushed into the car and made sure all the windows and doors were locked. Shohreh stood there, her hand to her forehead, looking at the sky and squinting. Then she walked in circles and smiled, and I watched her through the glass, turning and dancing in worship of it all.

BACK IN THE CITY, Friday afternoon, I waited across the street from the Artista Café. I smoked and paced, and when the professor stepped out I followed him. I caught up with him and held his elbow. When he saw me, he liberated his arm and stepped back, but before he could run or yell for help, I said to him: I just want to talk to you. No harm, everything is cool. I just want to talk.

I am busy, he said, and started to walk away.

I followed him, pulled out one of the stolen love letters, and started to read it.

He turned with his eyes open wide, and shouted, Where did you get that?

Let's talk, I said. I need to talk to you.

Give me back that letter, he said, defiant. He looked ready for a fight.

His reaction surprised me. You are not going to fight with me, professor, I said. You are a little too old for that.

Un fou, t'es malade, mon ami, un homme malade, he replied, and he started to raise his voice again.

I just want to talk to you.

I will call the police if you follow me, he said, and he held his leather briefcase in his fist, ready to swing it at me.

I do not understand, I said, why you let her do this to you. She does not care about you. She only talks about herself in these letters. And why do you lie to us? You do not teach or work as a consultant. You are on welfare. Why do you deny it? Tell me, please, what is wrong with being poor and in need?

The professor snatched the letter from my hand and started to walk away fast, and like a madman he shouted, Police, police, *un fou, un fou.*

And that was the last glimpse I had of the lost exile in his long, pitiful coat, his stolen case swinging and rubbing against one of its large pockets. He looked like a goner, a little lost imposter, a lonely spy walking out into the cold of the world.

I walked home, taking a left turn on Prince-Arthur Street. Some restaurants had ventured to put tables and chairs outside. It was a sunny day, and if you wore a light jacket you could safely sit and have a drink and a smoke outside and look at all the young women eager to reveal their summer legs, uncover their shoulders for the sun, and walk without fear on the last few batches of slippery ice, through the noisy slush and the shivery cold. I decided to sit and have a coffee and smoke.

I chose the patio of a café that was marked off by ropes dangling from one pole to the next. I lifted the collar of my jacket, lit a cigarette, and waited for the waitress to come. I blew smoke in the air and listened to the sounds of female shoes clacking along the street. The sun hit me in the face, and I wondered what had happened to those days when all I had wanted was to escape the sun. Now the sun did not seem that bad. I recalled a choice passage from one of the professor's letters: the morning his lady woke up early and walked with a towel to the sandy beach and noticed the birds. I wondered if people like that, always in a daze about beauty and sensuality, ever masturbate. What would their fantasies be like? Would they imagine a soft, handsome gentleman who walked around surrounded by flowers and floating smiles and deep and gentle voices? Were the colours more vivid in their dreams, the air just the right temperature, the towel and the sand the epitome of softness and delight? And yes, the songs they heard would all be good songs about mild suffering of the heart, nothing really tragic. I thought about how fantasies like that should rightly belong to poor girls with violent fathers and crazy mothers, but instead they were in the possession of the rich, the complacent, those who aspired to the old days of aristocracy and to chambermaids, swooning, and ballroom dancing.

Filth! I thought. I could shoot them all. I have a good aim. I never miss a shot. I could enter the professor's lover's dream and kill all those pretty boys, those older, sophisticated men with silk scarves around their necks. I could change the background music, halt the soft lapping of the ocean, shoot all the seabirds, and pull the towel from under sleeping swimsuits. I could also bring the professor with me and change him — make him look better and talk with arrogance, and give him better shoes, and lose his glasses and loosen his tie, and give him *un regard* so that he would always seem pensive, romantic, and suave, and of course rich. Then maybe that lover of his would be more attentive and loving to the old man.

THAT EVENING AT THE RESTAURANT, I knew that the man who had tortured my lover was about to arrive. The owner was looking nervous, and the cook pulled out his long knife to cut the good kind of lamb, and the waiter waited at the window.

Suddenly I remembered how, after my sister's death, I had avoided windows. I remembered sitting in the dark for days, stretching and measuring the length of my beard, inviting fleas and other little creatures to invade my hair and feed on my dirty skin. I found darkness in my bathroom and a cradle in my bathtub. I wept until I heard echoes in the drain, like the fluttering of sails, telling me to leave. I shaved and then I sailed away from that room, that house, that land, thinking that all was past, all was buried, all would come to an end.

Now I walked over to Sehar and asked her if she needed bubble gum and gave her a small wink. Yes, she said, go. I will tell my father that I sent you.

I walked across the street to the depanneur and called Shohreh.

It seems like the man is coming tonight, I said.

She asked me if the girl was there. Then she said, I will be there in half an hour.

Shaheed entered with his bodyguard, and the owner rushed to meet him. Everyone got busy. After half an hour I went to the basement, opened the back door to the alley, and put a piece of wood against the frame to keep the door from closing behind me. I opened the lid of the dumpster just outside the building and perched at the edge of the big green metal bin. I had never looked inside it before. I balanced my feet on the rim, and somehow the old smells, the gooey liquid that stained the bin inside and out, felt familiar, a déjà vu of old smells and dark landscapes, like the abstract pattern inside small coffee cups after the black liquid has been sucked down the abyss of tongue and throat. And I suddenly remembered every slice of vegetable that I had swept, that I had carried in garbage bags and thrown over the rim and inside that green metal bin. And when I looked behind me at the ground, the stained ground, I felt like I was high up, hanging from a tree or on the edge of a cliff, balancing with two extended arms. I almost forgot why I had come here in the first place.

Then I remembered. I searched for the bag that my lover had left me, and soon I found it. The gun was inside a white plastic bag, wrapped in many folds. I looked down towards the end of the alley and saw Majeed's taxi across the street, its signal light blinking like fear.

I hopped down and took the gun and went inside. I found some rope, cut it with a knife, and went straight to the bathroom. I tied the gun behind the toilet seat, wrapped it against the pipe, and left the knife on top of the tank.

I went back up to the kitchen. The owner was looking for me, and now he asked me to clean the kitchen floor with water and soap. I filled the bucket and got the mop and started to swing it like a slave in a dry field. I hummed and sang an old song that I had half forgotten. The smell of cooking onion rose from the stove. The cook was happily sprinkling spices, wiping his bloodstained fingers against his apron, chopping things on the counter, pouring water, covering the rice, and humming like a shepherd in a distant land. Through the opening that looked over the dining room, I kept my eye on the entrance.

Then I heard Shohreh's knock on the glass.

The bodyguard stood up and walked towards the door.

Shohreh asked for Sehar.

When Sehar saw Shohreh, she ran to the door, took Shohreh's hand, and pulled her to her table. The bodyguard went back and sat at the bar in his usual seat. He looked bored.

He moved his head occasionally, mostly to look at his boss. The owner talked to his daughter in Farsi, and the daughter answered back in English. She is my teacher, Sehar said to her father about Shohreh.

Shohreh had kept her sunglasses on. She was preoccupied and not attentive to the girl's talk. She kept glancing over at the table where the bald man ate. The man was oblivious to my lover's scent, to her long, covered thighs, her large, dark eyes. In the dungeon he had taken her from behind, on a metal desk that was cold in the winter and burned her skin in the summer. After he finished eating, he took a white napkin and wiped his dirty fingers, his wet mouth. He caught his breath, satisfied with the taste of the lamb.

I lifted my mop like a flag on a battlefield, and I heard the drums of Indians coming from the north. I bowed my head to the fire on the stove and circled around it. I said yes to the owner, and poured more water from my bucket onto the floor.

Shohreh released herself from Sehar's grip and went downstairs. I did not hear her fluid cascading against porcelain. I did not hear her laugh, cry, sing, shake her hips. But I did hear the cutting of ropes, the swinging of arms, and I heard the gallop of Persian horses ascending the wooden stairs. I heard the clang of pots and swords, the long knives, the cries of slaughtered sheep. I heard nature's stillness just before it sends its wind sweeping through the land.

Shohreh pointed the gun at the bodyguard and told him to stand still and to lift his hands in the air. It took a few seconds for the owner and the bald man to notice the gun, and in those moments Shohreh walked towards the table, calling the man by his name: Shaheed, she shouted. Shaheed! And she proceeded to talk to him in Farsi. She took off her sunglasses and laid them on the table and her eyes shone. Her hands stretched out and she pointed the gun at the man.

The owner mumbled and swung his head left and right, like a goat with its feet tied. Shaheed did not move. He did not look scared, or surprised. He was composed, calm, with an air of indifference. Arrogance showed on his face. He talked back to Shohreh and quickly glanced at his bodyguard.

Shohreh told the owner to move away from Shaheed, and the owner quickly hurtled towards the kitchen door, flying across carpets and tables. His daughter looked on, amused and unafraid, but her father grabbed her arm on the way out and she followed him. The cook dropped his big knife on the counter and peered through the kitchen opening.

Shohreh asked Shaheed to stand up. He hesitated, then stood up slowly. He picked up his napkin and wiped his mouth again, and then talked calmly to Shohreh. He extended his arm and took a little step towards her, asking her for the gun.

Shohreh moved back a few steps towards the kitchen door, shouted at him, and pressed the trigger on the gun. She missed. The bullet hit the wall and ricocheted onto the bar, breaking glasses. Everyone ducked except me and the bodyguard. Shohreh shook her head and screamed at the man. Shohreh! she shouted her own name, Shohreh Sherazy! She ordered the man to turn around and bend his upper body over the table, which he did.

I saw the bodyguard move towards the kitchen and slowly position himself closer to Shohreh. While Shaheed calmly talked to my lover, the bodyguard moved slowly into position behind her.

As I watched the bodyguard, I thought how he reminded me of a large man who once pushed me for no reason. I was in a bar drinking, and the man next to me wanted to talk about sports. When I told him that I did not give a damn about sports or chasing an invisible puck, he fell quiet. And then, for no apparent reason, he shoved me down from my stool. I fell on the floor and my drink spilled over me. The man looked back at the TV and continued watching his game. I left the bar and paced across the street. I hated the cold, and the wetness of the alcohol on my clothing made me feel even colder. When the man walked out of the bar and went down the street to his car, I picked up a large stone and flew at him with all four wings and hit him on the head. The man was so strong that it seemed as if he barely felt it. He turned and looked at me, smiling. I thought he was about to crush me, to step on me and twist his shoe sideways so that my cartilage would crack and pus would squeeze out of my entrails, but suddenly he collapsed. I took the stone again and threw it at the windshield of the man's car. I thought: Now when the bastard goes on a long drive down the highway, he will have a taste of what the insect thrown at him by the wind can do.

My lover's shots took too long and her aim missed, and her tears flooded onto the floor. Through the opening in the kitchen wall, I saw her kneeling with her arms extended, and I heard her voice changing. And I saw the man stand up straight and fix his tie. I saw him extend his hand again, and just when her gun took too long to fire, I watched as the bodyguard swiftly grabbed her hand and swung my lover across wooden tables and empty chairs. He swung her with ease, almost lifting her by the hands, and she dangled from his arms like a skinned animal on a loose rope. He swung her and she looked small and helpless, and her hair covered her face.

Shaheed came forward and touched her. He held her hands down by her thighs.

I watched all of this happen as if it were taking place somewhere far away. Everything was soundless. Everything was unreal, distant and slow. I walked back to the chef's counter and picked up the cook's knife.

The bodyguard had his back to me. I stuck the knife in his liver. He fell across two tables and crushed the candles with his body, and flying plates landed and shattered silently on the floor. The gun fell from his hand. I picked it up and aimed it at Shaheed. I shot him twice. I shot him right in the chest and he fell beneath his tablecloth.

I dropped the gun and walked back to the kitchen. I looked at the water that gathered and rushed towards the drain.

Then I crawled and swam above the water, and when I saw a leaf carried along by the stream of soap and water as if it were a gondola in Venice, I climbed onto it and shook like a dancing gypsy, and I steered it with my glittering wings towards the underground.

ACKNOWLEDGEMENTS

Special thanks to Lynn Henry, the Canada Council for the Arts, and Conseil des arts et des lettres du Québec.

Photo © Milosz Rowicki

ABOUT THE AUTHOR

Rawi Hage was born in Beirut, Lebanon, and lived through nine years of the Lebanese civil war during the 1970s. He immigrated to Canada in 1992. He is a writer, a visual artist, and a curator. Hage's first book, *De Niro's Game*, was a finalist for numerous prestigious national and international awards, including the Scotiabank Giller Prize and the Governor General's Literary Award, won the IMPAC Dublin Literary Award, and has been translated into several languages and published around the world. Rawi Hage lives in Montreal.